BLACKHEARTS

Also by NICOLE CASTROMAN

BLACKSOULS

BLACKHEARTS

NICOLE CASTROMAN

SIMON PULSE

New York   London   Toronto   Sydney   New Delhi

SIMON PULSE

An imprint of Simon & Schuster Children's Publishing Division
1230 Avenue of the Americas, New York, New York 10020
First Simon Pulse paperback edition February 2017
Text copyright © 2016 by Nicole Castroman
Cover photograph copyright © 2016 by Getty Images/Image Source
Also available in a Simon Pulse hardcover edition.

For information about special discounts for bulk purchases, please contact
Simon & Schuster Special Sales at 1-866-506-1949 or business@simonandschuster.com.
The Simon & Schuster Speakers Bureau can bring authors to your live event.
For more information or to book an event contact the Simon & Schuster Speakers Bureau
at 1-866-248-3049 or visit our website at www.simonspeakers.com.
Book designed by Karina Granda
The text of this book was set in Adobe Garamond Pro.
Manufactured in the United States of America
2 4 6 8 10 9 7 5 3 1
The Library of Congress has cataloged the hardcover editon as follows:
Castroman, Nicole.
Blackhearts / by Nicole Castroman. — First Simon Pulse hardcover edition.
pages cm
Summary: "A reimagining of the origin story of Blackbeard the pirate and his forbidden love
affair with a maid in his father's house"—Provided by publisher.
ISBN 978-1-4814-3269-6 (hc)—ISBN 978-1-4814-3271-9 (eBook)
1. Blackbeard, -1718—Juvenile fiction. [1. Blackbeard, -1718—Fiction.
2. Pirates—Fiction. 3. Love—Fiction.] I. Title.
PZ7.1.C46Bl 2016
[Fic]—dc23
2015012626
ISBN 978-1-4814-3270-2 (pbk)

For my mom, Doris,
for always telling me I should write.

And for my husband, Miguel,
for making it possible for me to do just that.

CHAPTER 1

Anne

Bristol, England 1697

After Anne's father died, her mother often said that sorrow was the only sun that rose for them. Her mother had since followed him into the darkness of death, leaving Anne to face the dawn alone.

That morning was no different, the thick clouds overhead were determined once again to release their pent-up frustration on her. In the crowded marketplace and its stalls, the air smelled of sweet water on damp stone and wood, accompanied by the tang of blood.

Other maids and cooks from the large homes in the city bartered and bought, their weary voices calling for pheasant, venison, and veal. Anne stood in line with her pail of fruits and vegetables, hoping she wasn't too late to get the better cuts of meat. At last she stepped up to the butcher, the many coins in her pocket reminding her of her errand's importance.

The butcher winked, his brown eyes almost black. "Good to see you, Anne. What'll it be today?"

"Master Drummond wants venison tonight," she said, inspecting the haunches and shoulders hanging from the stall's center beam. The butcher's eyes followed her with the same consideration. With his fair hair, some might have called him handsome, but she only saw his yellowed teeth and smelled his rank breath. If Master Drummond hadn't insisted she buy from this particular butcher, she would have found a different one long ago. He was at least twice her sixteen years, and though his apron was clean, the look on his face was not.

"Aye, his son is coming home, isn't he?" he said, leaning forward across the table. "Been gone a year at sea."

Anne took a step back, pulling her shawl more firmly around her, and finally met his gaze. "Yes, which means there's no time to waste. I must return to the house as quickly as possible. I'll take that one," she said, pointing to a fleshy red hindquarter.

The name Drummond was always on someone's lips, for Richard Drummond was one of the wealthiest merchants in the city. In four weeks' time one of the largest ships ever built, the *Deliverance*, would set sail from Bristol. It was Master Drummond's showpiece.

"Oi, you can't have that one. This one'll have to do," the butcher said, poking a knife into a thin portion of meat in front of him. It was old, the flesh tough and hard, the fat contracted.

Anne's face flushed with anger, and she wished for the

hundredth time that she could purchase elsewhere. "And why would I want that piece?" she asked sharply. "Do you know what the master would do if I served that for dinner tonight?"

The butcher grinned. "I know what I'd do," he said.

Gritting her teeth, she gave him what she hoped was a haughty look. "What else do you have?"

Unexpectedly, he grabbed her arm, pulling her close so that her pail hit the table, spilling the produce onto the cobblestones beneath their feet.

"Don't act so high and mighty with me. I've already told you. I'll give you the best cuts, but this time it'll cost you a little extra," he sneered. "I've been a patient man. If you want to please your master, you're going to have to please me first."

Like a dragonfly caught under glass, her heart fluttered. She'd become accustomed to his lewd suggestions, but the grip of his grimy fingers on her arm filled her with a new sense of panic.

"You can please yourself," she hissed, wrenching her arm out of his grasp. With shaking hands she quickly picked up the fruits and vegetables, not bothering to wipe the dirt from their skins. The butcher laughed, an ugly sound that made her stomach churn. She glared at him, turned on her heel, and barreled through the crowd in an attempt to put as much distance between herself and his stall as possible.

The devil hang him. If Master Drummond wants venison for his son's return, he should come down here and buy it himself. If the butcher tries to touch me again, I'll stick him like the pig he is.

Only after she was several rows away did Anne stop and lean against a brick wall to catch her breath, aware of the suspicious glances thrown her way.

Despite the fact that it was a major seaport, most of the inhabitants of Bristol were still unused to Anne's appearance. She was the illegitimate daughter of a prosperous English merchant and a West Indies slave, and people didn't know how to react to the mix of her mother's coppery skin and her father's blue eyes. It was obvious Anne didn't fully belong to either race, and others often viewed her with either distaste or distrust.

Wearily she straightened, her fingers reaching for her mother's small, gold watch hidden in her pocket, a habit whenever she was upset or distressed. She needed to find something else to cook for dinner, and quickly. With rows and rows of stalls, it would not be too difficult to find a new butcher, but she doubted she'd be able to find the same quality.

The church bell chimed the top of the hour, which meant Anne needed to head back to the manor, but there was no decent venison to be found. Desperate, Anne settled instead upon a clean stall near the edge of the market and bought two pheasants from a small, elderly woman with a hunched back and frail shoulders.

The woman took the coins Anne handed her and slipped them into her pocket, watching Anne intently the entire time. Anne ignored it, used to the scrutiny by now, after years of prying glances. "Do you ever have venison?" Anne asked, the poultry safely tucked beneath her arm.

The old woman nodded. "Aye, but we sold out first thing this morning."

Just my luck.

"I'll be back in the future," Anne assured her, before heading into the busy horde. From now on she would buy from the old woman's stall. Anne was the only one that Master Drummond sent to the market. There was no need for him to discover where Anne acquired his meals—she did not understand why he took such an active interest in his purchases anyway.

Part of her hair escaped her thick braid and cap, and she impatiently stuffed the stubborn black strands underneath, thinking of all the work that had yet to be done. A party of six would be eating dinner that afternoon, and she needed to get the pheasants home as quickly as possible.

Her feet turned in the direction of the harbor. Shrimp was a favorite treat of Master Drummond's, and she had enough money left over. Although it wouldn't be a lot, it might be enough to dampen his ire. If she could not secure the shrimp, she feared he might send her back to the workhouse, where she'd have to labor alongside the rest of the city's penniless inhabitants in exchange for handouts. The thought sent a shiver running down her back.

As Anne approached the docks, the sound of seagulls intensified and the bells on distant boats could be heard more clearly. Her father had sometimes brought her here very early in the morning or late at night, when not many people were about. He'd said that the presence of the sea gave the very skies a special quality, one that could not be duplicated.

There was freedom here. It flowed through the air and lifted the sails of the vessels as they left. How often in the last five months had she been tempted to stow away, sail off, and leave this life behind? Her mother had filled her head with stories of the West Indies, and her father had always promised to take her to her mother's island one day.

The familiar sights and sounds of the waterfront drew Anne in. It was hard to take a breath without inhaling the scent of salt and fish, and no one could speak without having to raise their voice over the cries of the gulls. Anne managed a smile, her first one all week.

The fishmonger she usually bought from saw her coming and straightened, returning her smile. "Good morning, Anne. You're a bit late this morning, aren't you?"

She nodded regretfully. "Yes, indeed. I don't have much time, but I need some shrimp," she said, referring to the small barrel behind him, full of the plump, gray crustaceans. "Two pounds should do."

He flinched. "I'm truly sorry, but those have been purchased."

Fear sharpened Anne's voice. "What? The whole barrel?"

"Aye. Someone came in and bought the lot."

"But I must have two pounds. Surely you can spare some," she said.

"They're not mine to spare. Though, you can ask him yourself, if you like," the fishmonger said, pointing at someone over Anne's shoulder.

She turned in time to see a large figure approaching. He was at least a head taller than she, with a broad chest, and muscular legs clearly visible in the brown breeches he wore. A cutlass hung from his waist, beneath his short jacket. He was tanned, and the hair on his head and the beard on his face were as black as the thatched roofs surrounding the dock.

She took an involuntary step backward as he stopped beside her. He gave her a cursory glance, his green eyes bright, before turning his attention to the fishmonger. His voice was smooth and low when he spoke. "Instead of taking them myself, I'd like you to deliver—"

Desperation drove Anne to interrupt him. "Please, sir. Might I have a word with you?"

Once again those green eyes turned in her direction. This time he afforded her a more complete perusal, and she swallowed the distaste in her mouth. He was no gentleman. His appearance suggested a simple sailor, someone who could not possibly afford the entire barrel.

"Yes?" he asked.

"It's about the shrimp. I was wondering if I could take two pounds from the top and pay you for them."

A woman came from behind and called to the fishmonger. He turned to help her, leaving the shabby sailor and Anne to their conversation.

When he had first approached, she'd thought him much older, for he was taller than most men. On closer inspection, she realized he couldn't have been more than nineteen. His expression warmed as he considered her. He was interested, clearly, but Anne wasn't sure if it was her proposal or her appearance.

"There is more than one stall that sells shrimp," he said.

She was not to be deterred. She'd already lost one battle this morning and could not afford to lose another. The last cook who hadn't provided the master's favorite meal for a special occasion had been fired and kicked out onto the streets.

As much as Anne disliked living in the Drummond household, it was preferable to the gutter. And if she went to another household, there was no guarantee she could secure enough funds to begin a new life. "Yes, but this man has the most honest scales and the freshest fish. Since I am unable to buy from him, I have no choice but to ask you. Surely you would not miss two pounds," she pressed.

The corners of his mouth lifted, and his green eyes twinkled. "Ah, but I would. Have you considered oysters as a substitute?"

Anne pursed her lips. Master Drummond hated oysters. "No, it must be shrimp. Please, I have a very important meal—"

It was his turn to interrupt. "I, too, have an important meal, for which I need the entire barrel."

No doubt trying to impress some girl and her family. "I have enough coin. How much would it take?" she asked briskly.

He paused for a moment, still considering her. She shifted uncomfortably beneath his gaze but refused to back down. The crowd surrounding them thinned, evidence that time was wasting. Her eyes begged him to comply.

"Perhaps I've been too hasty. We could discuss the price," he said, reaching boldly for her arm.

An image of the butcher flashed before her eyes, but this time there was no table to separate her from her attacker. Jerking free of his hold, Anne brought the pail forward, hitting the sailor soundly between the legs. He dropped to his knees, the breath escaping his lungs with a pained *"Ooof,"* his eyes no longer twinkling.

"Keep your hands to yourself, you filthy sea rat! Even if you were to offer me the full barrel, I wouldn't go anywhere with the likes of you!"

For the second time that morning, Anne rushed away from an unwelcome advance, cursing softly beneath her breath. She felt the sailor's eyes following her, burning a hole into the back of her head, but she didn't turn around. He was in no condition to give chase, at least not now.

Hurrying from the docks, she reached once again for her mother's pocket watch. A shiver ran down her spine and she sent up a silent prayer, asking that Master Drummond's heart would be softened and that she wouldn't find herself on the receiving end of his fury.

Anne also prayed that her path would not cross again with that of the sailor's, for if it did, she knew with certainty that she would not leave the encounter unscathed.

CHAPTER 2

Anne

When Anne arrived home two hours later, anxiety tightened her chest as it always did when the large gray manor came into view. It was cold and unfeeling, much like its owner, as if each wall were carefully designed to suppress joy.

Sheltered in the grassy downs several miles from the center of town, the property lay behind an ornate wall and gatehouse. It was rumored that Master Drummond had chosen this residence because his wife had fallen in love with the nearby woods. Anne knew the nine bedchambers and seven chimneys of the stone structure by heart, for on more than one occasion she'd been forced to clean them all.

As she entered, the estate buzzed with activity. Everyone appeared to be elbow deep in chores and preparations. Margery, the housekeeper, bickered with the elderly gardener about the roses for the table settings. Margery had gray hair and a pronounced limp (for one leg was shorter than the other), and as head of the kitchen, she took her duties seriously. If Mrs. Drummond had still been alive, Margery would have been second in command to her.

The two housemaids bustled about with dusting cloths, trying to shine the brass and polish the silver. Even the three-legged cat had something to do as it scurried away to devour the unlucky mouse clenched between its teeth.

"Well, it's about time you showed yourself. What were you doing for so long?" Margery pounced as Anne hung her shawl on a peg near the back door. "Did you go out into the woods and kill the deer yourself?"

Steeling herself against the housekeeper's anger, Anne turned to face her, the lie ready on her lips. "There was no good venison to be had today. Master Drum—"

Margery's eyes narrowed, and she cuffed Anne on the side of the head. Luckily, she never used much force.

Anne's cap flew off, but she caught it with her hands as her thick braid fell down her back, setting loose several more strands of hair.

"What? No venison? The master said he wanted venison for tonight, what with his son being gone for so long. The next time he requests it, make sure you get to the market earlier."

Anne nodded, preparing herself for a second strike. She didn't mention that she'd been up since before dawn. Any *earlier*, and she could have milked the cows for the farmer down the road.

"It's a good thing I made the master's favorite tartlets. At least you did right with the shrimp," Margery said, limping over to the fireplace to stoke the embers.

"Shrimp?" Anne asked, her head snapping up.

Margery gave Anne an odd look. "Aye, shrimp. I didn't think I'd given you enough for a whole barrelful, but that'll feed the lot of them, to be sure."

Confused, Anne left the pail and pheasants on the table and followed Margery into the pantry. There on a shelf was a barrel of shrimp. The same barrel Anne had seen earlier that morning.

Margery read the surprise on her face and hesitated. "You did ask the fishmonger to deliver them, didn't you?"

What was the right thing to say? Anne truly could not explain how the shrimp had gotten here. She was merely grateful that they had, for it meant that she would have a roof over her head, at least for one more night. And it meant that she could keep the leftover coins still in her pocket.

Every time Anne went to market, she saved whatever change she had left, for Master Drummond did not pay her nearly enough so that she might eventually afford passage on a ship bound for the West Indies. She'd also taken to pilfering the odd spoon or empty goblet from the household.

In a few weeks' time she would sell it all and leave on the *Deliverance*. Surely no one would expect her to be so bold as to depart on her master's ship.

Margery waited. "Well?" she asked.

"The fishmonger delivered them," Anne said, not quite phrasing her statement as a question.

"That's what I'm telling you, girl. Are you daft?"

Anne pictured the young sailor on his knees, his green eyes flashing fire, promising revenge if he ever caught up to her again. Had he simply given them back to the fishmonger? Why would he do that? The sailor had told her *he* had an important meal. It didn't make any sense for him to change his mind.

Even if he had, why on earth would the fishmonger have brought the whole barrel to the house? Anne had told him she needed only two pounds, not the whole lot.

Masking her confusion, Anne brushed past Margery and emptied the contents of her pail. "I'll get to the shrimp as soon as I dress the pheasants and start the vegetables," she said, a knot of unease forming in her chest. What would the fishmonger demand in return, she wondered. Would she have to look for another stall at the docks as well?

Pushing those unsavory thoughts aside, she worked quickly and efficiently for the next few hours. An excellent cook, Anne's mother had taught Anne how to prepare delicious meals, and Anne took special care to make sure things were done according to Master Drummond's specifications. Most of the time there weren't any problems.

That day, Margery had hired a young girl to help with the cooking. Normally Margery and Anne were able to handle all the duties in the kitchen themselves—Master Drummond typically ate alone and never had much company. But the return of the master's son was an important occasion, and Anne was grateful for the extra help.

Twelve-year-old Ruth peeled and chopped the potatoes with practiced ease. She was slight in stature and pale, her light blond hair plaited down her back in a thin rope. Anne felt the girl studying her as they worked.

"Do you have any family?" Anne asked, trying to fill the awkward silence between them.

Ruth dipped her head, her small hands flying. "Aye, ma'am."

"Any brothers or sisters?"

"Aye, ma'am. Three brothers and two sisters."

"Are you the eldest?" Anne asked.

"No, ma'am, the youngest. My sister Elizabeth is the eldest. My grandfather is the gardener here."

"Ah, so that's how you came to get the job."

Ruth nodded.

Trying to extract information from her was painful. Anne bit her lip, working silently for a few minutes. Once the vegetables and pheasants were roasting, they turned their attention to the shrimp. Anne showed Ruth where the cistern was to gather water to fill the large pot.

"All right, then. We just wait for the water to boil, and then we'll add the shrimp. Have you ever tasted shrimp before?" Anne asked.

Ruth shook her head. "No, ma'am."

"Please, call me Anne," Anne said gently. "I'm not much older than you and much too young to be called ma'am."

"Yes, ma'am," Ruth said automatically.

Anne laughed. "Tell you what. Once the shrimp are ready, I'll let you try one. It can be our secret."

Ruth's brown eyes lit up, and she gave Anne a timid smile. "Yes, ma—"

Anne raised an eyebrow at her.

"Yes, Anne," she said.

"Good girl. But don't tell Margery."

"Don't tell Margery what?" came a shrill voice behind Anne.

Anne's back stiffened. "That I might have added too much salt to the water." It was the first thing that came to mind.

"Well, that's easily fixed. Go and get fresh water," Margery said gruffly.

Making a face at Ruth, Anne dutifully took the heavy pot and dumped the perfectly good water out the back door, effectively washing the step for the second time that day. Instead of making Ruth take the trip down to the cistern again, Anne filled the pot herself. It was cool and dark in the lower story, and she enjoyed the solitude.

While there she heard a commotion coming from upstairs. The master's son, Mr. Edward, had apparently returned. He had been expected the previous evening, but a storm had delayed his arrival, and Master Drummond had not been pleased, especially with company coming later that afternoon.

Anne stayed where she was. If he was anything like his father, she certainly wasn't in a hurry to greet him. The master was a cold and angry man, preoccupied with improving his social status in the community, and he was well aware that many aristocrats mocked him behind his back. Wealth wouldn't be enough if Master Drummond were ever to attain the higher circles to which he aspired, which was why he'd arranged for his son to wed Miss Patience Hervey, the daughter of a local baron.

Although Anne had yet to meet either party, she thought it might be a most fortuitous match. She'd heard it said that God had made men and women, and then he'd made the Herveys. The family was known for their overbearing and overconfident manner.

Margery had said the master would have liked nothing more than to set his sights higher and have his son marry the daughter of an earl or a duke. But a baron was one of the few peerages that could descend through female lines, and by Mr. Edward's marrying Miss Patience, any Drummond offspring would be titled.

Once Anne returned to the kitchen, she set the pot in the hearth. It would take some time for the water to boil. She looked around for Ruth, but the girl was nowhere to be found.

The two housemaids were in the washing kitchen, fighting over the flowers in one vase, each girl wanting to take the large red blossoms to the respective guest rooms.

"I heard the young Miss Patience likes red roses," Sara spat, her slender fingers white from holding the vase so tightly. She was a handsome girl with dark hair and wide brown eyes.

Leaning back, Mary, the plumper of the two, shook her head, her blond curls shaking. Her normally pretty face had turned pink from exertion. "I don't care. The baroness should have them."

Rolling her eyes, Anne marched past them on her way outside. She debated about telling them that the female members of the Hervey family would most likely bring their own lady's maids, and any attempt on the housemaids' part to take over that position would surely be wasted.

She had no sooner finished her thought than there was a loud crash from behind her, followed by two shrill cries.

Now they've gone and done it.

Anne returned to the scene and discovered both girls crying and wringing their hands. There were glass shards everywhere, and the water was forming small puddles on the stone floor. The stems and blossoms of the flowers were unharmed, and Margery swooped in and plucked them up, turning on both girls. She gave them each a swift smack upside the head. Both Sara and Mary clutched their ears, recoiling from Margery's rage.

"What do you think you're doing? We don't have time for this kind of nonsense. Sara, you clean up this mess. Mary, you go and find another vase, and don't you dare touch any of the tartlets in the pantry. Those are for dessert." She pointed an accusing finger at Anne. "Where were you earlier when Mr. Edward arrived?"

"I didn't know my presence was needed."

Margery took a threatening step toward her, the glass crunching underfoot. "Don't act so smart with me. Take the young master some water, since you're so fond of the cistern. He'll be wanting a bath."

Relieved to leave the bickering behind, but loath to face the new master, Anne headed down the cold, stone steps once more, grumbling to herself. It took her twelve trips up the many flights of stairs to fill the large brass hip tub in the young sir's second-story chamber.

By the time she was finished, her back was drenched with sweat, her face flushed with heat. The last few buckets had been filled with steaming water. Master Drummond insisted they keep a pot of water in the washing kitchen for such purposes. He was fanatical about cleanliness, as it was next to godliness in his eyes.

There was still no sign of the young master, and Anne stuck her arm into the tub, swirling the water to mix the hot with the cold. She was tempted to climb in herself, and laughed out loud at the thought.

A low voice behind her stopped her heart cold. "So, you've changed your mind, have you? Come to talk to me about the price of the shrimp after all?"

CHAPTER 3

Teach

The girl jumped to her feet, the backs of her legs hitting the tub. Water sloshed over both sides, soaking her dress and shoes. No sound escaped her. She simply stared at him, her mouth gaping like a cod on a hook.

Teach smiled grimly as he closed the door with a firm hand. His footsteps were measured as he crossed the distance between them, despite the fact that he walked with a slight limp.

"So, *Anne*, you thought you got the better of me," he said softly, enjoying the look of fear on her face. She reminded him of a rabbit caught in a snare. Served her right after what she'd done to him.

Her eyes widened. She was clearly surprised at his familiarity with her name.

"Oh, yes, I already know who you are. Imagine my surprise when the fishmonger told me you worked in my father's house."

Anne's mouth snapped shut, but she did not move.

20

"I've been looking for you. You weren't downstairs when I arrived." He could not have planned their reunion any better himself.

Anne licked her lips nervously.

"You're not so confident now that you aren't armed, are you?"

Her eyes flicked to the bucket near her feet, but Teach snatched it away before she could wrap her fingers around the handle. Like a snake about to strike, he blocked her escape. She stumbled to the other side of the tub, using it as a shield. A smile crossed his face, but it lacked mirth.

"How long have you worked here?"

"Five—" Her voice came out as a squeak, and she cleared her throat. "Five months."

"I could have you punished for what you did," he said, watching her closely.

She nodded. "Yes, you could."

"After that, I could have you fired."

"Yes, you could. But I'd rather you didn't," she said.

"And why not?" he growled.

She held her breath but said nothing more.

Scowling, he leaned forward, his hands gripping the edge of the tub. "By Jupiter, you're an arrogant maid. How did you ever land in my father's house? More important, how in the world have you managed to stay for so long?" Teach was surprised his father had employed someone of mixed race. Richard Drummond was not known for his tolerance and open-mindedness.

Any reply Anne might have had was cut off by some commotion coming from the hallway. It was Master Drummond's voice, calling out for his son.

"Damnation!" Teach breathed, closing his eyes briefly. His father had terrible timing.

A hesitant sound brought his head up sharply. Anne had moved, and his eyes pinned her to the spot. Pointing a finger at her, as if she were a child for him to command, he said, "Stay," before striding to the door. He rested his hand a moment on the knob, feeling like a guilty schoolboy called before the headmaster.

The minute his head was turned, Anne took the opportunity to slip through the side door that connected to his sitting room. He listened as she fled into the back hall and down the stairs.

Although Teach would have liked nothing more than to chase after her and continue their conversation, *Master Drummond's* voice demanded his immediate attention. He would deal with Anne later.

Straightening his shoulders, he pulled open the door and stepped out to meet his father. It had been a little more than a year since they'd last seen each other, and time had not been kind. Richard Drummond was still a handsome man, even in his advanced years, with his square jaw and rugged looks, but there was no denying the signs of age. New wrinkles spread out from his eyes, and dark circles smudged his cheeks beneath.

"It's good to see you, Father," Teach said, wondering if the older man would embrace him. A part of him hoped that he would. His father had not been down in the courtyard to greet him upon arrival, and Teach had tried to hide his disappointment.

"You need to hurry," Drummond said. "You're late, as usual."

Teach nodded, doing his best to control his temper. He should have known better. His father had never been an affectionate man. Teach hadn't wanted to come home in the first place. He would have remained at sea, but his father had threatened to cut him out of his will if he did not return.

Ever since he'd set foot on land this morning, Teach had been met with nothing but obstacles. First in the form of the arrogant maid. Now with his own father. He wondered if his inheritance was worth all of the trouble. "It couldn't be helped. The storm was too strong to attempt reaching the shore."

"But when you landed this morning, you didn't come home immediately, did you?"

Teach was convinced his father had some mystical ball through which he looked and controlled everyone else's life. It was useless to lie. "No, you are correct. I went to see the ship."

"And?" Drummond asked.

"It's a beautiful vessel and will serve the fleet well," Teach said, choosing his words carefully.

It was clearly the correct thing to say. His father's face beamed with pride. "They thought a ship that large couldn't be built," he said, his tone arrogant.

Teach nodded. "Yes, even William said—"

Drummond frowned. "William? You mean the Earl of Lorimar?"

Too late Teach realized his mistake. He stuttered, regretting his hasty response. "Yes, I—I saw William . . . I mean, I saw Lorimar briefly." The world of the English peerage was confusing, with its many names and customs, and Teach had a hard time bringing himself to call his former schoolmate by his proper title. Thankfully, William did not stand on ceremony, at least not in private. In fact, it was William who had first started calling him "Teach."

As the only son of the Duke and Duchess of Cardwell, William had been given a courtesy title at birth, the Earl of Lorimar. Upon his father's death, William would then become the next Duke of Cardwell.

"What was so important that you went to see your friend first?" Drummond demanded, clearly not pleased.

Teach winced. If it hadn't been for Anne, he would have been home sooner. As it was, he'd been so angry at the time that he'd decided to head to William's, since the duke's estate was closer to the center of town. "He said in a letter that he had something important to tell me."

"And? What was it?"

"William—I mean Lorimar—was accepted into Cambridge," Teach said, saying the first thing that came to mind. In truth, he'd not kept up any correspondence with William.

Drummond exhaled loudly. "Yes, I already knew that.

Surely that could have waited until this afternoon? The earl will be dining with us, after all."

Teach shrugged. "I was unaware of that until I spoke to him. And he is on the route home. I'm sorry, Father."

"Yes, well, so am I. I'm not sure I've ordered enough food to satisfy his hunger." He gave his son a shrewd look. "Does he still enjoy his sweets?"

"He looked . . . well," Teach said, aware of his friend's tendency to eat anything within sight. "It appears he has his weakness firmly in hand." "Firm" might have been a bit of a stretch, but William had lost some weight since the last time Teach had seen him.

Drummond was clearly unconvinced. "I still don't understand what you hope to gain by his acquaintance. I should have put a stop to your friendship long ago."

"Mother liked him well enough," Teach said.

"Your mother always saw the good in people, whether it was there or not. If she could see what Lorimar has become, I'm quite sure she would agree with me. He doesn't take anything seriously; he's lazy and under the misconception that you can cure the world of its ailments simply by throwing a pastry at it."

Teach knew his father's dislike of William had more to do with William's father than with William's affinity for overindulgence.

The Duke of Cardwell had been opposed to the *Deliverance*, claiming its size would give Richard Drummond an unfair advantage over the other merchants when it came to commerce and trade. In the end the duke had lost the argument, and he'd also lost Drummond's respect.

Teach decided to keep his mouth shut. He suspected the only reason his father had invited William was so the earl could relay to the duke how impressive the ship was and what a grand vessel it had turned out to be.

Drummond pulled out his gold pocket watch to check the time. "You must shave. Miss Patience and her family will be here shortly," he said.

He wished he had more time to prepare for her arrival, but there was a part of Teach excited to see Patience again. Although she was a baron's daughter, when the two of them were alone together, she acted more like a scullery maid, allowing him to do things no lady of noble breeding should agree to.

But at the moment he was exhausted and wished for nothing more than to soak in the tub and rid himself of weeks of filth and grime. As much as he loved being at sea, there were benefits to coming ashore. "Can you not write and ask them to come tomorrow?"

His father snorted. "They are already on their way and should be here within the hour. You've known about this for quite some time, Edward. Why do you insist on provoking me?"

"I do not control the skies, Father. You cannot blame me for weather postponing my return," he protested.

"I blame you, because you insisted on this foolishness in the first place. What did you hope to learn by spending a year at sea? Nothing has changed since you've been gone."

"Everything has changed! When will you realize I am no longer a boy and start treating me like a man?"

"When you behave like one," was the cold response.

"How can I behave like one when you're still making my decisions for me? It's time you allowed me to determine my own fate, Father." Although Drummond didn't know it, Teach planned to be aboard the *Deliverance* when it set sail, with or without his father's consent.

Drummond drew himself up to his full height, forgetting that his son had surpassed him long ago. "What nonsense. The baron and I have discussed this at length, and even Miss Patience is in agreement. The sooner the two of you are wed, the better it will be, for everyone involved." Not waiting on his son's response, he turned on his heel and strode away.

Left alone in the hallway, Teach watched his father's back, resentment boiling within. He should have known it would be like this. His father had always pushed him to be more mature than his friends. Perhaps that was why Teach had always enjoyed William's company. Although he carried the title of an earl, William acted every bit like the eighteen-year-old he was, and his father, the duke, did not seem to object.

Richard Drummond did. He claimed he wanted only the best for his son, and no child of his would work on a merchant ship. He'd eventually agreed to let Teach try it out for a year, thinking it would rid Teach of his "unhealthy obsession" with the sea.

But his father's plan had backfired.

Teach was more determined than ever to set sail once more. The boy looked longingly out the window at the swirling gray sky, wishing for the hundredth time that the storm had postponed his return for at least one more day.

CHAPTER 4

Anne

Downstairs in the kitchen Anne was having the same thoughts, but for entirely different reasons. Anne pulled up sharply at the look on Margery's face, her heart pounding in her chest.

"They're here! They're here! The baron and his family are here. Quick, make sure Sara and Mary have the chambers ready. No, wait, have you added the shrimp yet? The water is boiling." Margery turned in a circle, wringing her hands in her apron, her limp more pronounced than ever. "No, no. First I need you to check the pheasants. Oh, we should have venison. The master wanted— Stop! What in the world happened to your dress? You were supposed to set a bath for the master's son, not take a dip in it yourself."

Margery's mouth continued to run, and Anne had a hard time concentrating. Anxious, she constantly checked over her shoulder, convinced the young Mr. Edward would come charging after her.

It took considerable effort on her part to focus on the tasks at hand. Her movements were jerky as she took the birds from the spit. She nearly dropped them, and burned her thumbs in the process. Tears sprang to her eyes, and she dunked her seared flesh into a bucket of water near the door.

The chaos surrounding her matched her insides, and it was all she could do not to run from the house.

He was here. The ragged sailor whom she'd hoped never to see again had reappeared, to live in this very house.

He was the master's son.

And he was angry.

How long could she hide from him? How long would it be before he exacted his revenge?

The next hour was torture, as Anne was forced to listen to Sara's and Mary's constant chatter with a combination of pity, fear, and disgust. They went on and on about how they wished they were a baron's daughter and how they'd heard that the young master had come downstairs to await dinner, looking very sharp, and what a fine pair he and Miss Patience would make, as they were both so handsome.

By the time the platters of food stood ready and waiting, Anne's head pounded. Margery had already spoken with the master about the meal. While he wasn't pleased, Margery said he hadn't said much else, occupied as he was by his houseful of guests.

Anne was grateful for the distraction they created.

Five months ago Henry Barrett, her half-brother from her father's marriage, had brought her to the Drummond household to work. Given a choice between starvation and employment, she'd naturally stayed. Henry had said he would make her pay if he heard she'd caused any problems for Master Drummond. Hitting the master's son between the legs with a pail was certainly problematic.

She wondered how Henry could possibly carry out his threat. No one knew they were related. Henry's mother had died when he was an infant, shortly before Andrew Barrett had brought Anne's mother back from one of his trips to the West Indies. Anne was born two years later. Although Andrew Barrett had provided a roof over Anne's head and taught her to read and write, he had never openly claimed her as his daughter, and as a servant, she rarely had need of a surname.

Nevertheless, she didn't wish to test Henry. She'd often been the target of Henry's anger and had spent much of her childhood locked in a closet. It was his favorite form of punishment and one of the reasons Anne enjoyed spending her time outdoors.

Sara and Mary pushed each other aside, each one trying to glance into the small looking glass that hung near the back door and check her appearance. They straightened their caps and collars, pressing their lips together in the hope that they would stay red. The two of them would assist Margery with the serving of the food.

Mary had a steady beau, a sailor by the name of John, and was soon to be married, though her engagement did not seem to prevent her from flirting with Tom, Master Drummond's groom. More than once Anne had noticed bits of hay sticking out of Mary's hair, despite the fact that involvement among staff was strictly forbidden.

The moment Sara and Mary left the kitchen with the first course, Anne escaped out to the garden to hide the coins she'd kept from that morning's trip to the market, her skirts whirling about her ankles. The rest of the chores demanding her attention could wait. She had a favorite place on the other side of the back wall, in a shelter of trees. It was there that she kept a small chest with her growing treasure.

Within the property, the level ground, clipped hedges, and molded trees all showed the master's desire to reshape nature to his specifications. But in her little corner, through a low archway, two willow trees grew together, wild and untamed, their branches hanging down, the leaves forming a curtain behind which she could hide. Her space was an unoccupied piece of land that led out of the city, one that very rarely received any traffic.

The chimney tops of the manor were barely visible from her vantage point. Anne remembered the first time she'd found the spot, the same day she'd arrived at the house more than five months ago. It had been after supper, and Margery had slapped her for dropping one of the dishes. Anne had taken off, determined to leave that awful house. She'd made it only as far as the two willows, for she'd realized she had nowhere else to go. A girl with no funds, and no family to claim her, she'd been helpless and at the mercy of Master Drummond.

She had decided she would scrimp and save money, even steal if she had to, in order to leave this place. Somewhere out there, Anne hoped she had family—people who would accept her, despite their differences. Although she'd been born and raised in England, not on one of the far off isles of the West Indies, that was where she planned to go.

Once the coins were safely tucked away in the chest, Anne returned it to its hiding place in the trunk of the tree. She hoped to visit the market within the week and sell more of the items she had stolen. The goblet and two silver spoons she'd sold had already earned her a tidy sum, but not enough to start her own life elsewhere.

Anne sat down on a small stump, relieved to be away from the house. The air surrounding her smelled like freshly cut hay, and a small beetle crawled on the ground. She watched its progress through the blades of grass, until a cry pierced the air.

It was Mary, and her voice was frantic.

"Anne! Anne!"

Groaning, Anne quickly ran back through the low archway and into the garden, unwilling to let Mary find her secret hiding place.

Mary clutched a hand to her chest, her cap falling from her

head. "There you are! Where have you been? I've been looking all over for you."

An exaggeration, Anne was sure. "I've been collecting rosemary," she said, wondering at her ability to lie to everyone in this household. Until five months ago she had never told an untruth or stolen anything in her life. There was something about this place that almost demanded it.

"Quickly, you must come and help Margery and me serve dinner."

"But I've never done that before. I wouldn't know what to do," Anne protested, taking a step back. Although her father had never required her to work, she'd never been present when he entertained guests. She had always eaten in the kitchen with her mother and the rest of the household servants. Anne had been caught between two worlds, unsure of her exact place in either of them.

Mary shook her head, grabbing Anne by the wrist and pulling her along. Shorter than Anne, Mary was strongly built. Anne dragged her heels, but Mary didn't seem to notice, intent as she was on hauling Anne to her doom.

Ignoring Anne's protests, Mary made it back to the kitchen and threw Anne through the door, barring her escape.

"Here she is, Sara. Tell her what you told me," Mary said, picking up a tartlet from the table and taking a large bite.

Sara sat on a stool near the fireplace, her face wet with tears. "It wasn't my fault! She tripped me! She tripped me, she did.

She saw the young sir watching me, and she was jealous."

Anne could barely comprehend what she was saying. "Who tripped you, Sara?" she asked. "Tell me what happened." Surely it couldn't be bad enough that it would prevent her from finishing the dinner service. Sara was far too sensitive to work as a maid, Anne thought irritably.

"Aye, I'll tell you what happened. It was Miss Patience. She isn't as pretty as we thought. She's ugly inside, and it shows. The young sir winked at me. He winked at *me*, he did, and she didn't like it."

Although Anne had yet to see Miss Patience Hervey, she *had* met the young master of the house and could understand how Sara would catch his eye. Mary, too, was pleasing, despite her generous middle.

Sara sniffed and wiped her nose with her sleeve. "She tripped me, and I dropped the soup onto the young master's lap. Master Drummond was furious! Oooh, I've never seen him so furious before."

In this house, people had been fired for less grievous acts than pitching a bowl of soup into someone's lap. Master Drummond often let maids or butlers go without so much as a warning if their collar wasn't stiff enough or if their shoes weren't polished. It depended on his mood and if he was feeling charitable or not.

Anne patted Sara's back in an attempt to calm her, just as Margery flew in. She pointed at Anne, her hand shaking.

Whether it was from rage or exertion, Anne could not tell. "Go and get changed. Quickly now. Wash up!"

"But I've never had to help with a meal. Surely you and Mary—" Anne's head snapped back from the impact of Margery's hand.

"I said now! Take a bucket, wash yourself, and be back down here in two minutes. The young master has changed, and the guests are ready for their next course."

The appearance of Mr. Edward had turned the entire household on its head.

Anne raced upstairs, her ear still ringing, and hastily tore off her dress and shift. The water splashed onto the floor as she filled the washbasin and quickly cleaned herself. Moments later, as she retraced her steps wearing a fresh dress and apron, a pit settled in her stomach.

With one last look at Sara's shaking form, Anne twisted her unruly braid under her cap and followed Mary and Margery toward the dining room, like a sacrificial lamb prepared for slaughter.

Even with her limp, Margery moved with amazing speed. Anne was breathless by the time they reached their destination, afraid she would be sick over the polished floor. With each footstep her anxiety rose, till it was all she could do to remain upright.

The sound of muted voices could be heard through the door. Silverware clinked against the porcelain tableware, and a woman's shrill laugh pierced the air.

Margery turned to Anne and whispered, "All right, now. Look

lively. You watch what Mary's doing and simply do as she does."

Anne nodded, her stomach twisting.

Straightening her shoulders, Margery turned and pushed open the door. She became a different person entirely, at once confident and discreet. Anne had a hard time reconciling the image of this competent woman with the hissing witch who'd slapped her not ten minutes ago.

Anne felt the young master's eyes on her the moment she walked in. A flush crept into her cheeks, and she kept her head averted. The walls of the dining room were covered with lavish frames filled with maps made by the most sought after cartographers. The charts marked the routes of Master Drummond's merchant fleet. Unlike in other prominent households, there were no portraits of distinguished ancestors here, as the master himself was the son of a soap maker.

Mary stepped up to the table to clear away the soup bowls, and Anne had no choice but to follow her example.

The conversation swirled around the room, and Anne took surreptitious glances at the guests, noticing with irritation that Mary had left her to clear Miss Patience's place. Miss Patience was quite the sight in her light blue dress, which boasted a broad neckline and long sleeves. It was corseted so tightly that she seemed to have trouble handling her cutlery. Her blond hair was a mass of curls, cascading elegantly over one pale shoulder. Despite her elegance, her features were pinched, like the sharp pleats in Anne's best dress.

Curious about the young master's appearance, Anne looked over, and gave a start when she saw his handsome face, now devoid of the shabby beard. His hair, too, had been trimmed and just reached the collar of his longcoat. He raised an eyebrow at her when he caught her staring.

She stumbled slightly and moved on.

When the baron's daughter saw Anne at her side, she jerked away as if scalded, dropping her spoon onto the floor.

Talking ceased, and everyone turned to look.

Bending to retrieve the spoon, Anne willed the ground to swallow her whole.

Nobody spoke.

Iron bands squeezed Anne's lungs, and the bowls clanked slightly in her shaking hands.

"What interesting help you have. I've heard people from the islands bring all kinds of diseases with them. I find it charitable of you to allow one into your household," Patience said.

Master Drummond gave Patience a small nod. "My staff have learned and understand the benefits of cleanliness and the importance of a sound moral character."

The air was heavy, the room quiet. Anne waited for someone to say something, *anything* to break the awful silence.

Margery stepped forward to announce the next course, creating a much appreciated distraction. As everyone turned to admire the roasted pheasant and boiled shrimp, a pair of green eyes followed Anne from the other side of the table. As if Miss Patience's and Master Drummond's words hadn't been humiliating enough, of all people, *he* had had to witness them.

Anne was sorely tempted to see what would happen if she threw the china at their heads, and it was only with the greatest effort that she took the other bowls from Mary and returned to the kitchen.

Sara scrubbed the pots and pans, looking up when Anne entered. Depositing the dishes onto the kitchen table, Anne clutched the back of the chair, her heart beating out of her chest.

"Got to you, too, did she?" Sara asked, her expression sympathetic.

Anne nodded.

"Did you go and spill anything on anyone?"

"No, nothing like that," Anne said, unwilling to share exactly what had transpired. Sara would hear it from Mary soon enough.

Sara frowned. "Watch her. She's a crooked one, she is. Miss Patience will smile at your face and reach around and stick a knife into your back if you're not careful."

Although Sara and Anne had never seen eye to eye before now, for once Anne agreed with her. "The devil hang them, I don't want to go back in there," Anne muttered.

When dinner was over, there would be a few hours of reprieve before they were forced to serve a light supper later that evening.

Sara shook her head. "But you must. Any minute now I expect the master to send me packing. Please, Anne. You've got to do it for me," she begged, her voice plaintive.

Smoothing the front of her dress, Anne didn't mention that Miss Patience was only one of her worries. If the young master continued to watch her every move, she'd go mad before the end of the day.

What was the worst that could happen if Anne left this place? If she did run away, where would she go? She didn't have enough funds yet to travel, and there was no guarantee she would be able to improve her situation in a different household in England. At least with Mary and Sara, she knew what she had.

Neither of them had been overly kind to her since her arrival. In many prosperous families it was fashionable to have servants of a different race to indicate wealth and rank. The girls had initially thought Anne's chief function was to look decorative. Mary was the worst and had made all sorts of callous remarks about Anne's hair and skin color, not caring if she was within earshot or not. Margery had sometimes joined in. Their cruel comments had stung. Anne had done her best to ignore them, but she'd been overwhelmed and depressed by her new situation.

Over time Anne had learned when to keep her mouth shut and when to strike back, for if she aimed at two, she would not hit a single one.

Now they all simply lived under the same roof. They were neither friends nor enemies. They simply existed.

"You have to get back in there, Anne," Mary said, arriving in the doorway and holding an empty platter in her hands. "I can't do it myself. The master will have my head if you don't."

Anne often wondered what they would say if they knew she was the daughter of another wealthy merchant. It was obvious Anne was educated, whereas the two maids were not, just one more thing that set Anne apart from them.

She could have shared her background, but had decided to remain silent. After all, it hadn't stopped Henry from kicking her and her mother out onto the street once Andrew Barrett had died a year ago. Her mother had been forced to take a job in the home of an earl, a less than ideal situation that had eventually led to her death. With no discernable skills, Anne had been forced to clean alongside the poor inhabitants of the city.

No one had come to their aid then. Why would strangers care about her now? Especially in this cold house.

"Please, Anne. Will you do it for me?" Sara asked, her voice pleading. Her mother was sick, and it was up to Sara to earn money for the family. She could not afford to lose her job.

"All right. I'll go."

Sara gave her what she no doubt thought was an encouraging smile but actually resembled a grimace, before turning back to the dishes.

Impulsively Anne slipped into the pantry and scanned the different earthenware jars that lined the shelves. She settled upon a small, red one. Ginnie pepper. Her mother had often used it in her cooking. The seeds were very hot and dry. She grabbed a few and slid them into her apron pocket, determined to return to the fight with her own form of ammunition.

CHAPTER 5

Teach

The dining room door swung open, and Teach watched as Anne reentered, her back straight, her expression closed. She kept her gaze on the carpet, crossing to the buffet and following the other maid's movements.

He wondered what was going through her mind at the moment, amazed she had the nerve to come back after Patience's and his father's comments. His father no doubt believed he was helping Anne by allowing her to work in his household.

Patience was another matter. Teach noticed the frown on his betrothed's lips, a sure sign of her unease. He was quite certain it had more to do with Anne's beauty than with her suitability as a maid, or her race. Patience did not take well to competition, especially in the form of a house servant.

When Teach had been younger and had first been attracted to Patience, he'd found her caustic nature amusing. He'd never been on the receiving end and had often laughed at her cutting remarks when she'd discussed other members of the aristocracy.

But now he recognized her comments for what they were: a way to make herself feel better when confronted with a rival.

Despite his irritation with Anne, even he had to admit that Patience's words had been in poor taste.

"The food is simply wonderful," William said, taking a portion of potatoes from the platter in Anne's hands.

Anne hesitated before moving on to Patience.

"Drummond demands the best," Lord Hervey boomed, taking a hearty bite of pheasant. "Have you not seen his ship?"

Lady Hervey laughed, a shrill sound like breaking glass, much like her daughter's laughter. "I, personally, have not. Would you be so kind as to show it to me?" she said, leaning toward Teach. "My own private tour."

Teach chanced a glance at the baron, surprised the baroness would speak to her future son-in-law in that manner. The baron didn't seem to notice his wife's boldness.

His daughter certainly did. Patience cleared her throat. "Mr. Edward doesn't have time for such things, Mama. We have much more pressing issues to discuss."

Lady Hervey leaned back in her seat, a frown between her brows. Teach could practically see the wheels turning in her head as she tried to come up with something to break the strained silence. It was clear from Patience's reaction that she was accustomed to her mother's flirtatious behavior. Only the baron appeared unaffected. If her daughter's marriage hadn't been planned for two years, Teach had the distinct feeling the baroness would likely have made a play for him herself.

It had been more than a year since Teach had last seen the Hervey family. He was trying to decide if they had changed so very much in that time, or if the change lay solely with him. Before, he'd found their eccentricities amusing. Now he was annoyed.

The maids retired to the side of the buffet, and Teach found his eyes drawn to Anne over the course of the meal. Her expression was oddly calculating. She appeared to be watching the group, waiting for something, but he was unsure what.

All he knew was that her expression did not match that of the other girl. The two could not have been more different. The plump one made eyes at William, blushing a pretty pink when he returned her stare. Anne looked like she wished the entire dinner party would fall off the end of a dock, with nary a boat in sight.

"Tell me about your year at sea, Mr. Edward," Lady Hervey said, reaching over and touching Teach on his sleeve.

"I wouldn't know where to begin," he said, his face lighting up at her request.

"Was it terribly difficult?"

"It was the most difficult thing I've ever done. In the past twelve months I've encountered more danger than some men experience their whole lives. We nearly sank in a storm off the coast of Jamaica. We were attacked by a Spanish sloop with ten guns and a crew of fifty, and barely made it to port before our captain died from his injuries," he said, aware he held the entire room captive with his voice. "Yet if the chance were to present itself, I would leave again tomorrow."

Teach wasn't sure who appeared more displeased at his statement—Patience, Lady Hervey, or his father. Anne, for one, looked thrilled. She was no doubt wondering if she could go to the docks herself and commission a captain and a ship if it meant she would be rid of him. Teach's irritation with the girl took on illogical proportions. She definitely needed to be taught her proper place in this household.

"But surely you don't mean that," Patience said, leaning forward and revealing a dangerous amount of décolletage, no longer content to let her mother steer the conversation.

It was Drummond who spoke next, his face hard. "No, he does not mean it. Edward's time at sea has passed. I granted him one year, to get it out of his system," he said, glowering. "He had a bit of excitement and adventure, but now it's time to get serious again about his future."

Lord Hervey took a sip of wine before turning to Teach. "You spent several years at Eton, didn't you? A most excellent school. I remember my days there," he said fondly, clasping his hands in front of him. "What was your favorite subject?"

Teach shrugged but made no comment, knowing his father would not take kindly to his saying he cared more for navigation than Latin.

Drummond sat up straight. "At my request Edward was exposed to many different subjects, and he enjoyed them all. He excelled at Greek and Latin. Mathematics also appeared to be to his liking," he said. "He read the works of John Milton and other renowned authors. While I do not approve of Milton's disdain for Catholicism, Edward learned a great deal."

Lord Hervey slapped Drummond on the back. "If he went to Eton, it was more likely gambling and drinking that he learned."

Only the slight tightening of his lips displayed Drummond's displeasure, but he was discreet enough not to correct the baron's statement.

It was William who added a bit of levity to the conversation. "Oh, no, he was a model student. Despite my attempts to lure him into shocking dens of greed, your son stayed clear of the gaming tables and drinks so that the rest of us had something to be good at," he said, with a self-deprecating smile.

Some in the party laughed, and the moment passed.

Teach shook his head, wondering how much longer this inanity would continue. He did not feel well and wished to retire as soon as possible. His head pounded, and he was uncomfortably warm. But it was the lesser of two evils to obey his father and simply remain where he was, a helpless bystander in this farce.

Not to be forgotten amidst the talk of personal edification, Patience cleared her throat. "Who is John Milton?"

Teach groaned inwardly. She was a baron's daughter. How could she *not* know of Milton? Teach's mother had often read Milton's works in the evening. He remembered sitting near the fire, listening, inspired by the prose so full of passion for freedom and self-determination.

He glanced at his father, wondering not for the first time if he was still intent on joining his line with the Herveys'.

The fork in Drummond's hand stopped midway to his mouth, for Teach was not the only one surprised by her lack of knowledge. "John Milton was a poet," he said, speaking as if to a child.

Patience nodded, pretending understanding. In truth, Teach knew she cared far more about her appearance than her education. She could paint a pretty landscape or stitch an altar cloth, but she'd once told him that literature and poetry would likely blemish her complexion with concentration lines.

Teach felt an inexplicable need to break the uncomfortable silence. "Don't worry, Miss Patience. I'd be happy to introduce you to the works of Milton. *Paradise Lost* is one of my favorites, and I believe you'll be a very quick study."

"I look forward to it," she said, smiling, no doubt remembering the last time they had been alone.

William spoke up. "That's Teach for you," he said, a grin on his face.

"Teach?" Drummond asked.

William nodded. "That's what we called Edward at school.

If you were willing to learn, he was always willing to *teach* you."

"Well, I'm a very willing pupil," Patience said.

Lady Hervey glanced between the two of them, a frown on her face. "I wrote a poem once, when Patience was just a child."

"Oh, no, Mama, please—" Patience began.

Ignoring her daughter's protest, Lady Hervey launched into her text. "Patience is a virtue, virtue is a grace. Both put together, make a pretty face."

William choked on his food, his face turning red. Drummond and Lord Hervey smiled politely. Lady Hervey beamed as if lauded with praise. It took considerable effort on Teach's part not to burst out laughing, for he could not tell if the mother had been trying to outshine her daughter or praise her with that poem. In either case, the poem was a disservice.

His gaze found Anne. It was apparent by the frown on her face that she thought the entire group beneath her contempt. It didn't help his temperament that he partly shared her sentiments.

At the moment the group did appear silly, their comments trivial and unimportant. The fact that a *maid* recognized it did not sit well with him.

He pierced a potato with his fork and chewed with vigor. How dare she stand there and look back at him like that? He could feel her judgment of everyone, himself included, and found he was on the defensive.

What was so wrong with the people seated at the table?

Yes, Lady Hervey and her daughter had led sheltered lives, and seemed rather ignorant, but it was not their fault. It was a result of their station.

And, admittedly, mother and daughter were not above competing with each other. It was sometimes hard to tell who flirted more with the male members of the party. But Teach didn't mind it so much when he was on the receiving end. Who wouldn't want two beautiful women fighting over him?

And William could be a bit overbearing, but that was because he was the son of a duke. There were three things in life William could not live without. Bad poetry, sugary treats, and women. In his case, two of those vices prevented the attainment of the third. William recognized his flaws and was often self-deprecating, the complete opposite of Teach's father, which explained why Teach had always enjoyed spending time with his old school friend.

In truth, the Earl of Lorimar was no more of a gentleman than Patience was a gentlewoman.

By the time dessert was served, Teach was as tightly wound as a top. He declined the tartlet placed before him and gritted his teeth, waiting for the meal to be over.

The other guests, unaware of his suffering, dug into their desserts with enthusiasm.

Across the table, Patience's eyes grew wide with the first bite. While everyone around her enjoyed the dessert, the veins in her neck began to bulge, and tears streamed down her face.

She emptied her goblet and motioned for Anne to pour more.

"I'll have to go and fetch some, miss," Anne said, her lips twisting into what appeared to Teach to be a smug grin.

From his vantage point, it looked as though the decanter in Anne's hands was half-full, but she left the room so quickly, he couldn't be sure.

He jumped up, but when he reached Patience's side of the table, he did not quite know how to ease the situation. William, too, stood next to them, for once at a loss for words. By the time Anne returned to the dining room, Patience's face was a deep shade of red, and she was fanning herself with her napkin, gasping for breath.

Lady Hervey was bent over at the waist next to Patience, pushing the tartlet around on its dish. "I don't see anything. I can't imagine what it could be."

Anne removed the offending plate and returned it to the sideboard. Lord Hervey insisted on calling a doctor. Drummond was the only voice of reason, contending that a doctor wasn't necessary.

"She simply ate something that didn't agree with her," he said. "Perhaps she is not used to the variety of cinnamon the cook uses."

It took Patience three more goblets of wine before she stopped choking and was able to recover somewhat. Everyone took their seats once more.

After that, Drummond kept a tight rein on the afternoon's proceedings. The conversation revolved around the *Deliverance*, and everyone recognized just how passionate Richard Drummond was about his ship.

By the time the meal was over, Teach wasn't the only one sorely in need of a drink.

Everyone stood, the men moving in groups toward the library, the women to the drawing room. Teach held the door open as William exited. He made as if to follow him, but stopped in the doorway.

Mary and Anne moved in to clean up the table. Mary was nearest the door that led from the dining room to the kitchen and slid out before Anne could stop her. The door swung shut behind her.

Teach heard Anne curse, clearly annoyed, her arms full of dishes. She held out her hand for the knob but couldn't extend enough to reach it. Teach crossed the floor behind her, reached over her, and pulled the door open.

Trapped between the door and his body, she froze. He knew he was using his size to intimidate her, but nothing else seemed to work where she was concerned. She was as bold as a badger and just as fierce. He could feel the heat emanating from her.

Anne swallowed, turning to meet his gaze.

"What did you put in the tartlet?" he demanded.

Her face paled, and her blue eyes flitted to the door on the other side of the room before meeting his gaze again. "I don't know what you mean."

"Don't lie to me. You put something in Miss Patience's apple tartlet. I want to know what it was."

"Margery was the one who baked the tartlets. I suggest you go ask her," she said.

"We still have unfinished business to discuss."

"You should concentrate on Miss Patience," Anne said. "Just like fair Eve in *Paradise Lost*, she is the one searching for knowledge. Not I."

Teach was surprised that Anne knew the details of the poem, but he kept his features guarded. "Are you saying you're above temptation?"

Relief washed over Anne's face when she saw something over Teach's shoulder. "I'm saying I don't have to partake of the fruit to understand the difference between good and evil."

Teach glanced at the room behind him, annoyed when he saw who it was. The scowl on Patience's face no doubt matched his. "This isn't finished between you and me," he whispered through clenched teeth.

As if emboldened by Patience's presence, Anne scooted beneath his arm and backed out through the door, her eyes flashing defiance. "In that case I'll be sure to keep my pail handy."

CHAPTER 6

Teach

The sun was warm overhead. Too warm, and Teach felt sick to his stomach. He leaned against the rough wood of the gardener's shed, fingering the large red bloom in his hand. He'd never cared much for roses but knew Patience liked them.

He moved impatiently from one foot to the other, wishing he'd chosen a different spot to rendezvous with his fiancée. The rose garden had been her idea. Not very original, but after two hours of interruptions by both Drummond and Lady Hervey, he was willing to go just about anywhere to get some time alone with her.

Twirling the flower in his hands, he wrinkled his nose at the scent. It was heavy and cloying, so very different from his mother's favorite blossom. He remembered how she used to decorate the house with delicate snowdrops, their light perfume filling the rooms. When they bloomed, it was like a blanket of white, signaling the arrival of spring.

After her death five years ago from a prolonged illness, his father had ripped up that section of the estate, letting the entire staff go. For several months Drummond had lived in seclusion, allowing the house and grounds to deteriorate. Teach had been off at school at Eton but had come home and managed to talk his father into rehiring the gardener and acquiring new staff. He'd pointed out that his mother would have been appalled at the estate's condition, and it hadn't taken long for the neglect to be repaired.

Now there were stone figures standing as sentinels throughout the gardens, much like the stone wall around Drummond's heart.

At length Teach heard Patience's voice, and he straightened, anticipation coursing through his veins. It had been too long since their last tryst. Although he didn't feel well, he was sure Patience could renew his spirits.

As long as she didn't say much.

Except she wasn't alone. Walking beside her was a young girl, her ear held in a painful grip by a tight-lipped Patience. "Where is he?" Patience demanded.

"I told you, my grandfather isn't here," the girl wailed, leaning her head to the side in an effort to lessen the pain.

Teach took a step forward. "What's going on?" he asked, uncomfortable at the sight of Patience using unnecessary force.

The girl's ear was bright red, and she had tears in her eyes. "What's your name?"

"Ruth, sir."

"Let her go," he said.

Patience's mouth dropped open. "Why?"

"Because you're hurting her."

"I asked her where her grandfather, the gardener, was, because I wanted to speak with him," Patience said.

"Please, sir. He's worked here for several years and won't work for anyone else," Ruth said, a single tear sliding down her cheek.

"But when Edward and I are married, he would still be working for a Drummond." Patience turned on Teach. "Tell her. Convince her that her grandfather could make more money if he came to work for us."

Teach didn't appreciate the fact that Patience was already planning to take one of his father's staff with her when they married. And he didn't like her talking about their upcoming nuptials so soon. He'd arrived only a few hours ago. "You heard her. Her grandfather enjoys working here. Now let her go."

"She merely said he's worked here for several years," Patience insisted.

"But she also said her grandfather won't work for anyone else."

"But my father is a *baron*."

There it was, the insidious reference to the aristocracy. Teach recognized the disapproval in her voice. He'd heard enough at school to recognize it. William was the only aristocrat who didn't seem to mind Master Drummond's low birth.

"Excuse me, sir, but Master Drummond would like to see you." The voice came from behind them.

The three turned and saw Anne standing there, a cross look on her face. Patience released Ruth's ear, and Ruth ran to Anne's side, her small hand finding Anne's.

"How dare you," Patience said, her eyes narrowing.

Anne ignored her and nodded to Teach. "Your father would like to see you in the library, sir."

Frustrated, it was all Teach could do not to yell at the sky. He swore his father planned his interruptions. "Tell him I'll be there shortly."

Anne pursed her lips. "He thought you might say that. He said you are to come immediately. It is important and has something to do with the *Deliverance*." Her message delivered, she turned on her heel and returned to the house, Ruth stuck to her side.

"Are you going to let her talk to you like that?" Patience demanded, her hands on her hips. "If she were my maid, I'd have her dismissed at once, with no severance and no recommendation for another situation. Who does she think she is, the little . . ."

Patience's voice droned on and on, but Teach paid her no attention. Anne had been quite discourteous, but he would have been more surprised if she'd been civil. She didn't bother hiding her dislike, and would need to be reprimanded at some point.

But his mind was occupied with more pressing matters.

Like what his father wished to discuss with him. Teach had often hinted that he would like to captain one of his father's ships, but his father had never taken him seriously.

Perhaps he'd had a change of heart.

Teach dismissed himself from Patience and followed after Anne, vaguely aware of Patience hurrying after him.

"If I didn't know better, I might begin to think you didn't want to spend time with me," Patience said.

"That's not true. I'll come find you later." Teach felt a twinge of guilt for dismissing Patience so quickly. He would make it up to her, he assured himself, but refused to dwell on the matter. It didn't take much for Patience to get upset. Then again, it didn't take much to make her forget her anger.

At the door to the library, Teach paused and took a deep breath. Lifting his hand, he rapped three times with his knuckles.

"Come in."

Teach stepped inside the book-filled room, inhaling the familiar odor of leather and the clean, sharp scent of linseed oil. The dark wood paneling gleamed in the afternoon sunlight streaming through the windows. Drummond sat in his favorite leather armchair decorated with brass studs. In his hands he held his worn, dog-eared copy of the Bible.

Ever since Teach had been little, his father had retired to his library at this time in the afternoon to read several chapters and drink his favorite tea. He must have just gotten settled, because the tea tray was noticeably absent.

"You wanted to see me?" Teach said, wishing his voice hadn't broken on the last word. At forty-three, his father was still a formidable figure.

Drummond held up a finger and continued reading. When he was finished with the last verse, he closed the book and set it on the table beside him. "Yes. I wanted to ask you to keep an eye out for me."

"An eye out for what?" Teach asked, puzzled. What did this have to do with the *Deliverance*?

"I believe some things in the house have gone missing, and I would like you to see if you notice any of the staff acting oddly."

"Acting oddly," Teach repeated.

"Yes. I've checked each of their rooms numerous times, but I haven't been able to find anything."

"Father, you didn't."

Drummond raised his chin. "I most certainly did. This is my house, and those are my things. Nobody steals from me and gets away with it."

"Have you asked Margery?"

"Don't be ridiculous. She might be the one doing it."

"But are you sure they're missing? Perhaps you are mistak—"

"Do not insult me. I know what I'm talking about. A goblet

is gone, one that I gave your mother that she admired. And I cannot find my favorite spyglass, the one with the silver-and-gold inlay. Someone in this house has taken them, and I intend to find out who it is. If you can't assist me with that simple request, then you're not the young man I raised you to be." Despite the cutting edge to his words, fatigue showed in Drummond's hollowed cheeks, and Teach felt a stab of compassion for him.

"All right, Father. I will keep an eye out for the thief." Teach didn't think anything would come of it, but it wouldn't hurt to make sure nothing was amiss. It would also give him an excuse to watch Anne more closely.

"Good. Thank you. Now I wish to discuss something else with you. As you know, I've spent quite a bit of time working on the *Deliverance's* completion. Nearly two years of my life."

"Yes, I know."

"Now that its launch is almost here, I find myself looking toward the future."

Teach's pulse accelerated, but he knew better than to say anything. He remained motionless, his hands locked behind his back.

"I've decided to step down as the head of the company and leave its maintenance to my solicitors."

This was not the conversation Teach had expected. "But they know nothing about seafaring," Teach blurted out.

"True, but then, neither did I when I began. Knowledge can be acquired."

Teach should have stayed with Patience. Preparing for an argument, he drew himself up to his full height. "Knowledge doesn't need to be *acquired* when I'm fully capable of running things myself. I've just returned from a year at sea and would be more than qualified to take over for you."

"What do you mean?"

"I mean, I know what it takes to be a merchant. From the office work you taught me before I left, to the running of the ship itself. I can help you if you would let me."

"Are you saying you want to become a captain?" Drummond asked, clearly horrified.

"Why not? I'm as capable as the next person."

"But you're going to marry Miss Patience. Does she know you want to command a ship?"

Teach shrugged. "Well, no, not yet—"

"Good. She never will."

"Your father never stood in your way."

"Because my father could not afford to give me a better life. If I'd stayed home instead of joining that merchant crew, my mother would have died. I could not stand by and watch her starve to death." It was rare that Drummond showed any emotion other than anger or disdain, but whenever he mentioned his mother and how she'd always given him her portion of their meager meals when he was a small boy, the look in his eyes softened and the lines in his face were not as pronounced.

Teach was filled with a mixture of sympathy and frustration. It was truly amazing what his father had accomplished in thirty years. At the same time, it was maddening that he refused to let Teach determine his own future.

A knock at the door prevented further discussion.

"Yes?" Teach and his father called out simultaneously. Anne entered the room with Drummond's tea. She walked to the small table situated between them and set it down.

"I don't wish to have this conversation again," Drummond said, his mouth tightening.

Teach shot Anne a dark look. He didn't want to have it in front of *her*, but his father never noticed his staff. The only time he paid any attention to them was if they did something wrong. Like stealing silver from him.

"Father, please—"

"You will not set foot on the *Deliverance*. Is that understood?" Drummond fairly boomed.

The full teacup dropped to the tray, and Anne, clearly startled by the outburst, bit her lip as the scalding water splashed over her hand. Teach cringed and moved to help her, but Drummond waved them both away. "Go. I'll pour my own tea. I don't wish to discuss this any further."

Teach practically wrenched the knob from the door in his haste to exit the room. Outside, he whirled on Anne the minute the door was closed behind them.

"Are you all right?"

"Excuse me?" she asked, wide-eyed.

"Let me see your hand."

She held it behind her back. "It's nothing."

"It is not. That water was hot enough to boil an egg. Now, show me your hand."

With obvious reluctance she held it out to him. The skin was an angry red in one spot, and small blisters were already forming. He dragged her several steps to a small sideboard. Atop was a large vase with several red roses resting inside. He threw the roses down. "Is it fresh?" he asked her.

Anne nodded. "Yes, from this morning."

"Good," Teach said, and stuck her hand into the water. He had seen quite a few burns in the last year. Working on the ship, several sailors had had to take turns manning the kitchen. More than one had left the encounter scarred for life.

For some reason Teach felt responsible for her injury. If he hadn't pressed his father about captaining the ship, he wouldn't have become so upset. "I'm sorry my father startled you."

Anne glanced down at her feet. "He meant you, didn't he? About not stepping foot on board the *Deliverance*?"

It was a strange question to ask, for a maid would never be banned from a ship. More than likely, she would never set foot on one in the first place, unless she was accompanying a lady. "Of course he meant me." Teach couldn't help the bitterness that crept into his voice.

The look she gave him could be described only as pity. "And yet you're his only son," she said, almost to herself. Shaking her head, she withdrew her hand, and then cupped it inside her apron so as not to drip water across the floor. "I . . . I'm sorry. If you'll excuse me, I need to get back to work."

Teach watched her dart away. Only after she was gone did he realize he had yet to put her in her place. It would have been the perfect opportunity, for the two of them had been alone.

Oddly enough, he wasn't as keen on it as he had been before. He had a disconcerting feeling that despite their short acquaintance, Anne, the maid, understood him better than Miss Patience, the baron's daughter, ever would.

CHAPTER 7

Anne

The next morning Anne stood in the kitchen, kneading the dough for breakfast scones, her arms covered in flour. She was not usually one to make a mess while she cooked, but the kitchen appeared as if the flour bag had exploded. She continued to pound the table and form the round shapes.

The rest of the house was quiet. Neither the masters nor their guests were awake, and she was grateful for the reprieve.

The burn on her hand was no longer painful. Anne had been so shocked yesterday, thinking Master Drummond had meant *her* when he'd actually meant his son wasn't to step foot on one of his ships.

She'd stood between the two of them and thought Master Drummond had figured out her plans to get aboard.

Thankfully for her, that wasn't the case. Unfortunately for Teach, Master Drummond controlled him, like everyone else under his roof. And Teach appeared just as helpless to do anything about it.

To be banned from his father's own ship, she couldn't imagine what that must feel like. Nor did she want to.

It was almost enough to make her feel sorry for him.

Still, Teach had a roof over his head. He would always have plenty of money to spend and food to eat. And he would soon be married to the daughter of a baron.

From what Anne had seen of Miss Patience, she wished Teach luck. He would certainly need it.

Throughout the evening meal the previous day, Miss Patience had taken every opportunity to make Anne look like a fool or drop things. Several times she had even attempted to send Anne sprawling.

Margery eventually took pity on Anne and had Mary serve Miss Patience the cold meats and cheeses instead.

Teach sat on the opposite side of the table, and Anne was unsure which situation was worse. He'd guessed correctly that she had placed something in the tartlet, although he would have a hard time proving it. Anne had thrown out the seeds as soon as she'd returned to the kitchen, and had vowed not to try anything so foolish again.

The rooster in the yard crowed, signaling sunrise. Sara walked into the kitchen and regarded Anne for a moment. "Do you need some help?" she asked.

Anne stopped to catch her breath, blowing a thick strand of

hair out of her face. "Thank you, I would appreciate it."

Sara nodded and grabbed a rag, then cleared the eggshells and excess flour from the table. At least one good thing had come out of Anne helping serve the meals. Sara was kinder to her now than she had been in the past few months. Unsure how long Sara's behavior would last, Anne was grateful to her for the moment.

While Sara finished cleaning, Anne baked the scones, and their hot buttery scent filled the air. Once they were ready, she covered them with a cloth. After pulling out the scraps of cold meat from the previous night's meal, as well as a carrot, she walked out to the stable, signaling to the cat. The master didn't care much for animals, but Margery had proven a valuable employee, so he allowed her to have her pet if she kept it away from the main house and fed it in the stable.

Margery had saved the cat from some street urchins who'd been torturing it, and had nursed it back to health. Anne suspected the housekeeper cared more for the cat than she did for her fellow humans.

Hurrying to the low brick building on the other side of the courtyard, Anne glanced up at the clear sky overheard. The air was brisk.

Leaving the door ajar to allow some light into the dark interior, she dumped the meat onto the floor and watched as the cat pounced, her back rippling with pleasure. From her pocket Anne pulled out the carrot. Then she approached the stall that housed the young master Drummond's horse. The stallion pawed the earth when he saw her and nipped at the treat in her hand.

Patting his black neck, Anne breathed in his smell. "You weren't meant to be cooped up like this, now, were you? Barely a chance to get out, with your master gone to sea. What would he do if I took you away from this place?"

"Perhaps you should try it and see what happens."

Gasping, Anne clutched her chest as she spun around. Leaning against the wall in the shadow of the door was the young master himself, dressed in a riding jacket, breeches, and riding boots.

"You should have made your presence known," she said, hating the breathlessness in her voice but unable to stop it.

"And ruin all the fun?" he asked, strolling toward her.

"It's not right to sneak up on someone."

"I didn't sneak up on you," he said, his eyes not leaving her face.

Taking a few steps to the side, she attempted to reach the doorway. "I have work to do."

Once again he blocked her path. "Your work can wait."

"I don't think Margery or your father would agree."

"I don't care what Margery or my father thinks. I've been looking for you. Now stand still. I'm getting tired of this constant cat and mouse," he said.

"Well, I'm tired of being chased," she snapped, forced to tip her head back and look up at him.

"Then stop running," he said. "I merely wanted to inquire after your hand."

In the dim light, half of his face was hidden in shadow. The other half looked tired and ashen. Gone was the arrogance from the previous day. He didn't appear as intimidating as before, with his shoulders now slightly hunched.

Anne spoke without thinking. "Does your future wife know you've been looking for me?"

His eyes widened in surprise, and he paused for a moment, before a look of annoyance crossed his face. "You forget your place," he said.

"And you, yours."

He laughed shortly, his teeth flashing white in the gloom. "Tell me, Anne. How old are you?"

"Sixteen."

"And where did you serve before coming here?"

"Why do you ask?"

"Because I want to know how you've made it this far with that tongue in your head. You don't speak like a common maid, and you certainly don't act like one. I intended to give you a good tongue-lashing, yet I find myself on the defensive where you're concerned. Why is that?"

"Perhaps you are too used to people bowing to your believed superiority, and don't understand when your presence is not desired."

"'Believed superiority'? Good Lord, you almost act as if you were the lady of the house and I were no more than a common footman."

Her back stiffened. "I'm sorry it appears that way, sir, but I refuse to be *treated* like a common maid," she said, for it was the truth. Her father had never required her to work. Anne's mother had been the one to insist that Anne at least learn how to cook, although she'd often been overruled by Andrew Barrett's stronger personality.

Stepping around the young master, Anne prepared to return to the kitchen, but his hand shot out and he grasped her wrist, his skin warm against hers. A bolt of awareness shot through her, and Anne stumbled backward, her head hitting the door of the stall. Tears sprang to her eyes from the pain.

His voice when he spoke was weary. "Please, I'm sorry. Don't run away again. I've just spent the last twelve months on a ship and have quite forgotten how to behave. I promise to leave you alone, if you'll simply stay put for one moment."

Rubbing her head, she gazed at him warily. This could be some kind of trick.

"What do you want?"

"Don't look at me like that," he said.

"Like what?"

"Like I'm the very devil himself."

"Thus far you have not proven yourself otherwise," she muttered.

"Yes, well, you're not exactly the innocent, now, are you?"

Her head shot up at his words. "What do you mean?" Did he know she'd taken another piece of cutlery last night? She hadn't planned on doing it, especially not after the tea incident with Master Drummond. But after that miserable supper, she knew she could never give up her plans to leave.

"I mean, you are as much at fault for our present situation as I am. In the market you attacked—"

"That's not true! You assaulted me—" she began.

"I didn't wield a pail," he countered.

"I acted in self-defense."

"You misunderstood my intentions."

She laughed out loud at that. "I'm quite sure I did not. I might be untested, but I know enough about men like you. There was no way I would let you take me anywhere to 'discuss' anything."

The young master gave her a long look. "Do I frighten you?" he asked at length.

Determined not to show him just how much, she shook her head. "No," she lied.

"Why not?"

"Because you are not the master of this house. Your father is, and I serve him." *Though, not for much longer.*

He raised one sardonic eyebrow. "And do you like serving him?"

"It does not matter whether I like it or not," she replied.

"But you choose to remain here. You could seek a situation elsewhere, and yet you do not."

"There is no guarantee that my next position would be an improvement," she said.

"What if someone were to do just that?" he asked.

"Do what?"

"Promise you that if you left here, your life would be greatly improved."

Anne shifted, uncomfortable with his line of questioning. "No one can promise me that, for no one can predict the future."

The stallion whinnied in the stall, tired of being ignored. Teach approached his horse and stroked the neck, like Anne had done just moments before. "Do you ride?" he asked.

Surprised by the sudden change in topic and by his apparent civility, Anne responded without thinking. "Yes, my father taught me."

"Was he a groom?"

Too late, Anne realized her mistake. It was rare indeed for a maid to know how to ride a horse.

She was saved from answering when William opened a door farther down the row of stalls. "Teach, there you are, old chap. I've been looking all over for you. When is breakfast—" He broke off when he saw Anne standing there, a sly grin lighting his face. "Ah. I'm sorry. Was I interrupting something?"

Teach did a poor job of masking his displeasure. "Forgive me, William. I needed some exercise and was about to take an early ride. Would you care to join me?"

William dragged his eyes away from Anne. "Before breakfast? You know how I feel about my tea and crumpets in the morning."

Teach snorted. "How could I forget? Though, instead of reaching for a cheesecake, I suggest you get out and enjoy the morning air."

William reached defensively for his waist and attempted a laugh. It sounded forced. "You always were an early riser. Now I understand the appeal."

"You would have earned better marks in school if you'd decided to give it a try."

"Well, I'd like to try now," William said, casting a meaningful look in Anne's direction. "You always beat me to the punch, don't you, Teach?" There was a hint of bitterness behind his words.

"You may leave us, Anne," Teach said.

Shuddering, Anne slipped through the door closest to her. William was a most disagreeable fellow.

And he was Teach's closest friend. Her mother had often told her that good clothes did not make an evil man more kind, and in William's case it was true.

She needed to remember to keep her thoughts to herself. Ever since Teach had arrived, she'd been far more outspoken than her position allowed. Her father had enjoyed her outspokenness and had even encouraged her to express herself openly, but Anne doubted anyone in this household appreciated it.

Teach and his guests would be gone soon. Only two more

days here at the Drummond estate, and then they would journey to the countryside, to the Herveys', where Teach could continue to woo his future bride and his old school chum could annoy their maids for the next fortnight.

Until they left, she planned to keep a civil tongue, avoid Miss Patience's feet, and make sure she was never left alone in Teach's company.

Anne had no talent for planning. If she had, she would have stayed behind in the kitchen later that afternoon instead of venturing outside the garden walls. The master and his guests had just returned from a picnic and had gone upstairs to prepare for supper.

She took that moment to steal away, knowing that everything was ready and waiting for the evening meal. Beneath the shelter of the branches of her favorite tree, she rested against the trunk and closed her eyes. It felt good to get away from the flurry and commotion of the house, if only for a few moments. She was so exhausted, she could hardly think straight. Despite having lived here for more than five months, she still considered it a strange house and was constantly stressed and tense. These short breaks of solitude were what helped keep her going, and she relished every second she could find.

Her rest was short-lived, for she heard the sound of a horse and approaching voices.

"You should not have waited for me, Miss Patience," a familiar voice called out. "I told you I would return momentarily."

"But I wanted to have a word with you, Edward. In private." Miss Patience's voice was breathless.

Anne was not surprised Miss Patience used his Christian name. It was obvious to all that they admired each other. As Miss Patience neared, Anne could make out her shape through the leaves. She was dressed in a handsome gown of deep blue.

The young master sat astride his stallion, still dressed in his riding clothes. Anne had been under the impression that all of the occupants of the house were either changing or resting. Apparently she'd been mistaken.

Teach slid down from the saddle as Miss Patience walked up to him. "And I told you, now is not the most opportune time. Perhaps it could wait until later," he said.

Anne froze. The trunk of the tree no longer seemed an adequate hiding spot for her small money chest. She sent up a silent prayer that neither of them would notice her and that the shade of the willow branches was sufficient to conceal her presence.

"I don't understand. It's almost time for supper. Where did you go?"

"To retrieve my book," he said, his voice weary.

"Your book?"

"Yes, my book. I made the mistake of allowing William to look at it while we were out this afternoon, and he misplaced it. I didn't want to wait until tomorrow to recover it."

Miss Patience laughed, obviously unsure if she'd heard him right. "You were prepared to miss supper because of a silly book?"

The lines of tension in Teach's body were visible in the evening light. He had a faint growth of stubble, and his skin was sallow.

"I have no appetite," he said.

Miss Patience took another step forward. "Are you unwell? Perhaps I can think of a way to make you feel better." She gave him a sly look, running her fingers up his arm. "If you'd like, we could stay out here and discuss *Paradise Lost*. William said it's all about Adam and Eve in the Garden of Eden. Since we were so rudely interrupted before, we could make this little spot our very own Eden."

Anne did not imagine the shudder that ran through Teach. He took Miss Patience's wrist and removed it from his shoulder. "I think it would be best if you went back inside. Your mother would not like you being out here without a chaperone."

"Do you think I care?" she asked.

"You should. It's not prudent for you to be in a man's presence without an escort."

Anne rolled her eyes. No one ever worried about *her* safety when she went to the marketplace all by herself. Was it possible she had more freedom than Miss Patience?

"You weren't concerned about that yesterday afternoon when you agreed to meet me in the rose garden," she said.

"I know. And I apologize for that."

"What is there to apologize for? Nothing happened," she said.

It was impossible for Anne to determine if Teach was disappointed or not. He gave no response.

"You used to enjoy our private conversations, Edward. What has changed?"

Teach ran a hand through his hair. "Being gone for a year has . . . changed me, as I'm sure it's changed you. We should spend some time reacquainting ourselves—"

"What nonsense is this? *Reacquainting* ourselves? You used to enjoy our kisses just as much as I did," Patience purred, leaning closer, her body pressed against the length of his. "We need to discuss our engagement."

"I've only just returned home. Surely there's no rush."

She took a step back, her bottom lip jutting forward. "Not for you, perhaps. While you've been off enjoying your adventures, I've been forced to remain at home, searching for some kind of entertainment. Now that you're back, I no longer need any distractions."

He frowned, a small muscle working in his jaw. "Is that all I am to you? A distraction?"

"Don't be ridiculous. You know I care about you. Only yesterday you were willing to meet me in private. What has changed? Do you not still find me attractive?"

In answer, Teach's shoulders hunched forward in a violent spasm. Anne jumped to her feet, tempted to call out, but there was nothing to be done. Teach turned his head too late, spewing his portion of the picnic down the front of Miss Patience's dress.

Anne's hands flew to her mouth.

Miss Patience froze, a look of horror spreading across her face. The only sound to escape her lips was a repeated whimper, like a sick pup, her bottom lip quivering.

Teach was no help, for he continued to retch by her side. At least he'd had the decency to turn himself slightly, so that she was no longer in the line of fire. The damage, however, was done.

The two stood next to each other, each one caught up in their own misery. It would have been difficult to decide who appeared more upset at the moment.

Shaking with suppressed laughter, Anne watched as Miss Patience eventually turned in the direction of the house, slightly bent at the waist. With mincing steps she disappeared through the archway back into the gardens, muttering beneath her breath the entire time.

Only when the young master dropped to his knees was Anne brought up short. By now, dry heaves racked his body, but still he did not stop.

Anne vacillated for a second more before sweeping the branches out of the way and going to him. Until now the stallion had stood quietly by his side, but he whinnied and approached as Anne bent over his owner.

Sweat soaked Teach's brow as well as his shirt. His eyes widened in surprise when he saw her.

Reaching forward, Anne grabbed him under the arms and attempted to help him up, careful to stay out of range. After hesitating, he threw a heavy arm over her shoulders, leaning on her as she directed him back to the house. She picked up the reins, and the stallion followed behind.

Their advancement was slow. He was at least a head taller than Anne, and she felt like a child next to him. He certainly resembled an old man at the moment, not the vibrant young man he was. By the time they reached the stable, the sun was low in the sky.

The groom rushed out when he saw them, and Anne stepped to the side. "Here, Tom, take him to his room," she said, for she could not have made it up the stairs under Teach's weight. The two of them disappeared while Anne took the stallion back to the barn. Once she removed his saddle, she brushed him down and gave him fresh grain, before returning to the house.

Mary and Sara rushed by her, each carrying a bucket of water.

"Mr. Edward is sick," Mary said over her shoulder.

"Aye, he was sick all over Miss Patience," Sara said, unable to hide the smile on her face. "You should have heard her when she came in. She swears like a sailor when she thinks no one is near."

Margery came back down the stairs just then, carrying a dark blue dress. Even if Anne hadn't recognized it, the smell alone would have been enough to tell her it was Miss Patience's garment.

Thrusting it into Anne's arms, Margery said, "Here. Do what ye can with this. It's new, and the missus doesn't want to throw it away."

Anne retreated to the washing kitchen, grateful to be out of the chaos but resentful that she was left to clean up the mess. Miss Patience was nothing more than a spoiled child, and Anne was sick of everyone treating the girl as if she were a queen.

Once the water in the large pot had boiled, Anne removed it from the fire and dunked the entire dress into it. It would need to soak for several hours, if not a few days.

The mark was large, the color of burgundy, and despite the dark shade of the dress, Anne didn't hold out much hope of ridding the garment of the stain. She had packed their picnic lunch.

While salt and wine could get out a grease stain, she doubted that salt and grease would remove a wine stain. From the looks of it, the young master had had his fair share of the liquid that afternoon.

With a stout stick she stirred the water, lifting the material out every once in a while to check its progress. It was indeed a beautiful gown, although on closer inspection she saw that the material wasn't as rich as she'd first thought, the workmanship not of the highest quality.

Anne left the wash kitchen for a time to help Margery serve supper. Neither Teach nor Miss Patience was present during the evening meal, and the conversation was subdued. Lady Hervey picked at her food, while Lord Hervey and Master Drummond shot each other dark looks.

It was left to William to try to lighten the mood.

When Anne returned to the kitchen later in the evening, after the guests had retired, she removed the dress and held it up to the candlelight. Just as she'd suspected, the stain was still there, although it had faded somewhat. About to return it to the water, she noticed that the seam on one of the sleeves had come undone. She yanked at the thread, but instead of the thread breaking, the material simply continued to unravel. Glancing over her shoulder, she quickly returned the dress to the pot, feeling as if she'd been tricked.

The dress might have been new, and Anne could do her best to return it to its former splendor, but there was no denying that it was poorly made.

Much like Miss Patience herself.

CHAPTER 8

Anne

The carriage drove away the next day in the pouring rain, the last of the houseguests safely inside it, along with Master Drummond himself. He was going with the Herveys in an attempt to smooth things over between the baron's daughter and his son. Their estate was a few hours' ride from the city, and they planned to discuss in which Hervey property Miss Patience and Teach would live. Coming from one of the oldest baronies in the country, the Herveys maintained four separate properties.

Standing alone in the doorway, Anne stared after them, wondering what she'd done to deserve such a heinous punishment. She was to tend to Teach until he was well, because he was too ill to travel with the rest of the party. Lady Hervey and Miss Patience had practically pushed each other out of the way to exit the house once Teach's illness had been confirmed.

Anne was not sorry to see them go and hoped they would not return before she quitted the house for good.

Behind her, Margery clucked like a mother hen, handing her some tea. "Here you go, Anne. Take this up to Mr. Edward now. See if his fever is any worse."

Resigned, she took the tray from Margery's hands. "I don't see why Sara can't take it up to him," Anne said. "Now that the master is gone, she should be free to leave the kitchen."

Margery shot her a sharp look. "Last night the young master requested that you bring the tea up to him in the morning, not Sara."

With his father no longer at home, Teach apparently got what he wanted. Anne was quite sure the Drummond men wouldn't know what to do if somebody outside the family ever said no to them.

The back stairs were dim, the rain hitting the windows with an intensity that rattled the panes. The sky outside fit her mood perfectly.

Anne reached the door and tapped it with her foot.

There was no response.

Should I take the tea back down? Or simply leave it by his bedside and hope that he wakes up before it's too cold?

Pushing the knob, Anne stepped into the shadowy interior, the room so dark that she could barely make out a form lying in the bed. After setting the tea on the table, being careful not to wake him, she turned to leave, and tripped over something on the floor.

It was a book, the pages weathered and worn. Crossing to the window, she held it up to the sliver of light falling between the heavy curtains, so as to read the title. *A New Voyage Round the World* by someone by the name of William Dampier. This was most likely the same volume he'd gone searching for yesterday after the picnic. Right before he'd vomited on his bride-to-be.

This was not some silly book. A "voyage" meant "traveling other than by a land route." It meant the open sea.

It meant freedom.

Curious, she read a page, for it had been more than a year since she'd last held something this dear in her hands.

I first set out of England on this voyage at the beginning of the year 1679, in the Loyal Merchant of London, bound for Jamaica, Captain Knapman Commander. I went a passenger, designing when I came thither, to go from thence to the Bay of Campeachy, in the Gulf of

Anne did not face the bed but suddenly knew he was awake. The skin prickled on the back of her neck, and she turned slowly, guilt causing her features to flush.

Teach watched her, no longer reclining but sitting up in his bed, his features pallid. "Are they gone?" he asked, his voice hoarse.

It took her a moment to register his words, for she saw that his nightshirt gaped open at the collar, clinging to his chest, drenched with sweat.

He repeated his question. "The houseguests. My father. Are they gone?"

"Ye . . . yes," Anne stammered. "About a quarter of an hour ago, sir."

He nodded and closed his eyes.

Returning to the bedside, she placed the book next to the tray and poured him a cup of tea. "Drink this, sir," she said, holding it out to him.

Opening his eyes, he glanced in her direction. He took the cup but had trouble holding it, and she did not release her grip. His hand clasped hers as he brought the cup to his parched lips. Her skin fairly burned beneath his touch, but he continued to drink like a person lost in the desert, seemingly unaware of any assistance.

Anne had trouble reconciling this image with the person who'd confronted her about the price of shrimp, and was surprised by an unexpected twinge of sympathy.

After replacing the cup in the saucer, she walked to the other side of the bed and wetted a damp cloth in the washbasin. His black hair was plastered to his brow, and she smoothed it away, just like her mother had done for her when she'd been sick with fever. She wiped the cloth across his forehead, and he turned in her direction, a relieved sigh escaping his lips as he watched her through heavy lids.

Anne pretended not to notice and wet the cloth once more.

"You're not going to run away again, are you?" he asked softly.

Every impulse told her she should, but for some reason she could not. "I should call a doctor," Anne said, still trying to cool his fevered skin.

He shook his head. "I don't want a doctor."

"But you need—"

"Read to me," he said.

Her hands paused, for his words were unexpected. "Sir?"

Leaning to the other side of the bed, the blankets pulled taut, he picked up the book. "Read to me. I know you know how." It was not a request.

Anne swallowed, the blood quickening in her veins. She remembered the familiarity with which he and Miss Patience had addressed each other. "It would not be right for me to read to you. You are betrothed to another."

His jaw clenched. "Which is exactly why there is no harm in it. You can rest assured that your virtue is yours to keep. I merely asked you to read," he said.

Anne bit her lip, returning the cloth to the basin. He was mocking her. He knew she'd heard his exchange with Miss Patience. It was clear his and Miss Patience's relationship was closer than either of their parents suspected.

Drying her hands on her apron, Anne searched her mind for a logical excuse not to remain. There were many.

Despite Teach's assurances, it would not be appropriate.

There were chores to be done.

Margery would come looking for her.

If Miss Patience found out, she would be livid.

Unfortunately, Anne did not give a whit about Miss Patience, and no matter if she read or not, there would always be chores to be done.

What could be the harm if she stayed? He was much too weak to get out of bed. He could be no threat in his present state, and she had been given specific instructions to tend to him.

If she left the door ajar as it was, there would be no cause for censure. He was to wed another; they simply needed to agree upon a date. There could be no harm in fulfilling his demand.

Teach waited, as if aware of the inner battle waging within her. In truth, Anne longed to find out more about William Dampier's voyage round the world. She imagined it was filled with glorious images and descriptions from destinations unknown.

"You may sit there," he said, pointing to the large armchair situated parallel to him.

Her mind made up, Anne took the book from his hands, walked back to the windows, and pulled the curtains aside. Settling herself in the armchair, she opened the pages once more.

Clearing her throat, she cast one last look at Teach. He gave her an almost imperceptible nod, and she began.

"Before the reader proceed any further in the perusal of this work I must bespeak a little of his patience here to take along with him this short account of it. It is composed of a mixed relation of places and actions in the same order of time in which they occurred: for which end I kept a journal of every day's observations."

For the next two hours Dampier's story wrapped the two of them in a foreign world. While other travelers at the time robbed and raided, Dampier wrote vibrant and detailed notes, describing the vegetation and bringing to life the inhabitants of the places he visited. Anne was transported in a merchant ship, similar to her father's, to the distant shores of the West Indies. She marched with the buccaneers through the jungles ahead of Spanish soldiers, raiding and pillaging small villages and large forts.

Anne felt Teach's gaze on her face. Eventually he closed his eyes, drifting in and out of sleep.

She was fascinated by Dampier's report of the Miskito Indians, a most remarkable race, and she was grateful he devoted several pages of his journal to their description. They were tall and strong, with copper-colored faces, long black hair, and stern expressions. Two Indians alone could supply an entire ship of buccaneers with food because of their fishing and hunting skills.

Anne paused, trying to picture such men. Her mother had told her stories about their ancestors, who'd come from the Spanish Main and settled on the island of Curazon.

Mapmakers had later changed the name to Curaçao, but the early Spaniards had referred to it as the *Isla de los Gigantes*, because of the Arawak tribesmen's formidable build.

There had not been enough gold or water to make staking a claim on the island worthwhile. The Dutch West India Company had eventually settled there in 1634, after the Spanish had left.

Because the land had been considered too dry to support large-scale plantations of sugar, coffee, or tobacco, hundreds of natives, including Anne's mother and her family, had been forced to raise food to feed the thousands of slaves awaiting shipment elsewhere.

Anne couldn't help wanting to know more about her mother's past, especially now that she was gone.

Teach opened his eyes. "Why have you stopped?" he asked.

She was unsure how to respond, afraid to reveal her true feelings.

He had an uncanny way of seeing through her, discerning her thoughts when she least expected or wanted him to. "You favor them, you know. The Miskito Indians."

"You've seen them?" she asked, incapable of hiding her enthusiasm.

He nodded weakly, a faint smile appearing on his face. "Oh yes. And if I were to ever command a ship myself, I'd want a whole crew of them. They're bold in a fight and excellent marksmen if supplied with proper guns and ammunition. They have extraordinary sight and can spot a sail at sea farther and better than anyone else I've met."

"I should so like to meet one," she said.

At that moment Margery appeared in the door, a disapproving frown on her face. "Excuse me, sir, but I need Anne downstairs in the kitchen to help with the cooking."

Teach's jaw tightened, but he merely nodded.

Disappointed, Anne closed the book and laid it on the bed beside him. "In case you want to continue reading," she said.

Teach shook his head. "No. When you bring me my dinner at noon, then we may continue the story," he said, loud enough for his words to reach Margery.

Nodding, Anne took the tea tray in her hands, attempting to hide her smile, but he caught her eye and winked. As Anne left his room, Margery closed the door behind her, but not before they heard a pleased sigh coming from the interior.

CHAPTER 9

Teach

Teach was asleep in his bed the next afternoon when he heard a commotion outside his room. He awoke, confused from a strange dream. In his dream he was the captain of a great ship and a large crew, but a sharp-tongued maid with copper-colored skin and thick black hair questioned his every command.

It was a surprise to wake to the sound of her voice. For a moment he thought he was still dreaming, until he recognized the sound of the other voice. It was Mary's, the blond maid in the house.

He waited, hoping their discussion would find an end, but it seemed to go on forever.

Too weak to move, he called out, "Anne? Anne!" It was no use. Groaning, he pulled the blankets up to his chin, willing the two girls to go away. Well, he hoped *one* of the girls would go away.

He wouldn't mind if Anne came to read to him again.

When she'd helped him out in the garden, he'd been rather surprised. Up until then their interactions had been anything but civil, yet she'd assisted him when he'd needed it most.

Even if he hadn't vomited on Patience, he wasn't convinced *she* would have come to his aid.

It was not the first time he'd been sick like this. The fever had a nasty habit of striking whenever Teach switched climates. Although it wouldn't last long, fever and chills would rack his body.

Rest was the only cure.

Outside his room the voices stopped. He heard footsteps marching down the hall.

Silence.

Teach tried to ignore the twinge of disappointment he felt. Anne should be coming within the hour with his food. He was looking forward to seeing her more than he cared to admit.

He was engaged, he reminded himself.

To Patience.

He had known Patience for several years now, and he was quite comfortable with her. She was like a well-worn shoe.

Teach cringed, imagining Patience's reaction to that description.

Anne was different. She intrigued him, for not only was she familiar with John Milton, but she claimed to know how to ride a horse. Patience had already proven she'd never heard of the poet, and the closest she ever got to a horse was when she stepped in and out of a carriage.

What could be the harm in getting to know Anne a little better? An acquaintance with her could prove useful if he hoped to help his father catch the thief in the house.

Closing his eyes, he began to doze off again, his thoughts turning once more to the sea and the mysterious maid under his father's roof.

There was a knock at the door.

"Yes?" he said, his heartbeat accelerating.

The door opened a moment later. Rolling over, Teach saw Mary coming toward him, a bowl of steaming broth on a tray. He frowned. "Where's Anne?"

Mary gave him a strained smile. "She's cleaning out the fireplaces in the guest rooms, sir," she said. "I brought you a little something for your sickness."

"Why can't you clean out the fireplaces?"

Mary's smile faltered. "I just thought that since Anne brought you breakfast, I'd give her a hand and bring you your dinner."

"You thought wrong. I made my instructions clear. Anne is the only one to bring me my food," Teach continued. His justification for the demand was that she had already been exposed to him. He didn't want to risk anyone else getting sick.

"But don't you want—"

"I want you to leave. From now on Anne is the only one to wait on me. You may go."

Mary still hesitated, clearly unwilling to give up so easily. She moistened her lips and glanced back at the door. He watched her through narrowed eyes.

"Are you sure there isn't anything I can do for you?" she asked, her voice full of innuendo, as she placed the tray on his bedside table.

Teach's head pounded. "Absolutely sure. Now I suggest you leave. Otherwise, I'll be forced to tell your beau, John, about your cheating ways."

Mary blinked in surprise at the rebuff. "I don't know what you're talking about," she said, holding her hand up to her generous bosom.

Teach took a deep breath, wishing, not for the first time, that he were still at sea. "Yes, you do. When William and I came back the day before yesterday from our morning ride, you and the groom were . . . how shall I say it? Otherwise engaged. If I catch you doing that again, I will have no choice but to let my friend John know exactly what kind of girl he plans to marry."

"I . . . Tom, he . . . he helped me . . . because I fell . . ."

Teach watched, unimpressed, as Mary tried to defend herself. She was clearly not quick-witted. "It appears you both fell," he said.

Scowling, Mary stomped toward the door, muttering something beneath her breath about seeking a different position elsewhere.

"Tell Anne to come here," he commanded before she closed the door with a loud bang.

Teach sighed, hoping Mary would make good on her threat and leave. He wouldn't be surprised if she turned out to be the crook. The less he knew about her exploits, the better. When he'd met John last year on the merchant ship, they had become close friends. John had mentioned that his girl was seeking a situation within a respectable household.

Unfortunately, there was nothing respectable about Mary, and Teach now regretted having asked his father to give her a job. Even if he hadn't been engaged to Patience, Teach would never have considered Mary as a prospect. She was too eager.

Teach liked a challenge.

He remembered fondly his first few attempts at wooing Patience. She'd played hard to get in the beginning, but he knew she'd enjoyed the attention. If there was one thing Patience *loved*, it was being the center of attention.

A knock at the door brought him back to the present. "Come in," he said.

Anne poked her head in, a wary look on her face. The girl was constantly on edge. He had the distinct impression that it took her a while to trust someone.

She stepped inside, rubbing her hands down her apron. It was covered with gray ash, and several strands of hair had crept out of her cap.

Teach's hand itched to touch them. She reminded him of

an exotic flower growing on the islands of the West Indies and seemed out of place in this cold, sterile environment.

"Sir?" she said.

His eyes met hers. Teach was aware how he must look, with his jaw covered with stubble, his face flushed. Everything was as she'd left it a few hours earlier, with the exception of one window being open, allowing a cool breeze to drift through the room. The chicken broth steamed in the bowl, filling the air with its scent. "You're late," he said, his voice rough.

She pointed to the tray at his side. "You have your soup," she said.

"Yes, but you are the only one I wish to bring me my meals. That includes breakfast, dinner, and supper."

"But surely the others are capable of bringing you your meals?" she asked incredulously.

"No doubt."

"If you'd like me to read to you, I can come later—"

"I do want you to read to me, and that is precisely why I wish for you to bring me my food, no one else," he said, pulling at the collar of his nightshirt. "Especially not that fool Mary," he muttered beneath his breath. "You're to let me know at once if you catch her anywhere near Tom, the groom. Is that understood?"

Anne bristled at his words. She opened her mouth as if to say something, but quickly shut it again.

"What?" Teach asked.

"Nothing, sir."

"That's not true. You were about to say something. Does it have anything to do with Mary?"

"It's not my place to say."

"It is if I'm asking. What do you know about Mary?"

There was a long pause before Anne spoke. He could see the uncertainty in her eyes.

"Out with it," he said.

"I have reason to believe that she engaged in an inappropriate relationship with one of your guests."

Teach's eyes widened in surprise. A guest? "You do? Why?"

Once more she hesitated.

"Come closer. Now tell me why you suspect that."

Anne took a few steps forward until she came to stand at the foot of his bed. Teach was keenly aware that he did not look his best. Sweat glistened on his brow, and he could feel the heat in his cheeks.

"Your father has made it very clear that he doesn't want any sort of *involvement* among the household staff. I'm sure that extends to your guests as well."

Teach squirmed beneath her steady gaze, remembering his earlier conduct. "I'm well aware of my father's rules. You don't need to remind me," he said.

Anne reached into her pocket, pulled out a small note, and handed it to him. "Your friend, the Earl of Lorimar, is not without fault in the matter, sir. See for yourself."

"William? You must be mistaken."

Anne scoffed, obviously not surprised Teach would come to his friend's defense. "Yes, William. He has clearly taken advantage of the fact that Mary, as a dependent in your household, has nowhere else to turn. He would compromise her position for his own enjoyment," she said.

Teach's eyebrows drew together as he read the note.

My darling,

I can scarce tell you how I felt when I first saw you in this house. I could almost not eat, for my stomach was truly in knots. You cannot imagine the depth of my emotions, and I myself am unable to fully convey to you how strongly I have come to feel for you.

Please tell me you feel the same.

Forever your loving,

William

Teach's own stomach was in knots, but for entirely different reasons. What a pile of rubbish. How many times had he told William to stop with this nonsense?

"Where did you find this?" he asked Anne.

"I found it while I was cleaning out the fireplace in the earl's room."

"And have you asked Mary about this?"

Anne nodded, folding her hands in front of her. "Yes, sir. Just before you called me in, sir."

So that was what the two of them had been bickering about. "And what did she have to say?"

"She insisted the note wasn't meant for her, claiming she cannot read."

Not many maids could read, but there were ways around it, especially if she was trying to impress an interested lover. "But you mean to tell me this note *was* intended for Mary?" Teach said at length. Teach had noticed Mary making eyes at William during the meal.

Anne nodded.

"Then she's even worse than I thought."

Anne blinked. "I beg your pardon?"

Teach closed his eyes, pinching the bridge of his nose. "I caught Mary kissing Tom when I returned from my early morning ride the other day."

"Again?" Anne asked, before clamping her hands over her mouth.

Teach snorted. "So this isn't the first time it's happened. Well, William hardly acted the jealous lover, even if the note was meant for her." In fact, William had appeared quite amused, and Teach had been forced to drag him away.

Anne's face burned with her embarrassment.

Teach did not bother to mask his impatience. "If it wasn't

Mary, then I have no idea who the intended recipient was. Perhaps he meant for *you* to find it."

Anne grimaced.

Ever observant, Teach frowned. "You do not like William?"

Anne shot him a look, as if cursing his watchful eyes. "It's not my place to either like or dislike your frie—"

"Oh, stop this nonsense," he said. "If I ask you a simple question, I expect an honest answer. Do you or do you not like the Earl of Lorimar?" he asked. He wasn't always this ill-tempered. There was something about this girl that touched on his nerves. She was unlike anyone else he'd ever met.

"I fail to understand how my opinion matters, sir."

"Well, for some reason it matters to me. Answer the question. Please."

She studied the floor, as if she wished for the flowers in the carpet to swallow her whole. "My father always told me, the enemy is dangerous who wears the mask of a friend."

"Are you saying William wears a mask? That he is not my true friend?"

"I would not seek out his companionship, sir," she said at length.

Teach was quiet. He was pleased by her confession, although he did not know why. William was one of his closest friends, was he not? As far as he knew, there'd never been any competition between the two of them. At school Teach had often laughed at William's antics, for William provided a nice foil for Teach's more serious nature.

William always joked and said Teach had what William wanted most: good looks, a sharp intellect, and the ability to command respect.

Teach argued back and said that William had what Drummond wanted most: a lofty title, a larger estate, and a life without labor.

Anne broke the silence. "You do not look well, sir."

His lips twitched. "I did not ask how I looked."

"I meant no offense, sir. I simply said it out of concern for your health."

He raised an eyebrow at her. "You're concerned about me, are you?"

"Naturally. As the master of the house—"

"Ah, but you said yourself I'm not the master."

Anne made a small movement. Teach could imagine her stomping her small foot in frustration.

"Now you're twisting my words," she muttered.

He relaxed against the pillows, a chuckle escaping him. He was actually enjoying himself. "What else would you tell me, Anne? What else about my appearance bothers you? Are my eyes too close? Is my mouth too large?"

"At the moment, yes," she said.

His laughter dissolved into a coughing fit, and his face flamed.

Anne stepped around the foot of the bed, to be of some assistance, but he waved her away. When he stopped, he leaned back, wheezing. Anne remained resolutely near his side. "I'm sorry, sir. I shouldn't have said that."

"No, no. You were quite right. I said I wished you to be honest. I should never demand honesty if I'm not prepared to hear it."

The fact that he had admitted defeat was telling. If he hadn't been so sick, Teach would not have given in so quickly.

Picking up the book from the table, Anne motioned to his soup. "If you like, I will continue to read for you. But only if you promise to eat," she said.

Teach bowed his head, much like he had when he'd been little and his mother had told him to finish his meal. "Very well. I will eat my soup. But only if you promise to always tell me what you're thinking."

"Agreed," Anne said.

Teach smiled, pleased with himself.

Anne sat down in the armchair beside his bed and opened the book once more.

CHAPTER 10

Anne

For the next five days Anne divided her time between the kitchen and Teach's room. Whenever she passed the housekeeper, Margery's mouth turned down and she sniffed her displeasure. Sara and Mary were beside themselves, wondering why Anne was able to get out of so many chores while the two of them had to compensate for her alleged inactivity.

Anne would have disagreed. If anything, the three of them left her more than her fair share of work. She went to bed even later than usual to make up for the amount of time spent reading to the young master, and was up before dawn to head to the market and start the proceedings all over again.

While she was tired and overworked, Anne hadn't been this happy since she'd entered Master Drummond's service. Teach still burned with fever, although his face had regained most of its color and he wasn't as weak as he'd been on the first day.

Anne brought him broth and continued to wipe his brow, doing her best to nurse him back to health. Master Drummond had sent word that Teach was to travel to the Hervey estate as soon as he was well enough, for Miss Patience was eager to see him again. Anne told herself she was simply facilitating their reunion.

For his part, Teach was quite the model patient. He ate when she told him to eat, and slept when she told him to sleep. And he did not make any untoward advances, appearing to enjoy Anne's company. She believed he looked forward to the reading almost as much as she did. She grew accustomed to his attentive eyes, surprised that he didn't disturb her as much as he had when they'd first met. She was far too engrossed in the story.

Dampier's attention to detail was inspiring, providing a tempting glimpse of the riches and adventures to be found beyond the shores of England. Much of what he described resembled the stories her mother had told her.

When Anne read that Will, one of the Miskito Indians accompanying Dampier on his voyages, was accidentally left behind on a remote island, she was surprised by the depth of her despair. In a way she felt a certain kinship to the young man, for despite the many people surrounding her, she too knew what it felt like to be left alone.

Three years later, when Dampier returned to the island, he was astonished to see that Will was still alive. He'd waited to greet them and had killed and dressed three goats with cabbage leaves for the shore-going party.

Tears ran down Anne's cheeks unchecked, and with the edge of her apron, she wiped her eyes. Embarrassed by her show of emotion, Anne cleared her throat but was unable to continue.

Her mother had been taken from her own people but never given the chance to return. Although Jacqueline's life in England had been better than the punishing work she'd performed as a slave in the West Indies, she had still left a part of herself behind.

If everything worked out, Anne hoped to make the journey back to the island in her mother's stead.

Teach watched her, his gaze soft, but he didn't speak. The light from the candles created muted shadows in the room. It was late in the evening.

"I should stop here," Anne said, closing the book reluctantly.

"Please don't," he said.

She managed a tremulous smile. "I think it's a good note to end on. I'm not sure I could handle any more heartache."

Teach returned her smile. "Ah, but it turned out all right in the end, didn't it? The Miskitos are a hearty bunch."

"They sound very brave. And strong."

He continued to watch her. "I could easily picture you as a Miskito princess, dressed in animal skins from head to toe."

Anne's face flooded with warmth, and she stood, disconcerted by the light in his eyes and the boldness of his words.

Perhaps she should remind him of his father's rules. In the past few days they'd built up a rapport between them. He teased her openly, and while she wasn't as comfortable teasing him back, there was an undeniable connection between the two of them.

"You shouldn't say such things," she said, placing the book on the bedside table.

"Why not?" Teach asked.

"Because I am not a princess." She picked up the supper tray, preparing to leave.

He grinned, unabashed, clutching his hand to his chest. "Oh, forgive me. You're quite right. You're not a princess."

Anne shook her head at him, trying to suppress a smile.

"You're a queen. From now on I shall refer to you as Queen Anne," he said, giving her a mock bow, made even more ridiculous because he still lay in his bed.

"Good night, sir," she said pointedly.

Even from across the room he pinned her to the spot with his gaze. "You'll come back again tomorrow, won't you?"

"I'll do my best," she said, ignoring the tingle of anticipation that skittered down her spine.

"Until then, Queen Anne."

Down the hallway she ran into Margery, a basketful of sheets and linens in her arms. Margery glared when she saw the smile on Anne's face.

"Here," the housekeeper said, thrusting her load toward Anne. "I was just bringing these to you. You may go and make up the beds and also return some of the master's clothes to him."

"Now?" It was a quarter past nine in the evening. Anne's limbs felt as if they were made of lead, and she could think of nothing besides the comfort of her own mattress.

"Yes, now. Have something better to do, do you?"

Anne shook her head. "No, it's simply so late. Surely the beds could be made tomorrow morning."

She did not see the back of Margery's hand until it connected with her cheek, the force of the blow causing Anne's eyes to water. Nearly dropping the tray, Anne staggered backward as a cup fell to the floor. It shattered at her feet.

Margery shook with rage, the basket resting on her hip.

"Don't talk back to me, girl," she hissed. "I'm still in charge around here, despite what you think."

The door to Teach's chambers flew open, and he stood there, his nightshirt stuffed into a pair of breeches, his feet bare. "Is everything all right?" he asked, holding a candlestick aloft.

Anne bent quickly and picked up the broken porcelain, her back to him, the skin below her left eye stinging.

"Fine, sir. The clumsy girl simply dropped a cup," Margery said.

"What do you have there?" he asked her.

"Sheets and linens, sir. As well as some of your shirts an' breeches. I was just about to bring them to you."

"Surely that could wait until morning," he said.

At last Anne stood, but she kept her face averted. She felt

rather than saw the ominous look Margery shot in her direction.

"Aye, it could, sir, but with Anne being gone so much these days, there's simply no time to rest if we want to get everything done."

The old witch made it sound as if she and the others were overworked. Without the master in the house and with Teach still sick, the cooking had been kept to a minimum. And Margery had both Sara and Mary to help her with the cleaning.

"Yes, well, why don't you take that tray from her, Margery, and return to the kitchen. Retire for the evening. I'm sure the beds can wait until morning."

"Why, thank you, sir. I greatly appreciate it," Margery said smugly.

It was all Anne could do to keep a civil tongue in her head as Margery smiled, an evil glint in her eyes. They exchanged loads, and Margery strolled down the hallway, toward the back stairs, humming a tune the entire time.

"Bring me my clothing," Teach said, holding out his hands.

Anne's chest tightened as she approached him, and she angled her face, careful to keep it in the shadows. But like a Miskito Indian, the young master was far too observant. He sucked in a deep breath when he saw her. Taking her chin in his hand, he brought the candlestick closer.

"She did this to you," he said, his eyes flashing. Taking Anne by the hand, he led her back into his room. She sat down in the now familiar armchair as he wet a cloth and dipped it into water, before holding it up to her burning skin.

Anne flinched.

He cursed beneath his breath, and a pulse beat at his temple. "I'll speak to her. I'll tell her that if she ever lifts a hand to you again, I'll—"

"You'll do what?" Anne asked, unable to keep her silence any longer. "Send her packing? Try to replace her with someone else? Who's to say the next person you hire will be any better?" Anne shook her head, pushing his hand away. "If you say anything to her, it will only make matters worse."

"This is my fault," he said, frowning.

"How? You could not help getting sick. You were too weak to—" Anne began, but just then she spied something unusual over his shoulder. In his haste to get up, he'd thrown the coverlet back. At the foot of his bed were two large stones, round and smooth. The sheets were marred with ash. Anne pushed Teach aside and felt one of them. It was still warm to the touch.

Turning on him, her eyes wide with shock, she pointed an accusing finger. "You lied about your fever?"

He straightened slowly, his expression masked. "Not initially. That first day you came to me, I was extremely sick. You saw that."

"Yes, but by the fourth day some of your color had returned."

He nodded.

"Were you still sick?" she asked.

He had the decency to flush. "I was truly ill in the beginning, but I might have nursed it along a bit."

"Why would you do that?"

"Because I needed an excuse to speak with you," he said, as if it were the most natural thing in the world.

Her heart skipped a beat. "About what, sir?"

"About anything. Everything. I enjoy conversing with you. Don't look at me like that. Is my request so distasteful that you'd choose to return to your chores rather than spend another minute in my company?"

Eight days ago she might have said yes. Now she wasn't so sure. "If I don't do my chores, no one else will, sir."

He waved his hand. "Margery can do them."

Anne nearly laughed out loud, pointing to the inflamed side of her face. "Yes, we've seen how much she enjoys that. Margery is the housekeeper. I'm simply the maid. I would never ask her to fulfill my duties."

"You said it yourself the other day, you're not a common maid, now, are you?"

Anne remained silent, for she did not know how to respond. She wasn't sure what she was most upset about—the fact that he'd prolonged his "illness" and she'd incurred the wrath of Margery as a result, or the fact that she'd enjoyed herself in his company and would most likely do it again if given the choice, despite the fact that he was to wed another.

Alarmed and confused, Anne prepared to flee, but Teach

reached out and caught her hand, his thumb smoothing the skin. The movement stole the breath from her lungs.

"This has to stop. You can't keep running away from me, Anne. I mean you no harm. Truly I don't. I've never met anyone like you before. You . . . intrigue me."

Anne withdrew from his touch. "You've just spent a year at sea, encountering untold dangers, and you find me interesting? I've never been anywhere. I've never seen anything." She might have been inexperienced, but she wasn't so naïve as to believe him.

"And that is precisely what is so fascinating. When you read, your face lights up. Those pages come to life for you, just as they do for me," Teach said. "Whether you are aware of it or not, you and I are alike, Anne. We feel things differently than others."

"That book . . . it's fascinating. Anyone would feel the same."

Teach took a step forward, and she immediately retreated, her legs hitting the bedpost, her eyes meeting his.

"That's not true. My father has refused to look at it, though I've offered to lend it to him. Patience could not be bothered to open it, much less read it. Not even William truly paid attention at the picnic, which was why he left it lying out in the field."

"Perhaps they're otherwise occupied—"

Teach waved his hand. "No one is more occupied than you, Anne. Not my father. Not Patience, and definitely not William."

"Then they have no need for escape," Anne said, before she could stop herself.

Teach's eyebrows drew together. "Is that what you wish for?"

Anne could not believe she'd been so careless, and her throat tightened on any response she might have given.

"Would it surprise you to know that I've sometimes wished the same thing?" Teach asked. "To leave this place and find out what life would be like on one of those islands Dampier describes so beautifully? Admit it, you've dreamt about it too."

It was pointless to deny it. Teach had an uncanny ability to see through any subterfuge with her. "But they're only dreams. They aren't real."

"They could be. I know you don't wish to live the rest of your life under my father's roof."

This conversation was far too dangerous. Anne searched desperately for a way to change its direction. "Every maid wishes for something greater. Take Sara, for instance. I'm sure she'd like nothing more than to stay home and care for her mother, but she has to work. That's her reality, as well as mine."

"But that's what I'm telling you. I realize you have to work. You're a maid, but you're also different, Anne. You must know that not many house servants know how to read, yet you do. I've also seen you glance at that gold watch in your pocket when you thought I wasn't looking, so you must be able to tell time. I've never met a maid who possessed such a treasure."

It was true. Most commoners measured time by the morning and evening church bells, the passage of the sun, or the movement of the tides. Anne's father had bought the watch on one of his trips to London and had given it to her mother. Before she'd passed away, she'd given it to Anne. It was the only thing remaining from Anne's previous life. That and her memories.

"I didn't steal it, if that's what you're suggesting," Anne snapped, a guilty flush creeping into her cheeks.

"I never suggested you did. I'm simply pointing out that you are unlike anyone else I've ever met."

"I'm sure Miss Patience knows how to tell time." Anne threw the words, like a pail of cold water to hit him in the face. They had the desired effect, and he stepped back, his expression masked.

"If that's all, sir," she said, taking up the linens and candlestick.

"Leave the linens for tomorrow. It's late."

"Yes, sir." Anne closed the door on her way out. Shaken, she headed to the west wing to start making the beds, disregarding Teach's instructions. As tired as she was, she knew she would not be able to sleep. Her mind replayed the events of the past few days, as well as Teach's professed interest.

He wasn't the only observant one in the household, and Anne could see a battle being waged. He was torn between wanting to please his father and wanting to make his own path.

Master Drummond dictated every aspect of everyone's life in this house, and Miss Patience was his choice for his son's bride. It didn't mean she was Teach's. It was not a stretch to imagine that Teach would look for any opportunity to rebel.

What would be more defiant than having a tryst with someone in his father's own household?

Not liking the direction of her thoughts, Anne hurried through the rooms, making the beds by the light of the single candle, trying hard not to picture the chamber she had just vacated.

She was halfway through the task when she heard footsteps in the hallway. Extinguishing the flame, Anne peered out through the half-open door, and spied Teach, dressed in a heavy riding cloak and boots, striding toward the back stairs, the candle in his own hands flickering with each step.

Curious, she followed him through the darkened house. Where was he off to at such a late hour? Not eight days ago he'd had a high fever. Now here he was, leaving in the middle of the night? Surely nothing good would come of this.

Tiptoeing down the stairs, she felt her way along the dim interior. In the kitchen all was silent. Margery had obviously taken his advice and retired. There was also no sign of Sara or Mary, and the embers in the fireplace cast an eerie glow about the room.

Anne reached the back door and was about to step out, when Teach came barreling out of the barn astride his black stallion. He flew past her, in the direction of town, the hooves echoing down the drive behind them. A dog barked in the distance, and Anne stayed where she was, staring after him until the sound of his departure faded away.

She could not help her small twinge of envy, or the strong desire to follow him. How she longed to ride into the night like that, with nothing holding her back. But it was as if she had a rope secured around her waist, anchoring her to this house. The only time she was ever allowed to leave was to run errands for Margery in the marketplace.

The closest she would come to freedom at the moment was when she slept, for there were no rules while dreaming.

With a heavy heart Anne climbed the stairs to her room up in the garret. With its slanted roof and crooked floor, it wasn't much compared to her old bedchamber in her father's house. She missed the soft bed and pale blue walls.

Her present space was a far cry better than the squalid hovel she'd shared with her mother, but it had come at the cost of her independence.

She'd spent far too much time in Teach's company the past few days, and needed to get to the city to try to sell some of the items she'd stolen. In less than three weeks the *Deliverance* would set sail. She saw her opportunity for escape as if it were the sand in an hourglass, and it was running out.

As Anne lay down, she attempted to wipe her mind clean. She was successful for the most part, but when she eventually drifted off to sleep, her last conscious thoughts were of black stallions and sparkling green eyes.

CHAPTER 11

Teach

The sky overhead was an inky black, lit by a sliver of the moon and a thousand sparkling stars. Adjusting the rough plank of wood, Teach slid it across the short gap stretching between the dock and the *Deliverance*.

She was broad in the beam and powerfully built, and Teach could picture her graceful bow cutting through the choppy waves on the open sea. As he boarded, a chill wind whipped his face, and he took a deep breath of the briny air, unable to prevent the smile on his lips. The boat swayed gently beneath his feet, and Teach stopped to close his eyes, his chest expanding in a moment of pure joy.

The ride through the empty city streets had energized him, for he hadn't slowed down, as if the very hounds of hell had been at his back. His father often called him reckless, but Teach liked to think he took calculated risks. This life was too short not to approach everything with zeal. His mother's untimely death had taught him that.

"Don't move, or you'll find yourself flat on your arse and my knife in your gut," someone growled from behind.

The smile on Teach's lips increased. "Is that any way to talk to a friend, John? Especially since I went to so much trouble to get you this post in the first place," he said, turning and extending his arm in greeting.

John let out a long breath and clasped Teach's hand in a crushing grip. John was built like any number of farmers or sailors walking the streets of Bristol, with a broad back and stout legs. And he was the best fighter Teach had ever seen, which was why Teach had written his father and told him about his friend. John had proven to be an excellent night watchman.

"Curse your eyes, Teach, you gave me a start. What are you doing here in the middle of the night?" John asked. His light brown hair was long and unruly, just like him. "Is Mary all right?"

"Yes. She's fine. This has nothing to do with her." Teach felt a twinge of guilt, wondering if he should tell his friend about the cheating maid. But he wasn't sure how to do it.

"I was thinking of coming by the house sometime to visit her, but whenever I send word, she says she's too busy to see me. You're not working her too hard, are you now?"

"Hardly. Instead of sending word, why not simply stop by and surprise her?" Teach knew it was a terrible suggestion, but perhaps

John would then see for himself what kind of girl he was marrying.

John smiled, transforming his formidable face. "I think I will, if I can find the time this week. I've missed her something fierce. Now, mind telling me why you're here?"

Teach walked to the mast and ran his hands along the smooth wood and ropes. "I couldn't sleep, so I decided to pay you a visit."

"You didn't come to see me."

"Of course I did. Why do you think I'm here?"

"You're in love with her, aren't you?" John asked, laughing.

"What?" Teach's head snapped up at John's words.

"You're in love with the *Deliverance* already. Don't bother denying it. I can see it in your eyes."

"Perhaps you're right," Teach murmured, his heartbeat returning to normal. He continued along the deck, his footsteps echoing through the night air. "How have you been? Have you had any trouble?"

"Nah, it's right quiet around here. A bit boring, if you ask me. But down the dock a ways, every once in a while, they get a bit of excitement."

"Really? How so?"

"Several men show up and empty the belly of a ship."

"That's nothing unusual," Teach said. "These are the docks, after all."

"Right, but why wait till the middle of the night to unload your cargo?"

Teach shrugged. "Maybe their laborers were delayed. The harbor master still has to inspect the ship."

"Aye, but it might be easier to hide things in the dark."

"Do you think they're hiding something?"

"I think they're unloading something they don't want nobody else to notice."

Intrigued, Teach took a few steps in the direction John had indicated, searching for any sign of movement in the distance. "Have you seen anything tonight?"

"No, nothing. I never know when they'll come."

"Do they ever bother you?" Teach asked.

John grinned, his teeth flashing in the dark. "I'd like to see 'em try."

"Well, let me know if they do. Or if you'd like more help," Teach said.

"I'll be fine, but you're more than welcome to stay for a bit."

Teach had left the confines of the house hoping to find a distraction from his home life and his impending marriage, as well as a particularly disturbing maid under his father's roof. Since he'd arrived home, the walls of the estate had seemed to be closing in on him for more than one reason, and he was searching for a way to let loose some of his pent-up frustration.

But since the *Deliverance* was simply another point of contention with his father, Teach wondered about his decision to come here. Perhaps a tavern would have been a better choice.

"Care to share a pint?" Teach asked. John was a simple,

hardworking type, and Teach enjoyed his company. In the past year he and John had become fast friends, much like Teach and William had been at Eton. Both William and John knew of Teach's struggle to please his father, while at the same time trying to assert himself and make his own decisions, and they were sympathetic to his plight.

But unlike with William, there was nothing about John that annoyed Teach.

"And have your father sack me? No thanks, mate. But drink one for me, will you?"

"Anything for a friend," Teach said, giving a mock salute and turning to leave.

"Hold on. You can't go into one of these taverns dressed like that. People might recognize you, and your father would hear about it for sure." After shrugging out of his jacket and picking up a large, floppy hat from the deck, John walked over and placed the items in Teach's arms and took Teach's cloak. Once Teach was back on the dock, John pulled the plank after him, preventing others from surprising him like Teach had.

"Stay out of trouble," John said with a final wave.

"Always," Teach replied before striding away.

Walking in the direction John had indicated, Teach scanned the area, but there was no movement at the moment, just the gentle splash of water hitting the stone dock.

Disappointed, Teach followed the unmistakable sound of a rowdy crowd coming from a tavern in the distance. It was several blocks away from the *Deliverance* but still within sight of the waterfront.

In the gloomy, smoke-filled interior, every corner was packed with lively games of cards, drawing plenty of interest from the raucous crowd, and Teach picked a seat near the back wall, enjoying his anonymity. The fact that nobody could recognize him beneath his disguise was reassuring. The floppy hat pulled down low over his forehead prevented anyone from getting a good look at his face, and the rough jacket John had provided fit in with the rest of the drunken horde.

There was no way Drummond would hear of Teach's activities, which was another reason Teach had sought out this particular establishment. Drummond would not have been caught dead in a tavern located in this part of town.

Teach, on the other hand, felt quite at home as he sipped an ale, enjoying the atmosphere and the revelry.

"Bring me another pint!" a large blond called out, his bulbous fist waving his mug in the air.

A bolt of recognition shot through Teach, and he looked in the direction of the booming voice. His old nemesis from Eton, Henry Barrett, sat at a table in the far corner. Teach frowned, debating if he should leave or remain where he was. During their years at school, Teach and Henry had come to blows more than once.

A short, ginger-haired companion attempted to wrestle Henry's bulky arm back down. "Come on, Barrett. You've had enough. Concentrate on the game," he said gruffly, sweat standing out on his brow.

Henry Barrett shook him off, like a giant swatting a fly, and shoved him back so that the small man lost his footing. "I'll tell you when I'm done," he bellowed, slamming the mug onto the table.

Someone helped the unlucky fellow to his feet while Henry picked up his cards and the game resumed.

A harassed barmaid struggled through the crowd, a frothy ale in her hands. She was almost to Barrett's table when she stumbled and fell forward. The drink doused a nearby sailor, who stood up, sputtering. Everyone's attention was drawn to the spectacle. In that same instant Henry rearranged two cards in the deck, which let Teach know the game was rigged and the cards were textured. Henry had been fingering them, giving the illusion of thorough shuffling, but what he'd really been doing was trying to find the match.

Teach whistled under his breath, not sure if he should be impressed by the boldness of Henry's actions, for the three other players involved in the game were by no means small. If they discovered Henry's deceit, Teach was quite sure Henry would leave the premises in a decidedly altered state.

Not that Teach would mind. After all these years Henry still had to resort to deception in order to win a single hand. He was as incompetent as Teach remembered. Teach wasn't worried about Henry recognizing him, for Henry had already enjoyed his fair share of ale.

If only William were here, Teach thought idly. William would take great pleasure in winning Henry's ill-gotten gains from him, for William was the superior player.

Drawing in a deep breath, Teach pulled John's coat more closely around his shoulders. After a few more hands were played, the game was over. Barrett reached out his meaty arms and drew the coins toward him. They fell into a drawstring pouch that he shoved into his longcoat.

Pushing back his chair, Henry slipped the cards into his pocket, before staggering toward the door. No one would know that he'd cheated. That didn't sit well with Teach, so he slipped out the back of the room, through the grease-filled kitchen, ignoring the angry calls of the cook. The stench in the alley nearly choked him. Henry Barrett walked down the middle of the street, his thick legs unsteady beneath his bulk.

Teach longed to settle the score with Barrett, and decided now would be the best time to do it. If fate had led him to the tavern that night, who was he to question it?

Swaying down the dark street, Henry appeared unaware of the stealthy figure following him. Shadows swirled around Teach's feet, and he clenched his hands, anticipation coursing through him as he thought how to best his opponent.

Luckily for Teach, Henry was the one who presented the opportunity. He approached a park, the outlines of the bushes and shrubbery creating enough cover for Teach to move closer.

Henry strolled toward a tree, clearly intent on relieving himself of his countless pints of ale.

While Henry was otherwise engaged, Teach drew forward, picked up a branch lying nearby, and poked the tip into Henry's back, all in one swift movement.

Turning, Henry scrambled to reach for his weapon.

Teach was too speedy for him. With deft movements he knocked Barrett's pistol away while at the same time pushing him to the ground.

Teach stood over him, clearly with the advantage. It took considerable effort on his part to refrain from laughing as Barrett looked up at him, fear and shock in his eyes, the smell of urine overpowering the air.

"I will take that purse," Teach said, flicking the stick in Barrett's face.

"Bugger off," Henry snarled. "That's not even a sword."

Teach clucked his tongue. "I never claimed it was. Now hand over the purse, and I will release you unharmed. If you don't, I will take you back to the tavern to explain the cards in your pocket."

Henry stared at Teach, peering in the darkness up at his face. "I know you," he mumbled, his speech slurred.

"Hand over the coins," Teach said, undeterred. The chances of Henry remembering this encounter were slim.

After a moment Henry reached into his pocket and tossed the drawstring bag several feet away.

Teach slid to the side and bent down, his eyes never leaving his victim. Once he secured the pouch in his hands, he hefted it, testing its weight.

In that instant Henry lunged forward, diving toward Teach's feet. Expecting just such a move, Teach sidestepped the tackle, but Henry still managed to hook an arm around one leg. Teach landed on his back, the breath knocked out of him. Momentarily stunned, he lay there until he saw the large rock in Henry's hand.

Teach scrambled out of the way and jumped to his feet. With a deft movement he grabbed Henry by the hair and slammed his fist into his face. Henry splayed in the dirt, like a pig on a spit, and didn't move again.

"You should have listened to me," Teach muttered, getting to his feet. He picked up his hat and dusted it off before retrieving the drawstring bag. He took out one coin and flicked it, and it landed near Henry Barrett's face. With one last disgusted look in Henry's direction, Teach turned and disappeared into the dark.

CHAPTER 12

Anne

When Anne got up the next morning, the sky was a light gray, the sun hidden just below the horizon. She discovered a note addressed to Margery on the small sideboard in the hallway near the kitchen. She would have read it if it hadn't been sealed. The handwriting was bold and strong, and Anne wondered when Teach had returned, for there was no question it was from him.

Was it a reprimand for Margery's behavior the previous night? A part of Anne hoped it was, even though she knew that would create more problems than it would solve.

Anne had not heard Teach return last night. Or perhaps it had been in the morning. She couldn't help wondering where he'd been.

When Margery saw the note, she ripped it open, clearly uneasy, and scanned the contents. With a sigh of relief she stuffed it into her pocket and turned to the three girls, who stood nearby awaiting their assignments for the day. "It appears the young master has an errand for me in the city. You will continue with your chores until I return."

Anne exchanged looks with Sara and Mary, but the three remained silent. Margery turned on her heel and started up the stairs.

In a matter of minutes the sound of the carriage could be heard as it drove away, taking Margery with it.

The girls collected their cleaning supplies, and Mary and Sara started whispering. "She forgot to tell us what to do," Sara said.

"Aye, she was off in quite a rush."

"What do you suppose the note said?"

"Don't know. Just be glad to have her out of the house," Mary muttered, her plump face flushed from the exertion of washing the hall floor.

Anne shook her head and left the two girls to their duties. She usually polished the furniture in Master Drummond's room but hadn't been able to get to it that week because of the time she'd spent tending Teach. She hoped to finish before he awakened.

The upstairs was silent as Anne began her labor. Starting at one end of the room, she worked as quickly and efficiently as possible. She'd been at it for some time when the sound of footsteps approached, but they were too light to belong to Teach.

Sara poked her head in the doorway as Anne knelt beside Master Drummond's armchair.

"Have ye seen Mary?" Sara asked.

Anne shook her head. "No, I thought she was with you."

"Aye, she was, but she said she left a candle burning in her room and ran to put it out. That was a while ago, and I haven't seen her since."

Anne was not surprised. With Margery gone, Mary would take any opportunity to shirk her responsibilities. "Have you checked in the pantry? Or perhaps the stable?"

Sara made a face. "Of course. I suppose I'll have to go and get her away from Tom again."

Shaking her head, Anne listened to the footsteps fade down the hallway. She didn't want to think about what would happen if Master Drummond ever found out about Mary and Tom. Somehow Mary had managed to keep her liaisons a secret even from Margery.

As Anne bent over to smooth one corner of the rug, her foot connected with the bottom of the bedside table, and something dropped with a solid *clank*. Turning, she discovered a turtle-shell spyglass, inlaid with silver and gold, wedged between the table leg and the wall. It was covered in dust. Picking it up, Anne felt her pulse accelerate at the find. From the looks of it, it was quite old, and the metal was tarnished, but Anne still recognized a valuable item when she saw one.

It appeared to have been there for quite some time. When she bumped the table, it must have dislodged it. She hesitated, weighing the object in her hands. It obviously meant something to Master Drummond. Otherwise it would not have been beside his bed. He kept only his most valued treasures closest to him, which was why the room was practically barren.

But the condition of the spyglass showed that the master hadn't thought about it for quite a while. It could have been hidden there for years without his knowledge.

For Anne, it could very well be the final piece she needed in order to afford a new life somewhere else. With a quick look behind her, she slid it into the pocket of her dress, her fingers slick with perspiration as she told herself he wouldn't miss it.

Wiping her hands on her apron, she stood, prepared to resume her work. Instead she froze when she noticed the large portrait hanging above the fireplace. It was of the lady of the house, Teach's mother, Mrs. Catherine Drummond. Anne had dusted it countless times before, admiring the burgundy dress and serene face, but she'd never felt those eyes staring back at her, accusing, as they appeared to be now.

Anne had heard stories from the gardener about Catherine Drummond. He was the only servant left who had known her, and he'd said that Mrs. Drummond had always gone out of her way to help someone in need, showing kindness even when there'd been no benefit for herself.

If Mrs. Drummond could see Anne now, what would she say? Would she encourage Anne, and give her money to help her escape?

Fingering the spyglass in her pocket, Anne pulled it out once more.

Or would Mrs. Drummond—

"What are you doing?"

Startled, Anne whirled, automatically hiding her hands behind her back. Mary stood in the doorway, glaring at her.

"I'm working. Which is what you should be doing," Anne said, her heart threatening to beat out of her chest.

Mary's eyes narrowed. "What are you hiding?"

Anne cursed the guilty flush that rose in her cheeks. "Nothing."

Mary raised an eyebrow at her. "Nothing? I don't believe you. Show me what you have behind your back."

"It's nothing. I was simply cleaning. You startled me."

"I cleaned this room yesterday," Mary said, looking unconvinced.

"I didn't know. No one told me it had been done." Anne glanced nervously toward the door, unsure how long the girl had been standing there.

Mary folded her arms over her ample chest. "What would Margery say if she knew you were polishing things when they didn't need it? There's enough work to go around without doing everything twice, don't you think?"

"What would Master Drummond say if he knew you were dallying with the groom?" Anne shot back, feeling more than a little defensive. "That is where Sara just found you, wasn't it?"

Mary's face flushed a deep red. "No, I was in the pantry."

"Alone? Or was Tom with you?"

"That's none of your business, now, is it?"

"No, but it is Master Drummond's business."

There was fear in Mary's eyes. "You have no proof."

Anne could not bring herself to feel any pity for the girl. "Mr. Edward said he caught you with Tom. I believe that's proof enough."

"Did he tell you that? Well, you better watch yourself," Mary sneered. "I don't think Master Drummond would take too kindly to you spending so much time with his son."

"Mr. Edward was ill, and both Margery and Master Drummond know it. I was simply doing my job."

"What makes you think I wasn't doing my job?"

"Because I've never heard of a maid working side by side with a groom before. And I'm quite sure Master Drummond hasn't either," Anne said.

With a toss of her head, Mary stomped off, muttering under her breath.

Exhaling, Anne slipped the spyglass once more into her pocket, her knees shaking. She would have to watch herself where Mary was concerned. The girl was trouble.

Until now Anne had done her best to choose less obvious objects, of lesser value, and she'd always made sure she was quite alone before she took anything.

The incident just now had been close.

Too close.

But Anne wasn't willing to give up the spyglass. Not if she wanted to reach her goal.

Drummond was notorious for his stinginess, and Anne was actually surprised that more people hadn't stolen from him. Or perhaps others had taken from him, but they'd been too smart to get caught.

With less than three weeks left to plan her escape on the *Deliverance*, Anne would have to be extra careful. If anyone was to be caught, it would definitely not be her.

CHAPTER 13

Teach

Teach had just slipped into a fresh shirt and breeches when an incessant pounding sounded at the front door. Closing his eyes, he was tempted to climb back into bed. His tongue was still thick and dry from the ale the previous night, and his efforts to erase Anne's image from his head had been futile.

He'd visited two different taverns on his way home, trying to figure out how he could talk his father into letting him command the *Deliverance* before he married Patience. But the more he drank, the less control he had, and it hadn't taken long before a pair of blue eyes had occupied his mind completely.

The pounding continued. Margery had gone into town. He'd sent her away to check several shops in search of his father's missing silverware. Although Drummond had told Teach not to say anything, Teach seriously doubted the elderly housekeeper was the thief. If anyone *was* stealing from the household, they would have to get rid of the evidence somehow and the shops were a good place to start.

What he'd really like to have done was dismiss Margery for hitting Anne. But any serious action would have to wait until his father returned.

There was no sign of anyone in the hallway, but he heard footsteps approaching in the entryway below. He had just turned the corner at the top of the landing, when he saw the color drain from Anne's face as she opened the front door.

In the light of day, it was clear the night had not been kind to Henry Barrett. His thick, pale skin resembled a loaf of bread before it was properly baked.

"They've got you answering the door now, have they?" Henry sneered.

Blocking his entrance, Anne scowled at him. "Maids are required to do a variety of jobs. I'm *certain* you remember my status in this house."

"You better watch yourself. I could make your life very uncomfortable if you're not careful."

Teach moved silently toward the stairs, his hands clenched at his sides, his vision momentarily clouded by rage at Henry's threat. It was clear he and Anne knew each other from somewhere. Had Anne worked in Henry's household before? No wonder she was so sharp-tongued.

"What do you want?" she asked, not bothering with any pretense of civility.

"I want to see that dirty bounder, Edward."

"He isn't here. I will let him know you called."

Henry shook his head and pushed his way past her into the large hall. He looked up at the rich tapestries and paintings adorning the walls, no doubt trying to determine their worth. "I saw him last night. I'd recognize him anywhere."

"And I you," Teach said with deadly calm, reaching the bottom step.

Henry and Anne both turned at his approach. Teach's mood didn't improve when he saw the slight coloration near Anne's eye. Margery would definitely answer for that.

"Should I get you some refreshment, sir?" she asked Teach.

"No, that won't be necessary. This won't take long," Teach said, barely managing to control his fury.

Taking her cue, Anne walked in the direction of the kitchen.

"What do you want?" Teach asked, turning to Henry.

"What you took."

Teach raised his eyebrows. "And what would that be?"

"My money. I know it was you near the tavern last night. You might have fooled the others, but not me."

"Really?" Teach drawled. "What if I told you I've been sick these past few days and haven't been out of the house? What would you say then?"

"I'd call you a liar! That was you, and I'm here to collect what's mine."

"Be careful what you say, Henry. I'm a fairly good shot, and

I won't have my integrity questioned by someone like you."

"And I won't be robbed by the likes of you. If you don't return my money, I'll report you to the constable—"

"And tell them what? I stole the money you stole from those men? Somehow, I doubt the constable would be very sympathetic."

"You have no proof."

"Oh, but I do. I returned the coins to their rightful owners. The men you cheated were quite interested to know about your deck of cards. You might want to avoid the docks for a time. I believe some of your friends might be looking for you."

While Henry sputtered to find the right words, Teach strode toward the door and pulled it open. If Henry didn't leave, Teach could not guarantee his safety. "Good-bye, Henry."

Henry sniffed, puffing out his chest like a peacock. He crossed the floor with less assured steps, and then paused on the step outside the door. "I want my money. I'll make you pay—"

The only response was the slamming of the door and Teach's colorful expletive. It was a good thing he didn't have his cutlass with him. He wouldn't have hesitated in cutting the oaf down.

Teach strode toward the back of the house to find Anne. For some reason, seeing Henry Barrett had clearly unnerved her, and he meant to get to the bottom of it. He found her leaning against the wall around the corner from the entryway, her eyes closed. She'd listened to the entire conversation.

"Anne. Are you all right?"

She took a steadying breath. "Yes. Yes, I'm fine, sir. Just tired, that's all."

"Liar," he said, searching her expression. "He upset you, didn't he?"

"He is rather unpleasant," she replied, straightening from the wall and heading toward the kitchen.

Teach walked alongside her. "I've known him for several years now. 'Repulsive' would be a more apt description." Tilting his head, he gave her a hard look. "What did he mean when he said he could make your life difficult? Did you work for him before?" The thought turned his stomach.

"What did he mean he saw you last night? When you left, did you go to the tavern as he claimed?"

Teach's lips twitched, and he leaned against the kitchen table. "I thought I heard you following me." He watched as she sliced into a loaf of fresh bread. Her posture let him know she wished he would leave. "All right, Anne, don't answer my question, but we both know the truth. At some point you must have worked in Barrett's household."

"It's a story I'm not ready to tell," she said.

"Did he hurt you?" *I'll kill him.*

"The past no longer matters."

"It does if he caused you harm."

Anne put the knife down and looked him in the eyes. "I do not wish to discuss Henry Barrett with you."

"Well, whether you wish to discuss him or not, this was not

the first time you've seen him. And unfortunately, knowing him as I do, it might not be the last." Anne's face showed her dismay. Teach was quick to reassure her. "Don't worry. If I give him his money, he won't have any reason to come back."

"I thought you said you'd returned it."

"I lied."

A slight smile played on Anne's lips as she resumed cutting the bread, and warmth spread throughout Teach's limbs, knowing he was responsible for it.

"You're impossible," Anne muttered.

"I'm a Drummond."

"Oh yes, I'm quite aware of that fact."

"You do realize this is just one more thing you and I have in common."

Anne shot him a curious look. "What is?"

"Our dislike of Henry Barrett."

"I don't think many people like him."

"True," Teach said. "Which is a shame. His father, Andrew Barrett, was a good man and one of my father's closest friends. Before my mother died, they did quite a bit of business together. They kept in touch off and on in the years since. When I left England a year ago, it was on one of Barrett's merchant ships."

The knife stopped moving. "You sailed on one of Andrew Barrett's ships?"

"Yes, although not many people knew about it."

"Why didn't you sail on one of your father's ships?"

Teach looked down at his boots. "Because I didn't want to be treated differently. If they'd known I was the owner's son, the experience wouldn't have been the same. I wanted to make my own path. On Barrett's ship I went by the name of Edward Teach. I arranged it with him, shortly before he died. Only my good friend John knew who I was." On board the *Deliverance*, Teach might continue with that tradition. It was why he was so comfortable here in the back of the house, talking to a member of his kitchen staff as if it were nothing.

Teach tried to picture Henry Barrett setting off to sea, performing menial jobs such as swabbing the deck and raising a sail, but not even he had that good an imagination. Henry was quite content to have things done for him. He was soft and compliant.

Not unlike William, Teach thought. Before, Teach had often found William's inactivity amusing, for William used any excuse not to exert himself. After seeing Henry Barrett, Teach was uncomfortable with William's and Henry's similarities.

"Does Henry Barrett still do business with your father?" Anne asked.

Teach's voice was gruff. "Not that I am aware of. This is the first time I've seen him since I left school. As I said, if I give him back his money, it should keep him away for a bit."

"How did you steal it?" Anne asked.

There was a strange look in her eyes that he couldn't quite decipher. "It wasn't as if it were *his* money. I'm quite sure he cheated every hand he played last night. What's the harm in taking something that never really belonged to him in the first place?"

Anne hesitated before answering. "Did you fight with him?"

"I simply took what wasn't his."

"Someone could have gotten hurt," she protested.

"What's this? Do I detect concern in your voice? Can it be that, despite your protests, Queen Anne has feelings for one of her subjects?"

Anne rolled her eyes but refused to be baited. "I hardly think this is a laughing matter. What if he'd drawn a sword? Or worse, a pistol?"

"He was in no position to draw anything," he said, remembering the shocked look on Henry's face.

"How can you be so sure? What if he'd had some hidden weapon?"

Teach shrugged. "He would not have bested me. I wouldn't have allowed it."

"You take far too many chances," she murmured.

"And you don't take nearly enough. I propose to change that."

Before she could inquire what he meant by his statement, Sara and Mary entered the house, covered in dust and carrying the floor rugs between the two of them. They stopped short when they saw Teach leaning against the table and Anne standing near him.

"Ah, I'm glad you decided to come inside. I would like to give you the day off," Teach said.

Sara's mouth dropped open, mirroring the look on Anne's face. Mary stared at him, as if he'd just grown horns. Or perhaps a halo.

It was Sara who found her voice first. "Have we done something wrong, sir?"

Teach shook his head. "No, quite the contrary. I was just telling Anne I think you've all worked very hard. I'm quite sure the house has never looked better."

The two girls preened beneath his praise. Anne's eyes narrowed, no doubt wondering what he was playing at.

Teach reached into his pocket, produced several gold coins, and handed some to each of them. It was Barrett's money, and he wouldn't miss a few schillings. "Here. I want you to take these and go into town to buy yourselves something new. Or useful. Or whatever it is you feel you can't live without."

Teach would have been hard pressed to determine who out of the three of them was more surprised by his actions. "I've never had this much money to spend on myself before," Mary said, a wary look on her face.

Sara gazed at Teach with adoring eyes. "Thank you, sir. Thank you ever so much."

Embarrassed, he brushed aside the praise, for he'd done it for only selfish reasons. He still thought Mary was a harlot, and Teach had decided to tell John the truth before it was too late.

"Think nothing of it. You just make sure you go and enjoy yourselves for the rest of the day."

"The whole day, sir?" Sara asked.

Teach nodded. "The whole day. But I don't want you resting upstairs. I want you to treat yourselves to something in town." He took a slice of bread and broke it with his hands. "But you can't mention this to my father. This is to remain between the four of us, do you understand?"

"Oh, don't worry about us, sir. We won't tell a soul," Sara assured him. "Will we, Mary?"

Mary shot a glance between Anne and Teach, her head tilted to the side, a shrewd look in her eyes.

"I'm sure John wouldn't mind a visit from you, Mary. He's eager to see you," Teach said.

Mary's lips moved, but Teach wouldn't have called it a smile. "Oh, yes, well . . . perhaps."

It was left to Anne to be the voice of reason. "What about Margery? She'll be back before long and wonder where we all have gotten to."

Sara's face fell, but Teach was unaffected.

"Margery won't say a thing. Where do you think she's been this whole time? She's in town as well. If you see her, tell her I sent you on an errand." Polishing off the piece of bread, he wiped his hands together, before reaching for the rugs. He'd told Margery to make a thorough search for the stolen items at the market and to take her time getting back. He'd done it only to get her away from Anne, but things were turning out nicely. Teach gave the girls a slight nudge. "Now go. Hurry. Put on a fresh dress and make yourselves scarce."

If their departure hadn't been so comical, scurrying up the back stairs, Teach might have felt sorry for Anne, for they did not think to ask if she wished to join them.

Nevertheless, he had ulterior motives and was glad they hadn't. Leaving Anne to tidy the kitchen, he replaced the rugs in their proper rooms.

In less than twenty minutes Sara and Mary were gone.

Anne had just swept the floor when Teach reappeared, a swath of wine-red velvet in his hands. She returned the broom to the pantry and cleaned her hands before drying them with a rag.

"Here," he said.

"What is it, sir?" Anne asked, fingering the smooth material. "Does it need mending?"

"Not that I'm aware of. Put it on," he said.

Her eyes flew to his face. "Why?"

"Because you can't go out riding in that dress of yours."

Anne took a step back and looked toward the door, as if to determine how far Sara and Mary were.

Teach's eyebrows drew together. This was not the reaction he'd been hoping for. "Well, don't just stand there. Go upstairs and put it on."

She stood rooted to the spot. "I'm not going riding, sir."

"Yes, you are. You're coming with me."

She swallowed. "Where?"

Impatiently he gestured toward the courtyard. "Out there.

In the country. You're going to get on a horse and ride." He'd thought Anne was different. Could it be that she disliked the outdoors as much as Patience?

"And if I choose not to?"

Teach gave her an incredulous look. "Why would you do that?"

"Because you've just given everyone the day off."

Teach ran his fingers through his hair. "Yes, I know I did. I did it for you."

Anne placed the dress on the back of a chair. "I would prefer to spend my day off alone."

Frustration flared in his chest. "Well, you don't have much of a choice. They've left you. I'm the only one here now."

She looked toward the door. "I could catch up to them. They can't be far."

He shook his head, his chin jutting forward. "No."

"You cannot make me stay."

"I have no desire to make you do anything. I was hoping you would choose for yourself." She opened her mouth, no doubt to protest, but once again he read her mind. "And don't tell me you can't ride. You said your father taught you." He folded his arms across his chest, blocking her only escape.

Anne laughed, the sound shrill with nerves. "You're mad."

"Not yet. But I'm getting there. What will it take to get you to spend the day with me?"

"I just spent the past several days with you," she reminded him.

"Ah, but that doesn't count. I was ill."

"You were not."

Being around Anne kept him on his toes. "Technically, I was for four of those days. But we spent only a few hours in each other's company. Today I wish to change that."

Anne was speechless. He was well aware he'd given her no way out of his trap. He lifted the dress from the back of the chair and placed it gently in her arms. "I promise to behave myself," he said, reading the tension in her face.

"You've confessed to being a liar and a thief. Why should I believe you, sir?" She stared at him, as if trying to understand why it was so important that they spend the day together.

The problem was, he couldn't explain it himself. He just knew he wanted to. "Because I'm telling you the truth."

"It wouldn't be proper. Your father has his rules—"

"Bugger the rules. I don't care if it's proper or not," he growled, determined to get his way. "And my father isn't home to find out. I would like to do something for you. Think of this as a reward for nursing me back to health."

"You gave Mary and Sara the opportunity to do what they wanted. Why can't you afford me the same courtesy?"

"Tell me the truth, Anne. Would you rather go into the city alone to buy yourself something new, or would you rather spend some time away from here, riding horses and seeing a bit of the countryside?"

"I would prefer to go to the city."

"Fine! I'll give you more coins after we return from our ride."

Anne paused for so long that Teach wondered if she had paid attention.

"If I do this, will you leave me in peace?" she asked.

He hesitated. Ever since he'd set eyes on her, he'd had no peace. Why should he grant her something that eluded him? "If after today you find my company so abhorrent, I shall leave you in peace for the remainder of my days in this house."

Something in her expression changed. "You give me your word?"

Teach held his hand up to his chest and bowed slightly at the waist. "I give you my word."

Anne nodded and took the red riding habit in her hands.

He had purposefully omitted the words "as a gentleman," for he knew she was not foolish enough to believe that.

CHAPTER 14

Anne

The person in the looking glass was a stranger, although the cap on Anne's head was recognizable. The bruise from Margery was not as terrible as she'd first thought, although the discoloration was obvious.

Anne could have counted on two hands the number of times she'd checked her appearance in the past year. During that time, she'd come to resemble her mother more than ever before. Gone were the rounded apples of her cheeks. Instead her face was now framed by high cheekbones, her neck long and graceful. And the dark circles beneath her eyes were not as pronounced today as they had been a month ago.

The riding habit was a little longer than she was used to, the close-fitting jacket made of superior velvet. Anne marveled at the color. Most of the ones she'd worn when she was younger had been either blue or green. Teach had told her this had been his mother's riding habit, and Anne admired Mrs. Drummond's confidence to wear such a vibrant shade of red, like wine fresh from a cask.

Anne told herself she dreaded the upcoming day she was being forced to spend with Teach, but in reality there was a light in her eyes and a flush on her face. Carrying the hat in her hands, she went out to the barn, excitement fluttering in her breast at the thought of the excursion.

While the coins were a most welcome addition to her funds, a ride through the countryside was irreplaceable. She liked to think Teach had forced her hand. In a way he had. She could have refused him, but then it would have just been the two of them alone at the house.

On horseback Anne would have the ability to get away from him, should he try anything inappropriate.

Anne met Teach as he led his black stallion out of its stall, Margery's three-legged cat following behind. What Anne assumed to be her horse was already tethered to the post.

Teach looked up as she approached. For a moment he froze, his mouth half-open as if he'd been about to say something.

In an attempt to hide her nervousness, she held out the hat to him. "Here," she said.

He cleared his throat and busied himself with the bridle, but not before she saw a spark of something in his eyes. "You'll need the hat."

"I cannot wear it."

He stopped what he was doing. "Why not? You can't ride in your cap. If somebody sees you, they'll wonder what a maid is doing out riding with her master."

Irritation flashed through her at his words, even though she knew he spoke the truth. "Whether I wear the hat or not, I will still be just a maid. Changing my appearance will not alter that fact."

"I don't understand your reluctance. The outfit becomes you. Simply put on the hat so we can ride."

She ignored the surge of pleasure at his compliment, knowing he said it only to achieve his end. "It won't work."

He ran his fingers through his black hair. "By Jupiter, you could drive a man to drink. Why? Why do you take every opportunity to argue with me? If I were to say that the heavens are blue, I daresay you'd contend that they were green. Do you take pleasure in provoking me?"

Admittedly, there was a small part of her that did just that. If she hadn't worked in his father's household, she would not have had to curb her tongue as much as she did. It was a constant struggle to control her feelings, thoughts, and actions. If she said what she was truly thinking, she would no doubt be whipped to within an inch of her life. "You asked me to speak honestly with you. I am simply telling you the truth. I cannot wear it, because it won't fit."

He looked about to explode from his irritation. "Why, in the bloody name of all that's holy—"

Before he could finish his outburst, she removed her cap. Her thick black hair fell around her shoulders, and she placed the hat on top of her head. It balanced there for a moment, before toppling to the ground. Picking it up once more, Anne tried again, this time jamming it down over her forehead. It was no use. The hat was too small, and she had too much hair.

"Now do you understand why I said I cannot wear it? It wasn't out of vanity or pride. I have no quarrel with you. It is simply not possible." After placing the hat on a hook near the barn door, she moved to gather her hair and restore the cap, but Teach stopped her.

"No, don't," he said, his voice gruff. "Let it hang loose."

She paused, noting the glint in his eyes.

He took the cap from her hands and then held out her horse's bridle instead. Not waiting for a response, he led his own stallion from the barn into the courtyard.

Drawing in a deep breath, she followed him. With the reins clenched in one hand, she walked toward the mounting block. The heavy skirts hampered her first attempt to mount, for she was out of practice.

"Allow me," Teach murmured, stepping up behind her.

"Where is the groom?" Anne asked, looking around.

Teach hoisted her into the sidesaddle. "I gave him the day off as well."

Of course he had. Anne had never met anyone like Teach. He was arrogant and driven, as was his father, but at the same time Teach was not above gestures of kindness or consideration, traits he had no doubt inherited from his mother.

Anne could still feel the imprints of his fingers long after he withdrew his hands. Her heart hammered in her chest, and she patted the horse's neck, pretending to calm *her* down as she stepped sideways. "What's her name?" Anne asked, waiting for Teach to mount.

Shooting her a mischievous grin, he said, "Queen Anne."

"You mock me," she said.

He raised his hands. "What? No, I tell the truth. My father bought her shortly before I returned."

"Your father doesn't believe in naming animals." Upon her arrival in the household, she had asked the others the names of the different horses in the stables. No one had answered, for no one had known.

"Precisely, which is why *I* have decided to name her Queen Anne."

"And your stallion's name? Is it something equally ridiculous? King Edward, perhaps?"

Teach's grin deepened. "Don't be silly. It's Kaiser. Now, are you ready?"

Kaiser, the German word for "emperor." "Yes, Your Excellency."

"Good. Then follow me," he called out, slapping his reins. The stallion leapt ahead, and they took off. "If you can!"

Smiling, Anne did as he'd commanded, catching up to him as he neared her favorite trees outside the property. That was the farthest she'd ventured in this direction since arriving in the household. Today would be different.

As the house faded in the distance, Anne leaned forward, her breath catching in her throat. It was as if she were flying. With the wind rushing through her hair, her skirts trailing beneath her, Anne was free once more.

Teach reined his horse and rode beside her, the look on his face matching hers. He could have outpaced her, for he rode astride, but he adjusted his speed to hers.

Both of them knew the impropriety of their actions. If anyone were to find out they'd left together, the consequences would be dire.

But for the moment neither of them thought about the cost.

For several minutes the only sound that could be heard was the horses' hooves as they ate up the ground beneath them, churning small clumps of earth.

On and on they rode, through fertile fields, toward the surrounding woodlands. Every once in a while they passed a farmhand, laboring in the crops, but the riders were too far away and too fast for the laborers to give them more than a passing glance.

It was sometime later when Teach reined in his horse, slowing down to a walk. It had been quite a while since they'd last seen or heard a passerby. The city of Bristol was well behind them in the distance. Anne pulled in beside him, aware of the flush in her cheeks and the tangle of her hair.

"That was . . . amazing," Anne said, unable to contain her

joy. It reminded her of spending time with her father, before he'd become ill.

"I'm glad you enjoyed it. While I was gone, I was almost afraid I'd forget how to ride."

Leaning forward, Anne patted her horse. "You can never forget something like this."

"You said your father taught you?"

"Yes, when he had access to horses," she said, hoping to steer clear of any personal conversations. She could have told him her relation to Henry, but she would soon leave Bristol in search of her mother's family, and the less people knew of her past, the better. "Who taught you?"

"My mother. She loved animals. When she was alive, the stables were full. We had chickens, dogs, and cats, all living harmoniously under one roof. After she died, my father had them either killed or sent away." Whenever Teach mentioned his father, a hard mask slid over his features, making him look much older and fiercer.

"So you didn't ride for an entire year?" she asked, trying to change the subject.

Teach paused, his head tilted to the side as he tried to remember. "It must have been at least six months," he said. "It was on Jamaica, and I rode along the beach."

Anne couldn't help a slight tinge of jealousy. "That sounds wonderful. Have you missed it?"

"Yes. But being away at sea was its own reward. I can't imagine doing anything else." As Teach spoke, there was a look of sadness in his eyes. She knew, if his father had his way, Teach would not be returning to sea anytime soon.

Sympathy pierced Anne's heart, for as long as Teach lived under his father's roof, Teach would have to do as he commanded.

They rode in silence for a time, each one lost in thought. The guarded feeling Anne had whenever she entered the Drummond household was gone now, replaced with a calm she hadn't known for quite a while.

"Let's stop here," Teach said, dismounting.

Surprised, Anne looked around, seeing no reason for them to stop. They were at least ten miles from the city. On their right, scattered across the ground were several large stones covered with lichen and moss, the tree line not far behind. It was not the kind of place she would have chosen to take a break.

"Can we not keep going?" she asked. She could have ridden for hours and not tired of it.

Teach shook his head, taking the reins from her hands. "Trust me. You'll want to see this."

Anne most definitely did *not* trust him, but she had little choice. Teach caught her as she slid down. Pulling away from him, she pretended to fix her skirts. In truth, she was flustered at his proximity.

Teach approached the woods and then entered through a slight opening in the trees. The scent of pines and wet leaves filled the air, and Anne breathed in deeply. He tied the horses to a large branch that looked as if it had been placed there. It's positioning was too careful for it to have simply fallen. A small stream flowed near their feet.

The trail upon which they walked was overgrown, yet still visible.

"What is this place?" Anne asked, her voice loud in the silent surroundings.

Teach did not respond. He continued to walk forward into the dense forest, sunlight filtering down through the branches and leaves.

"Sir?" she said.

"Please stop calling me 'sir.' That title is reserved for my father."

"Well, what shall I call you? 'Mr. Edward'?"

"Teach," he said.

"Your father would not approve," she said, noting with satisfaction the stiffening of his shoulders.

"Since my father isn't here to object, there's no reason you can't simply call me Teach. Now come. It's not far."

"What's not far?" she asked, deciding not to call him anything at all.

"This way."

Anne froze, the hair on her neck standing up as she realized how stupid she had been. She'd been so eager to escape the confines of the household that she'd ignored the hazards of going off alone with the young master. He was becoming far too familiar with her.

Teach, no doubt sensing something amiss, turned back to her. In three long strides he closed the distance between them. "Is something wrong?" he asked, scanning her from head to toe.

"I wish to return to the house," she said.

"Why?" he asked, clearly puzzled. "I want to show you something."

A hysterical laugh rose in her throat. "I'm sure you do, but I have no desire to see it." She spun around. Several leaves clung to her skirts as she returned the way they had just come.

Teach leapt in front of her, blocking the path. "You promised you would come with me."

"And you promised to behave yourself!" she snapped. What a fool she was! Anyone who could be friends with someone like the Earl of Lorimar was not to be trusted.

Teach's eyes grew wide. "What have I done?"

"You've led me here," she said, gesturing to their surroundings.

He waited expectantly. When she remained silent, he nodded. "Yes, I know."

"Well, what is this place?"

"Blast it, that's what I'm trying to show you." He raked a hand through his hair. "I am not in the habit of bringing helpless maids to the middle of the forest."

"I might not have a pail handy, but I would not characterize myself as helpless. Why can't I return to the house?"

"Because I simply wanted to show you something. Why is that so hard to understand?" His voice echoed around them, and a quail, upset by all the shouting, shot upward, wings flapping wildly to escape. After a few failed attempts at flight, it settled several paces away. Just because it had wings did not mean it could fly well.

She studied Teach's face, but his expression revealed nothing except for his annoyance. In return he continued to watch her, waiting for her to make a decision.

"All right," she said at last. Catching her lip between her teeth, she nodded, indicating that he should lead the way.

As they walked, Anne heard the distant sound of running water. The farther he led her into the forest, the louder it became. Soon they happened upon a small stone cottage with two chimneys, set in a clearing. The old rock wall surrounding it was in ruins. Teach proceeded past the cottage, toward a stone ledge. Holding out his hand, he motioned for her to join him.

His fingers clasped hers, firm and warm, and she took a tentative step toward the edge, gasping at the beauty before her. Far below, a river meandered through a rocky gorge. Both sides of the ravine sported uneven and precipitous cliff faces with a broken line of hawthorns visible near the water's edge. Upon closer inspection, Anne also recognized the golden leaves of the whitebeams.

"Well?" Teach asked.

She could only shake her head and cast a quick glance at him, noting the satisfaction in his features. "I don't know what to say," she said at last.

"'Thank you'? Or 'I shall endeavor to trust you in the future'?"

A grin tugged at her lips. "I would not go so far as that." Teach opened his mouth, but Anne continued before he could say anything. "But yes, thank you for bringing me here. How did you find this place?"

Teach leaned back against a tree, releasing her hand. "My mother had my father build this cottage for her. It was a place for her to get away."

His own mother had needed to escape the house, Anne thought. Somehow, she was not surprised.

"It's lovely," she said, no longer anxious that it was just the two of them. "She must have come here often."

He shrugged. "As often as her illness would allow. Toward the end she wasn't able to move much. My father would bring out a chair for her and set it right here." He indicated a spot in the center of the ledge. "She would hold the dog's lead in one hand. When she was ready to go inside, she'd release the dog, and he would go and find my father."

"Your father wouldn't sit with her out here?"

Teach tore a leaf from an overhead branch and ripped it to shreds. "My father can't remain still for too long. He never went far, but he could not stand to see her in that state. I think she preferred the solitude as well. He would go and look for willow bark or other roots and plants to ease her pain."

"No herbs or medicine could cure her?"

Teach's voice was bitter. "The doctors claimed nothing could have saved her."

Anne swallowed around the unexpected lump in her throat. Her own father had collapsed and died before any doctor could be summoned.

Teach crushed a spider beneath his boot. "Until then, he did what he could to make her time here on earth as comfortable as possible. But what good are linen sheets and feather beds when your body is racked with pain?"

Anne was reminded of her own mother's death. After Henry had kicked them out, Jacqueline had found employment in an earl's household. She'd been beaten when she'd refused the advances of the earl's son. By the time she'd made it home, she'd been bloodied and broken.

They hadn't had enough money at the time to call on a doctor. Anne had been so enraged, she'd nearly gone to the house and killed the man responsible. Only the fact that her mother had been in agonizing pain and had needed constant attention had prevented Anne from carrying out her plans. Her mother passed away three days later. A short time later, Henry found her.

What would be more frustrating? Knowing you had the means but couldn't utilize them? Or not having the means, and knowing there was nothing you could do to help the situation?

"I'm sorry," Anne said, wishing she could say something that did not sound so trite. She was all too familiar with empty words, having experienced loss of her own.

Teach stared woodenly at the ground. "I am too," he whispered, almost to himself.

CHAPTER 15

Teach

Teach could not believe that the girl sitting by his side was the same one who'd assaulted him with a pail in the market. Nor could he believe he'd brought her here, to his mother's favorite resting spot.

Not even Patience knew of this place, and Teach was unsure if he would ever show it to her. Something inside him balked at the idea, for he knew she would fail to appreciate its simple beauty. Patience would only notice what was lacking. It wasn't a grand residence. It was a cottage, with two rooms and a quaint porch. His mother had had no desire to ruin the natural surroundings with anything large or garish.

Perhaps Teach would keep it for his own, a secret getaway when married life to Patience grew to be too much for him.

Unnerved by his train of thought, Teach bit back a curse. He wasn't even married yet, and already he was planning trips without his future bride-to-be? It did not bode well for their union.

Neither did the fact that he was quite enjoying Anne's company. He recognized in her the same restless spirit that he possessed, and he was glad he'd chosen to spend the day with her. Teach could see that in her own way, she was beginning to trust him.

The rays of the sun peered down through the trees, warming the area where Teach and Anne sat. He'd taken the liberty of bringing two chairs from the cottage out to the ledge, and they watched the river flow through the gorge below.

Teach pulled out Dampier's book from his coat pocket and held it aloft. "Would you be so kind as to continue where you left off?" he asked.

Anne smiled, but shook her head. "No."

Shocked, he raised his brows at her. "No? I thought you liked hearing about all of their adventures."

"I do. It's like holding a dream in my hands. But you're no longer *ill*," she said pointedly. "And I am no longer required to wait on you hand and foot."

Teach grinned, liking the fact that he never knew what kind of a reaction he would receive from her. Just when he thought he had Anne figured out, she turned around and surprised him.

"All right. I'll read to you. What chapter were we on?" he asked.

"As much as I've enjoyed the book, I would actually like to hear more about your adventures. You mentioned at dinner the other day that you were attacked by a Spanish sloop and that your captain died of his injuries. If it isn't too painful, I would like to hear the tale."

Teach could not picture Patience showing any interest in his activities at sea. Nor his father. Even William, despite professing to be such a good friend, would sooner discuss affairs of the state than listen to any accounts of life on a merchant ship. "Well, I'm not sure where to begin. I left England four months prior to the attack, and we'd managed to trade all of the goods we'd secured. Our captain was a good man, handpicked by Andrew Barrett himself. Barrett expected integrity from all of his employees, whether they were a simple cook or a captain on one of his ships. I was impressed with the crew, for they were all decent men."

"You seem to hold Andrew Barrett in high regard," Anne said, folding her hands in her lap.

Teach nodded. "I do, and I was sorry to hear about his death. Henry brings dishonor to the family name."

Anne grimaced.

"I'm sorry for bringing up Henry. I forgot you used to work for him. That can't have been pleasant."

"No, I'm sorry. I interrupted your story." She gave him a small smile. "Please, continue."

"We'd just left the port of Tortuga and planned to rendezvous with some others in Barrett's fleet off the coast of Jamaica. It was near there that we spotted the first war ship. The Spaniards were dependent on the direction and strength of the wind, so we had an advantage, in that we could outmaneuver them. As they bore down on us, we attempted to get to windward, but were unsuccessful. Three of our sailors were hit by a barrage from the ship's guns as she passed."

Teach looked off to the woods, somber and thoughtful. "We shot back and managed to wound several of the sailors. With no one at the helm, their ship rounded into the wind and lay helpless. We continued to shoot every man who attempted to take the rudder, and targeted their sails until they were shredded."

Teach paused in his story to catch a breath. Glancing again at Anne, he noted the rapt attention she gave him, clearly fascinated and aghast by his account.

"What happened next?" she asked.

Teach frowned. "The Spaniards continued to fire, and our captain took two shots to the chest. It was at that moment that I noticed two powder kegs on the deck of the other ship. Knowing it was our only chance of survival, I ordered our helmsmen to bring us closer. The Spanish captain commanded everyone to hit the deck, and I took a shot. It wasn't enough to destroy their ship, but it gave us the distraction we needed to escape." Teach remembered with vivid clarity the sights and sounds of the men as some of the Spaniards had caught fire when the keg had exploded. He could still hear their cries as they leapt into the ocean in an attempt to douse the flames burning their flesh.

Anne reached out and touched his arm, seemingly aware of

his haunted reflections. "I'm sorry," she said. "I shouldn't have asked."

Teach looked down at the hand on his sleeve, overcome with a sudden urge to cover it with his own. Instead he cleared his throat and looked out across the gorge. It took him a moment to answer. "I have since come to terms with that event," he said, his voice raw.

"You saved their lives."

Teach met her eyes and saw in them understanding and compassion.

"Yes, by taking the lives of others."

"If it hadn't been for you, more men on your ship would have perished, yourself included," she said.

Teach shrugged. "If it's God's will for me to go, who am I to stop it?" he asked.

Anne gave a short laugh. "That might be, but God also gave you a brain and intellect. Would you rather have stood by and let them kill the lot of you?"

"All I know is that I never want to watch a man suffer like that at my hand again."

The silence that followed was pressing, and Teach realized that whenever the two of them spoke, he revealed more about his past than she did about hers. He was determined to change that.

"Enough about me," Teach said. "Tell me, do you have any family?"

"No one to claim me."

Teach was amazed at her ability to avoid answers. "What does that mean, exactly?" he pressed.

"My parents are dead."

He studied her face. There was an unmistakable look of sadness in her eyes, and he regretted his insistence that she clarify her statement. "I'm sorry for your loss, but that means there is no reason for you to leave my father's household."

"It does not matter whether I stay there or not. Once you marry Miss Patience, you will live with her at her estate."

His head jerked back as if he had been slapped. "Why do you insist on bringing Miss Patience into every conversation?" he demanded.

Anne frowned. "I only speak the truth. Am I wrong in assuming you will soon be married?"

His mouth twisted into a bitter smile. "No. If my father has his way, we will be wed within the year."

"And if you had your way?"

"If I had my way, I would leave tomorrow on the first ship sailing out of Bristol, regardless of its destination." *And never return.* Afraid that once more he'd said too much, Teach stood abruptly. "I believe we should go back."

Anne waited as he placed the chairs once more inside the cottage. He led the way through the trees, and they found their horses exactly as they had left them. Lifting her back up into her saddle, he allowed his fingers to linger slightly longer than necessary on her waist. She glanced at him sharply, but Teach pretended not to notice.

He did not truly desire to return to the house, but knew it would not do to remain any longer in the woods.

They rode back in relative silence. Teach was tired. Perhaps it was a lingering effect from his illness.

As the house drew nearer, he felt the familiar bands of tightness settling around his heart. Anne's own face mirrored his, for her eyes were no longer shining, and her cheeks were no longer flushed.

At the weeping willows on the outside of his father's property, Anne stopped and dismounted. "Just in case the others have returned, I do not think it's wise for them to see us arriving together. I will return the riding habit as soon as possible."

"You may keep the garments. My only concern is if they see you in them. They'll know we were together." He realized too late that he hadn't thought things through.

Anne bit her lip. "Perhaps if you went in first, you could arrange some kind of distraction? I could slip in through the kitchen and head upstairs to change."

If she entered through the back way, there would be too many opportunities for her to be discovered. Teach shook his head. "No, I will go in first and return the horses to the stables. You go through the front door and enter your quarters from the other side of the house. They'll be less likely to see you."

He paused. "Unless they've already determined that you aren't in your room."

"No, they aren't so concerned for my welfare that they would go and inquire after me." Striding away, she disappeared around the corner of the wall.

Teach led the horses in through the garden, searching for movement near the back of the house. There was no sign of the groom as Teach entered the barn and unsaddled the horses, giving them a cursory brushing before heading for the kitchen door. The irony of the situation wasn't lost on him. He'd sent Anne to the front of the house, and he was stealing in through the back.

Passing through the kitchen, he was on his way to the stairs when he first heard the shouting. It was Margery. Even from his vantage point down the hall, it was clear she was angry.

"Don't lie to me, girl!" Her words were followed by the distinct sound of a slap.

Teach rounded the corner, just as Margery raised her arm again. Anne reached out and caught Margery around the wrist, clearly unwilling to yield to yet another strike.

"Stop!" Teach thundered, his voice exploding throughout the entryway.

Both Margery and Anne turned to see him barreling toward them, his face contorted with rage. "If you strike her again, I will have you removed from this household. You will not find another position for as long as you shall live!"

Anne released Margery's suddenly limp arm.

Margery's mouth dropped open, the anger in her eyes dying like a flame dipped in water. "But, but . . . sir, I caught her sneaking into the house, dressed like that!" She pointed to Anne, still clothed in the riding habit.

Teach studied Anne's appearance from head to toe, looking for any more signs of ill treatment, but thankfully could see none. Rounding once more on the old woman, he leaned forward, speaking through clenched teeth. "It's a riding habit."

Margery blinked. "Yes . . . yes, I know, sir."

He raised his eyebrows at her. "Is that a crime?"

The housekeeper flushed beneath the obvious scorn in his voice. "No. Yes. She's . . . How did she get it?"

An answering fire flared in Anne's eyes. "I told you, it was a gift."

"Where have you been, dressed like that?"

"I don't see how that's any of your business," Anne snapped.

Margery straightened. "As housekeeper, it's my business to know exactly what is going on—"

Teach waved his hand impatiently. "She already said it was a gift."

"Yes, but you told me several things have gone missing, and—"

"You will not say another word," Teach growled. He'd given her specific instructions to keep silent about the stealing, but Margery was too upset to notice.

"If anyone's taken anything from your father, it would be that one. She's the by-blow of some foreign gutter wench and a sailor, no doubt raised on the streets." Margery turned on Anne once more. "And to think I trusted you. You can't even follow directions proper like. I ran into the butcher while I was in town. He said you haven't been to buy meat from him since the young master returned."

Anne jumped forward. "Because he wanted more payment than I was prepared to give! If you want his wares so badly, then I suggest *you* lie with him!"

Margery dove for Anne's face, her arms outstretched and her teeth bared. Teach was able to scoop Anne out of the way as she scrambled to get hold of Margery's sleeves, the two of them clawing like cats.

A pounding at the front door brought the argument to a halt. Teach, for one, was grateful for the reprieve.

Holding on to Anne's arm, he practically dragged her with him, keeping a stern eye on the housekeeper. "Margery, you will pack your bags at once," Teach said.

"But who will run your father's house in the meantime? Her?" Margery shrieked.

Teach hadn't thought of the particulars. He only knew he wanted to keep Margery away from Anne. His jaw was clenched so tight, it ached. "Return to the kitchen. I will discuss your position with my father. Until then, you are not to speak to Anne, do you understand? You are not to go near her."

Margery nodded, glaring at Anne before turning on her heel and stalking away, her limp pronounced.

Anne trembled, whether from anger or nerves, Teach was unsure. She tried to wrest her arm from his grip, but he tightened his hold.

"I still wish to speak with you," he muttered.

"And I wish to change."

Teach deposited Anne in a nearby chair. "Do not move." Wrenching open the front door, he came face-to-face with a small boy standing on the front step. The boy jumped at the look on Teach's face, and quickly handed him a small note. A handsome carriage was waiting in the drive.

"What's this?" Teach snapped.

"A letter from yer father, sir."

Teach reached into his pocket and pulled out a coin. The boy pocketed it and scurried away. The black carriage did not move, and the driver remained seated.

Closing the door with a little more force than necessary, Teach wished he'd chosen to stay in bed this morning instead of rising. Despite his enjoyable afternoon with Anne, it had already been a grueling day, and it was not over yet.

After ripping open the delicate paper, he scanned the contents.

I know you have recovered, and would like you to come to the Hervey estate at once. I have sent a carriage to collect you. Until this evening. Richard Drummond

Teach was not surprised by his father's words. Of course his father would know he'd recovered. Teach was actually surprised it had taken him this long to send for him. His father never had been one to favor sentiment over practicality. There was nothing in the letter about wishing to spend more time with his wayward son.

No, his father needed him to come and secure the betrothal with the Herveys.

Truly this day could not get any worse.

Looking down, he discovered Anne had already moved and was headed up the stairs at a fast pace.

"Anne!" he called out.

She cringed, stopping where she was, and turned slowly.

He took the stairs two at a time, and came to a halt at her side. "What Margery said . . . pay her no heed. I will have my father dismiss her immediately."

Anne met his eyes, her gaze firm. "I was not born in the gutter like she says. Nor was I raised to work in someone's household. I do not know what my father wished for me, but I do not believe it was this."

Teach chose his words with care, not wanting to upset her further. "I'm sure he wanted you to be happy, whatever you chose."

"He always told me he loved me, and said he would take care of me," she said, her eyes glistening with unshed tears.

"I'm sure he did, in his own way, but now that he's gone—"

Drawing a deep breath, Anne squared her shoulders. "My father was Andrew Barrett. My mother was his cook, Jacqueline. He brought her back with him from one of his trips to the West Indies. I did not *work* for Henry Barrett. We grew up in the same household together. He's my half brother."

Stunned, Teach leaned against the banister, his mouth open, but no words escaped. A thousand questions fought for supremacy, and it took him a moment to gather his thoughts.

Anne stood before him, her hands clenched, and looking every inch the sixteen-year-old girl that she was.

"Why didn't you mention it before?" he managed to ask.

"What difference would it have made? My father kept my identity a secret. Why, I do not know, but I had no wish to dishonor his memory. Henry knows exactly who I am, and yet he kicked me out of the only home I'd ever known. Why would I think a houseful of strangers would treat me any differently?"

"But surely if my father had known . . . Andrew Barrett was one of his closest friends."

"What makes you think I would be eager to share my story with someone residing under this roof? You said yourself, after your mother's death their contact was infrequent. Growing up, I heard the name Drummond once or twice in my father's home, but I never dined with guests. My parents were rarely seen together, and when I spent time with my father, he never spoke of business acquaintances."

"I still can't believe my father didn't know."

"When Henry brought me here, he told me to keep my mouth shut and not to cause any problems, or else he would return me to the workhouse where he'd found me a few weeks after my mother passed. As I did not wish to return to that lifestyle, I did as he said."

Teach's stomach heaved at the thought of Anne spending time in one of those filthy workhouses. "But surely you could have found a different position elsewhere."

"Doing what? I have no references. It took my mother weeks to find a job as a cook."

"I'll speak with my father. Come with me. Now. We'll go and tell him who you are."

Anne retreated up one step, shaking her head. "No. I will not go with you to the Hervey estate."

"You must. I'll find you a room somewhere at an inn. You can stay there until I speak with my father—"

"No."

"Why not?"

"I have no desire to see Miss Patience again."

Teach sucked in a quick breath. "So you wish to stay here with Margery?"

"I prefer to stay here rather than go to a strange inn and sit in a strange room all day. Or all night. At least here I can go to the city. I can get out."

"You can do that there. There's a small village—"

"And I will be more out of place there than I am here. I will not go with you."

Once again Teach was at a loss for words. They stared at each other for several seconds.

"Why are you so stubborn?"

"Why are you so persistent? I will not accompany you. Now if you'll excuse me, I wish to change." Anne turned and headed up the stairs.

Teach called out after her. "I'll instruct Margery to leave you alone. You will no longer perform any chores. Stay in your room—"

Anne shot him a dark look over her shoulder.

"All right, then simply stay out of Margery's way. I will tell her who you are and that you are no longer employed as a servant."

She froze on the top step, one hand clutching the banister. "Then what am I?" she asked in a voice that was barely audible. "And where do I belong?" Not waiting for an answer, she picked up her skirts and fled.

Teach watched her go, tempted to force her to accompany him. But deep down he knew she was right. Knowing his father's temperament as he did, Teach understood that it would be best to confront him alone, and find out how Anne had come to work in the Drummond household.

Unfortunately for Teach, he wouldn't reach the Hervey estate until later that evening. He could not summon any enthusiasm at the thought of seeing Miss Patience again.

Entering his room, he grabbed a small trunk from his wardrobe, and then threw several garments inside. Henry Barrett's words raced through his mind. *"I could make your life very uncomfortable if you're not careful."*

By the time Teach left his room, his face had settled into harsh lines. What kind of power did Barrett still hold over Anne? Or had that been an empty threat? Why had Barrett brought her there in the first place? He had to benefit from her position in the Drummond household somehow. Otherwise he would not have bothered taking her from the workhouse. A caring older brother he was not.

It was obvious that Barrett had lied to Anne, and more than likely he'd lied to Teach's father as well. Either way, it didn't matter. Teach would make Barrett pay. Stealing his purse had been just the beginning.

CHAPTER 16

Teach

The crescent moon hanging low in the sky cast just enough light to illuminate the Hervey estate as the carriage pulled up the drive. It was an ornate, rectangular building with ivy winding along the sides like spidery veins, and only a few rooms were lit from within.

Before when he'd come to visit, Teach had always respected its grandeur and opulence. It had reminded him of an elderly duchess who refused to age. Looking at it now for the first time in more than a year, Teach recognized it for what it was. A grandstanding showpiece with very little substance behind the facade.

The carriage pulled to a stop, and he jumped out, not waiting for the footman to perform his duty. The front door opened, and an elderly butler held a candle aloft, bowing when he recognized Teach's face.

"Good evening, Mr. Edward."

Teach nodded. "Abraham. How are you?"

Abraham's expression was unreadable as he answered, "Fine, sir. Thank you for asking."

The butler had been a fixture in the Hervey household for as long as Teach had known them, and Teach marveled that the old man still retained his dignity in this unconventional atmosphere.

"Tell me, has my father retired for the evening?" It was half past nine. Master Drummond was notorious for going to bed early. Only Teach knew that once he was in the safety of his room, his father would often read for hours.

"Yes, sir, as well as Lady Hervey. But Miss Patience and the Earl of Lorimar are still with Lord Hervey in the drawing room. Would you care to join them? Miss Patience heard you arrive and is expecting you."

Teach wanted nothing more than to see his father, but knew etiquette required that he make an appearance. "Very well," he said, unable to hide the resignation in his voice.

Abraham bowed slightly at the waist and turned, leading Teach down the hall. Opening the door to the drawing room, he announced Teach's arrival. William and Patience stood up from the divan as Teach strode across the carpet toward them. The baron sat in a large chair near a window, his head tipped back and his mouth open, a pronounced snore sounding through the room. Patience's face flushed a deep red, and her hands fluttered at her side as Teach drew near.

"Edward," she said. "You've come."

"Miss Patience," he said, bowing over the hand she offered him.

William's eyes were red, and it was clear he'd been drinking. His voice slurred as he said, "Glad to see you feeling better, old chap. You gave Miss Patience here quite a scare."

Teach shook his head. "It was nothing serious. I'm sorry I wasn't able to join you sooner."

"That doesn't matter, now that you're here. You missed our fête last night. I tried to tell Mama that we couldn't possibly have it, with you being so ill, but Lord Lorimar convinced me otherwise. We shall have to have another, now that you've arrived."

"*Lorimar* never was one to miss out on a party," Teach said, using William's proper title in front of Patience. In fact, William appeared to still be celebrating.

William made a face, heading across the room for a crystal decanter filled with amber-colored liquid. "My parents are hosting one of their own in the near future. You're both expected to put in an appearance."

"Don't drink everything at once. Leave some for Father," Patience said over her shoulder. Settling herself once more on the divan, she patted the seat beside her. "Well, now that you're here, we may begin finalizing our arrangements. We've decided which property would be best for us."

Teach stiffened at her words and remained standing. "*We* have?"

Patience laughed, but it sounded forced. "Of course you have final say, but I'm sure you'll agree with what your father chose. Now it's just a matter of deciding the date."

"Surely it can wait until tomorrow. Teach has only just arrived," William said, taking a large sip. He smiled, although it didn't reach his eyes.

"Ah, but I'm quite sure that it can't," she said. "I've waited long enough, and I don't intend to wait any longer. If you wish, you may retire for the evening, Lord Lorimar. I shall be quite all right now that Edward is here."

It grated on Teach's nerves that she continued to use his name with such familiarity in front of his friends. He hoped she wouldn't be quite so obvious when others were around. "I'm afraid we shall have to postpone our conversation, Miss Patience, for I am quite tired and wish to retire now as well."

The look on her face would have been comical if it hadn't been so disturbing. A mix between a scowl and a smile as she tried to hide her disappointment. "Tomorrow, then," she said, exhaling loudly. "Father. Father. It's time for you to go to bed."

Lord Hervey gave a start, a loud snort escaping his mouth as he sat up and looked around, trying to gain his bearings. "Ah. Edward. Glad to see you here."

Teach smiled. "Thank you for having me, Lord Hervey."

Miss Patience took her father's arm. "Come along now.

Let's get you upstairs." She turned once more to Teach and William. "I will see you both in the morning." Not waiting for a response, she swept out of the room, her mouth a thin line of displeasure.

Once the door had closed behind her, William whistled softly. "You're going to have to make it up to her, Teach. You shall have to pay extra attention to her, or I fear she will not forgive you. She requires a finer hand than yours," he said, as if the two were discussing a horse.

Teach sighed, unbuttoning his collar. "I know, but I just didn't have the strength for it tonight." He gave his friend an appraising glance. "You look well. Have you enjoyed yourself?"

William grinned. "Who wouldn't? While you've been lying in bed convalescing, I've been quite entertained by your lovely fiancée."

Teach frowned. "Entertained? How?"

"In your absence I have decided to begin Miss Patience's study of *Paradise Lost*. I hope you don't mind."

Teach wasn't quite sure how he felt. William was harmless, and always had been when it came to matters of the heart. As far as Teach knew, he'd had no serious relationships with anyone. "On the contrary. I'm delighted to hear you've finally taken your studies seriously. Your parents will be happy to know that their money did not go to waste."

"If I'd known how enjoyable it could be to describe the difference between good and evil, I would have tried it long ago."

William's words reminded Teach of Anne. He wished she'd agreed to accompany him. "I'm sure Miss Patience appreciates your time. Now, if you'll excuse me, I need to see my father."

William's eyes widened in surprise. "Are you quite sure you've recovered?" He reached forward, as if to gauge Teach's temperature. "When did you ever willingly seek out your father's company?"

Teach smacked his hand away. "I have to ask him a few questions."

"About what?" William asked.

"Nothing that concerns you. Not directly, that is. But I might need your help with something later."

William rubbed his hands together, a gleeful look on his face. "Oh, what do you propose we do? Are we going to break into someone's vault? Or do you prefer something less dramatic, like stealing their sheep? I've missed you this past year, Teach. My life has been deadly boring without you."

"I highly doubt that. You are quite capable of creating your own entertainment," Teach said, turning his back on his friend and heading for the door.

"I'm here when you need me," William called after him. "Just say the word."

"I'll remember that." Teach appreciated his friend's loyalty, even though he didn't know what their actions would entail. Teach himself was unsure. It all depended on his conversation with his father. If he found out Henry Barrett was indeed responsible for Anne's position in his father's household, he would make sure Barrett never stepped foot in his house again.

Upstairs the hallway was dim as Teach walked in the direction of the guest wing. He knew exactly in which room his father slept, for the man was a creature of habit. In fact, Drummond didn't like anything over which he had no control. Teach would have to proceed with caution if he wanted to find out as much as he could about Henry Barrett and Anne.

After knocking on the third door on his left, he waited, looking down the dark-paneled walls stretching away in the gloom. His father's voice called for him to enter.

"There you are," Drummond said from the large armchair positioned near one of the windows. Still dressed in his shirt and breeches, he held a book in his hands. A tall candelabra stood sentinel beside him, giving the room a warm glow. "I heard you arrive."

Teach closed the door behind him. "Yes, sir. Miss Patience wished to see me first—"

"As she should. I was beginning to wonder if we would be planning your funeral instead of your wedding. I was most concerned."

Teach nearly laughed out loud. If his father had been so concerned, why had he left with the Herveys instead of staying behind to help him? "Never fear. I have fully recovered."

He took a few tentative steps forward, disliking how his father always managed to make him feel like a disobedient schoolboy. "You had a visitor while you were gone."

"Oh?"

Teach nodded. "Yes. Henry Barrett."

Drummond's eyebrows drew together. "What did he want?"

"He said he had some business with you," Teach said, unsure if this was the best way to introduce the topic. Should he ask his father outright if he knew Anne was Andrew Barrett's daughter?

If Teach did, his father wouldn't take kindly to having his actions questioned by his son. On the other hand, if Drummond didn't know, he would be upset to think that someone had deceived him. Either way, Teach had to tread carefully.

"Did he?" his father asked, his frown deepening.

"Yes. He made it sound as though the two of you were in the habit of discussing business matters. Does he have anything to do with the *Deliverance*?"

Drummond snapped his book shut. "Hardly. I haven't had or wanted anything to do with him since he showed up five months ago with that girl."

Teach's nerves prickled with awareness. "What girl?" he asked.

His father stood and walked toward the night table. "One of the kitchen maids."

It wasn't a surprise that his father didn't know Anne's name. He never showed any interest in his hired help. Even Margery, who'd worked for him for years, was still a relative stranger.

"You mean Anne?" Teach asked, his stomach clenching.

Drummond stretched, rolling his neck from side to side. "Hmm? Yes, yes, I believe that's her name. Several months after his father's death, he came and said she had worked in his house, but he had enough kitchen staff and wondered if she couldn't come and work for me."

"Did he give a reason why?"

His father's face was thoughtful. "Andrew had had a cook, a woman by the name of Jacqueline. Your mother and I were quite fond of her cooking. When your mother was ill, Jacqueline sent soups and salves to help ease her discomfort. Normally I would never hire an islander, but Henry obviously knew I would take in anyone who had learned at the hands of that woman."

Teach struggled to keep his expression neutral, shamed and angered by his father's obvious prejudice. "Did he mention anything else about Anne? Her surname, perhaps?"

"Good heavens, no. Why would I need to know that? I don't make it a habit to learn everything about the help. I suggest you don't either."

"How long had it been since you'd last had contact with Andrew Barrett?"

Drummond was silent, fingering a small frame on the night table with the painted likeness of his wife. He'd had it commissioned when Teach had been a boy, and Drummond never left the house without it. It matched the large portrait hanging over the fireplace in Drummond's bedchamber back at the estate.

"A year or two before his death, Andrew sent me a letter asking me to look after Jacqueline and her daughter should anything happen to him. We hadn't had much contact for some time, but I told him I would."

Teach knew Andrew Barrett was one of the few men his father had called a friend. The two had been close, or as close as Drummond would allow.

"After his death I received a letter informing me I was the executor of an account under Jacqueline's name. I replied to the solicitor, who said he would send word once he learned more."

"But you didn't hear anything else?"

"No. When Henry came to the house with that girl, I asked after Jacqueline. Barrett told me she had decided to return to the West Indies for a time and had taken her daughter with her. I remembered Andrew once telling me the name of the town when Jacqueline had been born, and I sent a letter there, hoping to learn of their fate, but all to no avail. They're quite primitive, I believe."

"So you never heard from Henry Barrett again?" Teach asked.

"No. Perhaps that's why he came by."

"No, that's not the reason. He was looking for something."

Drummond's eyebrows drew together. "What was he looking for?"

"Nothing of significance. So Barrett told you that Anne had worked for him?"

"Yes, which was why I hired her to help Margery in the

kitchen. Since I'd failed to fulfill Andrew's other wishes, I felt it couldn't hurt to employ one of his servants. I had just fired my own cook and was on the lookout for a new one."

"Did Henry say anything else? Anything about Anne's background or where she came from?"

Drummond looked up. "Heavens, no. Nor did I ask. The girl is a servant. All I care about is that she performs her duties satisfactorily. Why the devil are you asking all of these questions?"

"Because Henry lied to you, Father. Anne isn't a servant. She happens to be Andrew Barrett's daughter."

His father's face turned red, and his eyes widened with shock. "Good Lord! That girl is Andrew Barrett's daughter?" he asked, clearly stunned.

Teach should have known better. He could accuse his father of many things, but Drummond would never have employed the daughter of one of his closest friends. Especially not when he'd been asked to look out for her.

"Why didn't she say anything?" Drummond asked. Teach was fairly certain his father had barely spoken a word to many of his servants, including Anne, and he could not imagine a sixteen-year-old maid asking to speak with the master of the house. It simply wasn't done.

"She doesn't trust easily. When her father died, Henry Barrett kicked them out onto the street. I believe they had a hard time of it, and no one came to their aid. Anne didn't think it would make a difference if you knew her true identity."

"They?"

"Yes, Anne and her mother, Jacqueline."

Visibly shaken, Drummond sat on the edge of the bed. "Where is her mother now?" he asked, his voice subdued, as if he already knew the answer.

"Anne said she passed away. I don't know how or when, but it must have been before Henry brought Anne to you."

Closing his eyes, Drummond leaned forward, his arms resting on his knees. "Oh no. Oh no. I see it now. Good Lord, why didn't I see it before? She has his eyes. His eyes," he whispered, almost to himself.

Teach was surprised at the depth of emotion on his father's face. "You couldn't have known. If Barrett didn't say anything—" Teach began, but his father wasn't listening.

"I've failed him. He asked me to look after her, after *them*, and I failed him."

Teach stepped forward, a surge of sympathy washing over him. "It's not your fault. You had no idea. Barrett never said she was his daughter—"

"No, but I should have seen the resemblance. The minute she entered my house, I should have noticed the similarities. The cooking, the attention to detail." His eyes had a distant look in them. "Anne is just like her mother and is as proud as her father. And I have failed them all."

The room was eerily silent. Teach's mind filled with visions of what he would do to Henry when he found him. Not just on Anne's behalf but also on his father's. And his own.

Drummond stood abruptly and paced the floor. "I must go back. I must return and make this right."

Teach nodded in agreement. "Excellent idea. Tomorrow, we shall both—"

His father's head whipped around, and he fixed his son with a penetrating glare. "No. Tomorrow I will return. You will stay here."

"But I want to go with you," Teach insisted.

"No. *You* need to make things right with Miss Patience. I've spent enough time under this roof and must return to Bristol at once. In less than three weeks' time, the *Deliverance* will set sail, and there is still much to prepare. You will leave the matter of Anne to me."

Teach glowered at his father, wondering how he could have ever felt sorry for him. Teach also wondered how he could ever convince the man to let him captain a ship, if Teach couldn't even talk his father into letting him return home. "If it hadn't been for me, you would not be aware of the situation," he pointed out icily.

Drummond's voice was just as cold. "And do you care to explain why you were conversing with the kitchen staff about their status in my household?"

"I've noticed Margery dealing rather harshly with Anne and was curious as to why. I believe you should get rid of Margery."

"Could it be you have other reasons for being concerned for Anne's welfare?"

"Don't be ridiculous. I'm engaged to be married," Teach snapped.

"Good. And don't you forget that. Drummonds are honor bound to keep their promises."

"It is hardly a crime to speak with subordinates, Father. You could learn a lesson from Andrew Barrett in that regard. He took an active interest in his staff."

"Yes. I've seen how active an interest it was," Drummond said. "Andrew was a good man, but there is no denying his questionable judgment at times. Nevertheless, I will do as he asked and care for the girl."

"But you still need my help watching the servants because of the thefts. If you're too busy, I can—"

"I haven't noticed anything else missing. Perhaps I was mistaken. Anyone would be a fool to steal from me. Now, if you'll excuse me, I wish to retire. I'll return home first thing in the morning."

Teach reached the door in swift, angry strides. "Good night, Father. Have a safe journey back," he snapped, closing the door solidly behind him.

CHAPTER 17

Anne

Anne clutched the pocket watch in her hand as she entered the drawing room. Master Drummond rarely asked to have a word with one of his staff. When he did, the person was typically dismissed. Anne's insides flipped uncomfortably as she closed the door behind her. She wasn't sure if she was still an employee, which made her even more anxious.

"You wished to see me, sir?" she asked, attempting to keep her voice level, pressing the pocket watch into her palm.

Master Drummond turned from the window. His sharp green eyes, so similar to Teach's, studied her. "Yes, I did. Please, won't you have a seat?"

Anne's heart pounded in her chest, but she did as he requested.

He sat down across from her. "I don't know exactly where to begin, as I have apparently made quite a mess of things. But

189

I shall attempt to rectify the situation." Taking a deep breath, he leaned forward and looked Anne squarely in the eyes. "I believe I owe you an apology."

If Anne hadn't been sitting, her legs would have given out beneath her at his words.

Master Drummond continued. "A long time ago your father asked me to look after his cook and her daughter in the event that something happened to him. When you came to this house, I had no idea who you really were. Henry Barrett merely mentioned that you'd been employed in his father's household. If I'd known you were Andrew's daughter, I would never have agreed to let you work for me."

The pocket watch slipped from Anne's hand and fell to the floor. Too stunned to move, she watched as Master Drummond picked it up and examined it, turning it over in his palm.

"I know this watch. I was with your father in London when he bought it," he said softly. Popping it open, he read the inscription inside, which said *For my Jacqueline*, before handing it back to her.

"Thank you."

Master Drummond sighed. "No. You have nothing to thank me for. At least not yet."

Anne remained silent, waiting for him to continue.

"Looking at you, I can't believe I didn't see it earlier. Andrew never told me he had a daughter *with* Jacqueline, but I should have guessed as much. He was lonely after his wife died."

Anne did not like the insinuation that loneliness was the only reason her father had turned to her mother. "They cared for each other."

Master Drummond's gaze did not quite meet hers. It was clear he was uncomfortable speaking about the relationship between Anne's parents.

"Your father sent me a letter, asking me to make sure Jacqueline and her daughter were looked after. He said he'd leave the money in a trust and I was to oversee it."

Anne's eyes widened in surprise, for this was the first she'd heard of such arrangements.

"When Henry brought you here, I asked after Jacqueline and her daughter. He said you'd returned to the West Indies. Clearly, that was not the case," he said.

She shook her head. "No, it wasn't. My mother and I were removed from the house hours after my father passed away."

"If only I'd known," Master Drummond said, sitting back in his chair, the wrinkles in his distinguished face more pronounced than ever, "I would have taken you in. I would have done everything for you that your father had asked of me. You have to believe me when I say that."

Anne was shocked that the repentant man before her was the same person who hadn't said more than ten words to her since she'd entered his household. At the moment she wasn't sure what to believe.

"When Henry first brought you here, he asked if I wouldn't

mind giving you a job because he had enough servants. Since I hadn't been able to fulfill your father's request concerning Jacqueline, it was the least I could do."

Anger curled through Anne's chest like a snake. Henry had lied to both parties, never suspecting that the truth would come out. "Henry told me you were a friend of his, and threatened to send me away if I caused any problems for you. I didn't know if you knew my real identity, but I decided it didn't matter."

Master Drummond's mouth turned down at the corners. "Your father must have suspected that something like this would happen. I have reason to believe that part of Henry's inheritance required you to be taken care of. And that is why he came to find you at the workhouse. I've sent a note to his solicitor."

"Taken care of how?" Anne asked.

"Knowing your father as I did, I imagine he applied a stipulation that Henry would receive his portion of your father's estate only if you lived under my roof. It didn't matter to Henry how you lived here, so long as he could prove that you were indeed living in this household. I'm afraid we've both been ill used by the boy." Master Drummond steepled his fingers, his mouth set in a flat line. "But you are not to blame yourself. Once we hear from the solicitor, we will get to the bottom of this."

Once again Anne was stunned. Teach had clearly done as he'd said and gone to his father upon reaching the Hervey estate. She was grateful that Master Drummond would take the time to set things right.

"I would like to make amends. You will no longer work in my household. Instead you will take up residence in one of the guest rooms."

Anne started to protest. "Sir, that won't be necessary—"

Master Drummond cut her off with a wave of his hand. "I insist. You will be taken to one of the finest dressmakers in Bristol this week. Your father would want it this way."

Anne felt a warmth in her chest, knowing that her father had cared enough for her and her mother to see to it that they would be looked after.

"What about Henry Barrett? Will you tell him what you've discovered?"

Master Drummond's mouth grew ugly and flat at the mention of Henry's name. "I will take care of Barrett," he said. "He will not bother you again."

Anne wished she could be as sure as Master Drummond, but she knew her half brother better than he did. Nevertheless, it was useless worrying about it now. She was still trying to come to terms with everything that had been said in the past half hour.

"We will move your things to another room once one can be readied."

There weren't many things to move. Aside from the pocket watch, Anne had only the few maid's dresses she'd obtained when coming to work here. She couldn't wait to see the looks on Margery's and Mary's faces when they discovered she was no longer subject to their every whim. Quite the contrary, they would now take their orders from her.

"I suppose I should start to look for another cook," Master Drummond muttered, ever practical.

A sudden thought occurred to Anne. "I beg your pardon, sir, but the day your son returned, Margery brought in Ruth to help with all of the cooking. Ruth mentioned she had an older sister, Elizabeth. If she's anywhere near as capable as Ruth, you'll be in fine hands."

Master Drummond studied her. "Hmm . . . I shall have to give your suggestion some consideration. In the meantime, I would like you to go and gather your belongings. Wait, no, better yet, I will have Margery bring your belongings. I intend to have a word with her. It appears some things have been happening in this house of which I was unaware, and for that I apologize. I would dismiss her, except she has been quite loyal. If I threw her out, I'm not sure she would find employment elsewhere. I hope you understand."

Anne stood, sliding her watch into her pocket beneath the apron. A part of her wished he would sack Margery, but clearly Master Drummond had undergone some kind of change. And Anne knew only too well how hard it was to find employment. Where could the housekeeper go at her age? "Yes, of course, and thank you, sir. I don't quite know what to say. This is all so . . . unexpected. And very generous of you."

Master Drummond shook his head as he too came to his

feet. "I have been far too remiss in my duties as master of this house. My wife would be appalled to see how things have changed since her death." With a bow, he turned and walked away, leaving Anne to stare after him, amazed at the turn of events.

Master Drummond made good on his word and moved Anne into one of the spacious guest bedchambers on the second floor. Once she was left alone, she ran her hand over the soft comforter and sheets on the large four-poster bed, comparing them to the scratchy wool blanket she'd left behind.

The blue curtains hanging at the windows were as beautiful as the clear sky beyond and reminded her somewhat of her room back home. Her father, although affluent, had never amassed as much wealth as Master Drummond. It would be impossible not to be impressed by the luxurious surroundings.

Clutching a pillow to her chest, Anne remembered with glee the shocked look on Margery's face when she'd discovered Anne would no longer be her inferior.

And it was a good thing Anne wasn't made of straw, because the look Mary had given her would have torched her right there on the spot. Every time Mary passed Anne, a wave of resentment rolled off her. Anne determined to be extra diligent where Mary was concerned. She wouldn't be surprised if the girl ended up stealing from *her*.

Sara had been the most pleasant, and Anne decided she

would make Sara her lady's maid. It had been Master Drummond's suggestion. Anne's status in the house was second only to Drummond's, or so he claimed. He recognized Anne's need for a female companion after they attempted to visit one of the dressmakers in the city, for it did not go as well as he had planned. The dressmaker had insulted him by assuming that Anne was his mistress.

Master Drummond decided then that he would bring the dressmakers to the house.

They came with bolts and bolts of fabric, from the smoothest silks to the richest velvets. Yards and yards of cloth in ivory, sand, light blue, and pink. Anne was overwhelmed with the variety and, at one point, tried to tell him that it wasn't necessary to have a gown in every shade.

"On the contrary," he replied. "I can't have you wearing the same dress every time you leave this house. What would people think? I'm your guardian, after all. And you may call me Mr. Drummond."

Since her father had never openly claimed her, Anne was reluctant to attach herself to the Barrett name. However, as an islander, Anne's mother had had no legal surname, and it had been Anne's father who had given her the Christian name of Jacqueline.

As much as Anne enjoyed her new position and all of the finery that came with it, she also knew that even if you washed a pigeon with soap, it remained gray. She was still the illegitimate offspring of a merchant and a slave. And beneath Drummond's kindness, she felt an undercurrent of disapproval. Whether it was directed at her or himself, she was not sure.

Perhaps it was her own guilty conscience. Her thoughts turned to her secret stash of coins and household silver, including the valuable spyglass. She resolved to go to the city and try to recover the pieces she'd already sold, and hoped they would still be at the small shop. She had not yet returned the stolen objects to the household, hesitant to return all of them at once, for fear of discovery.

Despite Drummond's assurances, Anne wanted to make sure she was never left destitute again. She could still remember the fear in her mother's eyes when Henry had kicked them out. In order to survive, both she and her mother had been forced to work until their bodies hurt.

Life had been hard, but quitting had meant death.

Anne was not about to quit now. If she needed to, for whatever reason, she could still escape on the *Deliverance* when it set sail, and start a new life elsewhere.

CHAPTER 18

Anne

In a pale pink dress and looking as regal as a queen, Anne walked along the busy Bristol street in the afternoon sun, Sara at her side. Aware of many disapproving looks and whispered comments following her progression, Anne regretted her hasty decision to leave the confines of the Drummond household, but she'd been driven mad by her inactivity for the past four days and had resolved to do something about it.

"You look like a princess, Miss Anne. Visiting from a far-off land. That's why people are staring at you so."

Although it was nice of Sara to say, Anne knew that was not always the case. Before, when she'd been dressed as a simple maid, she'd glowered and scowled at anyone who had dared stare at her. Now she was no longer a nameless girl among many, but wore the clothes of a lady. Some people might be less inclined to be discourteous to her face, but that did not mean they accepted her. She doubted they ever would.

As long as she remained in England, she would always stand out.

Due to the number of pedestrians crowding the streets, Anne and Sara had left the confines of their carriage to walk up Broad Street. Their destination was a shop located near the parish of Saint John, a place for travelers to offer prayers before a journey.

She'd had no idea how tedious her life would become when she'd accepted Drummond's generosity. While she didn't miss Margery ordering her around, Anne realized that being industrious had helped to pass the time more quickly, and now she found herself wandering through the large rooms of the house, not quite knowing what to do.

Drummond himself had been absent the past four days. Despite the presence of the other maids in the house, Anne was lonely, and she'd wished more than once that she still had Teach's book to read. Drummond's library was stocked, but nothing caught her attention like the story of Dampier's travels.

Thoughts of the book naturally brought Teach to mind, and Anne wondered when he would once again return home. Not that it was any of her business. He was where he belonged, since he and Miss Patience were to be married.

The thought of Teach and Miss Patience together left a bitter taste in Anne's mouth, and she did her best to redirect her thoughts whenever they turned to him.

"Are we almost there, Miss Anne?" Sara asked, noticeably unnerved by the number of pedestrians surrounding them.

Anne nodded. "Yes, but I'd like you to wait outside the shop for me. It shouldn't take long," she said. She hoped that it wasn't too late to retrieve the items from Drummond's household, for it had been a month since she'd sold them.

"I've never seen the streets so crowded before, miss."

"Nor I," Anne admitted. The atmosphere among the throng could be described as festive, with an undercurrent of expectancy, as if the crowd were waiting for something to happen. Anne didn't understand it and was therefore caught off guard. As far as she knew, it wasn't a holiday.

"How's your mother?" Anne asked in an attempt to distract the girl.

Sara frowned. "As well as can be expected. She's able to get up a bit, but she still has an awful lot of pain."

"Perhaps you should take some time off to tend to her," Anne suggested.

Sara's eyes widened. "Oh no. I can't afford to do that, miss. All my money goes to help her, to pay for the doctor. If I don't work, who will?"

Sympathy tugged at Anne's heart. "I don't mean for you to quit. I'm simply suggesting you take a few days to be by her side. Heaven knows I don't need you waiting on me hand and foot." Aside from this excursion, Anne hadn't gone out, except to walk through the gardens.

What she wanted more than anything else was to take another ride through the countryside, but Sara didn't know how to ride, and Anne wasn't sure she'd want Sara to accompany her even if she could. "I shall talk to Mr. Drummond about it. I'm sure he wouldn't mind."

"But I can't afford—" Sara began.

Anne took Sara's arm in hers. "Nonsense. I will help pay for any missed wages. There is no need for you not to be with your mother," Anne insisted, knowing how important it was to care for loved ones, especially when they were ill. Drummond had given Anne some extra coins, in the event that he missed something while filling her wardrobe. Like with everything else he did, he had thought of every last detail, and Anne wanted for nothing.

Except companionship.

By sending Sara away, Anne would be sacrificing the one person in the house with whom she could converse, but she would feel even worse if she kept Sara by her side for selfish reasons. In truth, it was only a superficial relationship, and a few days apart would not make much of a difference to Anne.

To Sara's mother it could make all the difference in the world.

"Thank you, An— I mean, Miss Anne. That's most kind of you."

Smiling, Anne remained silent, grateful that the shop front appeared up ahead. But a sudden shout amidst the crowd drew her attention. She and Sara exchanged curious looks as answering cries could be heard along the street. People shuffled back and forth, and more than one stepped on Anne's toes. Almost as one, the movement of the crowd surged forward, sweeping Anne up in its wake.

Alarmed, she drew Sara's arm more tightly through hers as they were jostled to and fro by the group surrounding them. "Stay with me, Sara," Anne cried, her voice rising as she tried to speak above the noise of the throng.

Torsos and shoulders bumped Anne from every side, and Anne heard the telltale rip of her hem. Unable to see above anyone's head, Anne held on to Sara and hoped the two of them would not be separated. She had no idea what had caused the chaos. She only wished she could find a way out of the crush.

"Miss Anne!" With a frightened shriek, Sara was torn from Anne's side, her eyes wide with fear.

Anne struggled to get back to the girl, but like a drop of water fighting against a current, it was no use. She lost sight of Sara's terrified face as more people pushed in around her. Her own heart pounding, Anne fought a rising tide of panic. Elbowing her way through the mob and gasping for breath, it took her several minutes to reach the front stoop of a shop. It was not her intended target, but at least she was situated above the rest of the onlookers and had a clearer view of what was going on.

Two sturdy horses pulled an open cart filled with five

rough-looking men. It was clear they were some sort of prisoners, for their hands were tied with ropes.

People jockeyed for a better position to see the cart, and the roar from the streets was thunderous. Anne couldn't tell if the crowd jeered or saluted them, for some people threw produce, while others threw flowers. Frantic to find Sara and get out of the city, Anne searched for any sign of the girl, but to no avail.

When the cart drew up in front of Anne, she couldn't help staring at the men contained inside. They weren't men at all. Beneath their scraggly facial hair and unkempt clothing, they appeared to be only a few years older than Anne herself, and an unexpected twinge of sympathy pierced her heart. She didn't know what they'd done, but the hardened expressions on their faces spoke of a world of adversity and suffering that far surpassed her own.

Raising her voice to be heard above the noise, Anne addressed an elegant woman pressed alongside her. "Who are they?" she asked.

The woman gave Anne an incredulous look. "Have you not heard? They're pirates. Caught stealing from several merchant ships and bringing their wares here to sell."

That was why so many people crowded the streets. No doubt hoping for a glimpse of the bandits. "Where are they taking them?"

"Back to a ship for transport. They've just been questioned by the local constable."

Anne stared after the retreating cart, wondering what had driven the occupants to choose such a life. Had they done it to escape something, such as poverty and hunger? Or perhaps they had longed for a better future and had done the only thing they could think of to attain their goals. "What will happen to them now?"

The elegant woman shrugged. "Most likely they'll be taken to Execution Dock in London and hanged," she said, her voice detached. "That's where all pirates go to dance the Marshal's dance."

Anne didn't know what the Marshal's dance was, but she knew it couldn't be good. The woman's indifference upset her, although she couldn't explain exactly why. Anne had never met those young men, nor did she know if they'd killed anyone. But their wasted lives were surely worth grieving. Did they have any family? Someone who would mourn their deaths once they were gone? If they'd been born under different circumstances, what could they have achieved?

Watching the progression of the prisoners, Anne and the rest of the crowd waited until they disappeared from view. Slowly the throng dispersed, allowing movement once again along the busy street. Carriages proceeded with caution, and pedestrians bustled about, the spectacle forgotten as they continued with their daily lives.

Anne remained where she was, trying to control her churning thoughts. Images of the five prisoners hanging from nooses taunted her, and she resolved to return Drummond's items as soon as possible. If someone had caught her stealing, she would have found herself in their position.

"Anne? What the devil are you doing here?" a familiar voice ground out beside her.

Anne's mouth went dry, and her heart clenched painfully in her chest.

Teach.

Turning, she met his thunderous green gaze, momentarily caught off guard by his proximity. She willed her tight throat to relax. "I . . . I, um, came into the city to do some shopping. With Sara. Oh, I have to find Sara!"

"I just saw her and sent her home in my carriage. She was beyond worried, but otherwise unharmed. Why did you choose to come to the city, today of all days?"

Relieved to know that Sara was all right, but annoyed at the criticism in Teach's voice, Anne decided to launch her own offensive. "I didn't know I needed to report my whereabouts to you. Your father doesn't request it of me. Besides, aren't you supposed to be with Miss Patience?"

Teach's jaw clenched. "She's ill and might be suffering from the same ailment that plagued me. I left her estate late last night and only just returned. I heard that you'd gone into the city."

So he'd decided to come after her. If he dogged her every move, she'd never be able to return the stolen goods. "As you can see, I'm quite all right."

"Were you harmed?" he demanded, his eyes raking her from head to toe, taking in her muddy and torn hem. "Who did this to you?"

"I'm fine. Sara and I were separated by the crowd. Someone stepped on my skirts, that's all." Anne's cheeks burned with embarrassment and frustration. "I didn't know the city would be like this. Otherwise I would not have come." She almost wished she hadn't.

"You saw them, then?" Teach asked

"Yes."

Teach muttered something under his breath. "You shouldn't be here."

He was the one who shouldn't be there. "If you'd like to return to your father's estate, please don't let me keep you."

"I'm not about to leave you here by yourself."

"You sent Sara home by herself."

"In the safety of the carriage. With my driver."

Anne was confused by the different emotions his presence stirred in her—attraction and resentment as well as yearning and exasperation. She'd never felt like this about anyone before she'd met Teach. It was a bit overwhelming. "I'm sure you have more pressing matters than to accompany me."

"I wouldn't say they're more pressing, but they do concern you. I was on my way to see *your* father's solicitor. He sent a note this morning. My father was busy, so I came in his stead."

"What did the solicitor say?" Anne asked.

"Only that he's had some news about Henry. Would you care to join me?"

"I still have some errands to attend."

"In that case, I'll accompany you."

Anne's heart dropped. "But the solicitor—"

Teach waved a hand. "He'll simply have to wait. He didn't specify a time for the visit. I've given my driver instructions to wait for me at Mr. Cogswell's office, once he's delivered Sara safely back to the estate. Now, where did you need to go?" Teach asked, preparing to take her by the elbow.

It was all Anne could do not to stamp her foot. Her cage might now be wrapped in silks and lace, but nevertheless she was still trapped by her circumstances. "I will go with you to see Mr. Cogswell." *And come back for the silver another day.*

"Are you sure?"

Anne nodded. She could not deny her curiosity about Henry. If her father had left instructions for her to be cared for, then she wanted to know what, exactly, that entailed.

CHAPTER 19

Teach

Teach gave instructions to the carriage driver to take them back to the Drummond estate, before sitting back against the plush velvet upholstery inside.

Anne stared down at the papers in her hands. Mr. Cogswell, Andrew Barrett's solicitor, had handed them over to her, along with the news that Anne was now an heiress.

"What are you thinking?" Teach asked.

She didn't appear to hear him.

The moment lengthened uncomfortably. "What are you planning?" Teach asked, unable to remain silent.

"What makes you think I'm planning anything?" she asked, not quite meeting his eyes.

"Because I know you. What do you intend to do with the money?" Teach tried to make his voice light, knowing how inappropriate the question was, but there was a sense of urgency behind his words. He truly did want to know what she was thinking. What she was feeling. The lack of emotion on her face was unusual, especially for someone as passionate as she was.

Andrew Barrett had left her a fortune. Three thousand pounds, to be exact. Mr. Cogswell had apologized for not knowing sooner about Anne's predicament and had confirmed that Henry Barrett had lied to him as well.

"Not that it's any of your business," she said after an interminable moment, "but I would take it . . . and . . . travel—"

"You can't leave! Where would you go? What would you do?"

"I would take the opportunity to start my own life somewhere, find some of my mother's people—"

Teach laughed out loud, a hint of desperation in his voice. "But you can't. You can't leave. You won't receive the money until you turn eighteen."

Anne's own voice rose. "So you mean to tell me I have no choice but to stay here?"

"Would it be so terrible?"

"For someone who doesn't feel like I truly belong, yes. What do you see when you look at me?" Anne asked.

A myriad of words flowed through his mind at her question. Strength. Intelligence. Beauty. Compassion. "I see you."

Anne's expression softened somewhat. "Because you've taken the time to speak with me. And to listen. But most people see only how different I am."

"It doesn't mean you have to leave."

Anne caught her lip between her teeth, but made no response.

Her silence frightened him. "Please, Anne. I know I cannot begin to understand how you must feel. I'm sorry you had to go through what you did. I'm sorry Henry Barrett lied to you. If I could, I would kill him with my own hands if I thought it would make a difference. I still might. But right now my father is in charge of—"

Anne held up her hand. "Yes, and you heard Mr. Cogswell. Your father plans to move my inheritance into his account. His account, not mine! As my guardian, he controls my life as much as he controls yours, except I have even fewer liberties than you."

"But that's only until you're eighteen."

"Which feels like a lifetime away. I must speak with Master Drummond and see if he will release the money sooner."

"But your own father wanted you to wait." *I want you to wait.*

"I refuse to be a burden to anyone. I simply wish to live my life as I choose, to go where I choose. What is so hard to understand?" Anne asked.

"You were born in this country, Anne. You have no idea what life is truly like anywhere else. I've been to the islands and have seen the way people live. It's a hard existence. You can't go alone. It's far too dangerous."

"I want to at least be given the chance."

The air in the carriage seemed to shrink, charged with oppressed tension. It reminded Teach of an uneasy calm before a storm.

Anne's breathing wasn't quite steady, her agitation obvious. "I do not mean to sound ungrateful, but I'm tired of others directing my life. I'm ready to take charge of it and see where my choices lead me."

Teach sat back, his unease sharpening into something else. He could not argue with Anne, for he was all too familiar with her hopes. How often had he longed to tell his father the exact same thing?

But Teach knew Drummond, better than anyone else, and as much as Teach understood Anne's feelings, he sincerely hoped that his father would be able to change her mind.

CHAPTER 20

Anne

The library was Anne's favorite room. The wide windows usually let in long slanting rectangles of light, warming the otherwise cold house. And there were, of course, the books to linger over, innumerable titles containing wonderful details of adventure.

At the moment, however, a stormy sky outside cast ominous shadows over the library's carpeted floor and obscured Drummond's expression. Anne hesitated in the doorway, unsure if she should follow Teach in, or . . .

"Father—"

"I see that trouble has again darkened our door," Drummond said, swirling a glass of amber liquid in his hand.

Anne stopped short, exchanging a questioning glance with Teach. Was it possible Drummond knew what she was about to ask him?

Teach continued a few more paces and stopped beside his father's chair. "Sir?"

"None of this would have happened if you had simply done as I asked," Drummond said, his mouth hardening as he looked up at his son.

"What's wrong?" Teach asked.

Drummond tipped back his head and downed the rest of his drink before he answered. "This will ruin everything. Everything that I've worked so hard to accomplish."

"What?"

"You've been charged with piracy."

Anne's stomach plummeted, every muscle clenching with fear. Any argument for her own cause fled from her mind, replaced with an image of those five men in the cart. Except, in their place she saw Teach.

"That's impossible." Teach's body tensed.

Drummond stood slowly, as if he'd aged ten years in the short time since Anne had last seen him. The grooves in his face were more pronounced than ever. He thrust a piece of paper at Teach. "See for yourself."

Teach took the paper and scanned its contents, while Anne moved silently to his side and read over his shoulder.

In support of our sovereign lord the king, upon oath, I present that Edward Drummond, late of Bristol, mariner, not having the fear of God before his eyes, but being

moved and seduced by the instigation of the devil, by force
and arms, upon the high seas, and within the jurisdic-
tion of the admiralty of England, did piratically and
feloniously set upon, board, break, and enter a certain
merchant ship . . .

Teach crumpled up the paper before Anne could read any further. "There is no basis for these allegations," he ground out, visibly trying to control his anger.

"Who dares accuse him of such things?" Anne asked.

"The constable did not say. There is to be an inquiry. I have arranged for my Bristol solicitor to meet me at his office, and will leave within the hour. I do not expect to return anytime soon."

"Shall I come with you?" Teach asked.

"No! You've done enough. None of this would have happened if you'd simply stayed home and married Miss Patience like I asked."

"You didn't *ask* me, Father. You never ask me anything. You either demand or command." Teach spoke with a boldness no doubt born out of desperation. Anne recognized the anxiety and frustration on his face, for they mirrored her own. These were serious allegations indeed. If found guilty, Teach would hang. The thought filled her with dread.

"If the baron or Miss Patience find out about these charges, it could mean the end of your engagement. They have sent word that they will arrive in two days' time to discuss a date for the wedding. I don't know how to stop them from coming."

Caught off guard by the news, Anne was unprepared for the sharp stab of jealousy that pierced her. Miss Patience would be returning. She chanced a glance at Teach, to gauge his reaction to his father's statement about Miss Patience, but his expression was closed.

"Miss Patience is ill," Teach said.

"She appears to be on the mend," Drummond snapped.

"I should leave you," Anne said.

"No, please don't. I must rely on you to make sure Edward does as I ask this time."

Teach rubbed the back of his neck. "Father, let me go with you. I'll speak to the constable and explain to him that those charges cannot possibly be true. I did not commit any crimes."

"You expect him to believe you?" Drummond demanded.

"Why wouldn't he?" Teach shot back. "I've done nothing wrong."

Even though it was not directed at her, Anne felt the full force of Mr. Drummond's fury, and she wished she'd waited until the morning to try to speak with him.

Drummond opened his mouth once again, but Anne stepped forward, hoping to defuse the situation. "Please, what is to be done?"

"Have you not heard of the men they apprehended earlier, the ones charged and convicted of piracy?" Drummond asked.

Anne nodded, sure she would not forget them for as long as she lived.

"The constable says, since their capture, he's had at least two new charges of piracy brought before him. It's the equivalent of a witch hunt." Drummond turned an accusing finger at Teach. "And if you hadn't insisted on sailing, I would not be in this predicament."

"What evidence did they have against those men?" Anne asked.

"They were caught unloading stolen goods from a ship late at night. It's suspected they've been attacking merchants near the continent for the last six months at least."

"But in the past six months, he was nowhere near these shores," Anne said. "That should be easy enough to prove."

"Yes, well, with everyone clamoring for justice to be served, the investigation will proceed, regardless of where he was. As I've said, I'm meeting with my solicitor shortly. Edward is not to leave the house until I return."

"You can't be serious," Teach said.

"I am. And this time you will do exactly as I say. I do not want you venturing into the city, for any reason. You are to stay here and wait for Miss Patience's arrival."

"And what should I tell her? How long will you be gone?" Teach asked.

"I have not the faintest idea, but I do not expect to return home until the matter is resolved satisfactorily. I will do whatever it takes to see these charges dropped, and will send word with a messenger once I have more information." With that,

Drummond turned on his heel and left the two of them alone.

It was several moments before Anne heard the sound of Drummond's carriage fading away. Teach remained where he was, staring at the floor, his mouth grim.

Anne wanted to say something, anything to comfort him, but wasn't sure what that should be. Glancing at the door, she almost wished for Margery to appear. But the house was silent, except for the occasional pop of the fire.

"My father thinks I'm the devil incarnate," Teach said, striding to the hearth. He stabbed the logs with the fire iron. Sparks flew up, illuminating his face with a dangerous light, as the evening outside darkened to dusk.

"You don't mean that," she said.

"Don't I?"

"No. He just wants to see that your name is cleared."

"Not my name, Anne. *His.* He's never cared about my thoughts or my dreams. It's always been about him and what he wants."

"He wouldn't have rushed off in such haste if he didn't care for you. He's a powerful man. If anyone can have the charges dropped—"

Teach flung the fire iron against the nearest wall. The wood paneling cracked beneath the force, and the rod clattered to the floor. He rounded on Anne and approached her, his steps purposeful. "If word of this gets out, which it undoubtedly will, then any chance my father had of the aristocracy accepting him will be gone. *That* is what he cares about. *That* is why he was so quick to act."

Had their relationship always been so volatile? Or had it deteriorated since Mrs. Drummond's death? "He is not as cold as you believe he is. Look at what he's done for me. He will get you out of this."

"How?" Teach asked, stopping in front of her. His face was grave.

She threw up her hands, her own fear making her voice sharp. "I don't know. I don't know how any of this will turn out, but we have to give your father time."

"You saw the men today, Anne. Time is not on my side."

Anne turned and strode toward the fire, her speech trying to keep pace with her agitated thoughts. "Concentrate for a moment. Who would want to see you suffer or possibly hang?"

"I can't imagine anyone would want to see me hang."

"Nor can I, but obviously someone does. Now think. Is there anyone you've angered recently?"

"Henry Barrett is the only person I can think of."

"Do you think he knows we spoke with Mr. Cogswell?" Would that even be possible? They'd left the solicitor's office barely an hour before.

"I doubt it. Henry is angry with me for another reason."

"Why is he—" As his words sank in, Anne closed her eyes against the prickling along her scalp. Teach had never returned the money. "Why? Why didn't you give it back to him?"

"Because he's a fool!"

"And it appears you're the greater fool for not thinking he would seek revenge. When he left, he said he'd make you pay."

"Do you really think he's capable of such a thing? He would accuse me of piracy simply because I didn't return a few coins?"

Anne noted the heightened color in Teach's face, and wished she could tell him no. But she wouldn't put it past Henry to have done just that. "I can't say for sure, but look at what he did to me," Anne said. "If it had benefited him to have me gone, I have no doubt he would have sent me away. Permanently."

Teach's eyes glinted, his chest expanding with a deep breath. "I'll butcher him. This time I'll kill him with my bare hands. If I'm going to hang for a crime, I might as well be bloody guilty of it."

CHAPTER 21

Teach

Teach's mouth was dry, and he strode to the sideboard to pour himself a drink. He noticed the trembling of his own fingers as he gripped the decanter. Despite Anne's and his father's assurances, he was unsure how the investigation would end.

Studying her over the top of his glass, Teach noticed that her face was ashen, and she fingered the watch in her hand, a sure sign of her anxiety.

"Killing him won't solve anything," she said. "And you said yourself you do not want another man to suffer by your hand."

"That was before I knew that Henry Barrett planned for me to suffer."

"Don't do anything rash."

"He should pay for what he did to you."

"Yes, but not by you. If you go after him now, it will be as good as admitting your guilt. We need to let your father know about Henry. Perhaps he can—"

Setting the glass down with a little more force than necessary, Teach cursed beneath his breath. Anne gave a start at the sound. He wished there were some way to soothe her, but his mind was already busy with plans.

"I have to go out," he said. "If anyone asks for me, tell them I've retired to my room."

She intercepted him on his way to the door, planting herself in front of him. "Your father said you shouldn't venture into town again."

"My life is on the line. Not his."

Anne grabbed Teach's arm. "Which is why you need to be careful. These charges are serious."

Teach placed his hand over hers. "And that is precisely why I must act. I cannot idly sit by and do nothing." He gave her fingers a squeeze. "I will return before daylight."

"Don't do this. He's not worth it."

"Would you absolve me of my crimes, Queen Anne?"

"If it were in my power to do so. But I do not believe you are guilty of any," Anne said, studying his face. "Yet."

"Trust me," he said, her hand still caught beneath his.

She looked as if she were about to argue further, but Teach stepped around her and exited the room.

On his way out the back of the house, Teach stopped in the

kitchen. "Please see that Anne has a hot bath, and prepare a tray of food for her." After the day that she'd had, Teach knew she could use both.

Margery's mouth turned down, but she merely said, "Yes, sir."

As much as he would have liked to stay behind and make sure Margery obeyed his orders, Teach didn't have the time. He needed to find his friend John, and find him quick. Despite what Anne believed, Teach had no intention of tracking down Henry Barrett and killing him.

Yet.

By this time tomorrow Teach wanted to know what kind of proof Barrett had to support his charges of piracy. It was a lie, all of it, but somehow Henry had managed to convince the constable. Teach had to find a way to dismiss any evidence and prove that Henry was a liar.

Instead of riding Kaiser, he decided to take an older carriage from the stables, one that hadn't been used recently. As much as Teach hated to admit it, his father was right. It would be better if he wasn't recognized or seen about town.

Wearing the floppy hat John had given him, as well as the old coat, Teach set out, thankful for the disguise.

By the time he arrived at the *Deliverance*, it was dark and a thick fog had rolled in, cloaking the docks in a sheltering mist. Teach didn't wait to search for a plank to board. He took a running jump and leapt onto the deck.

John appeared almost immediately, no doubt drawn by the

sound of Teach landing and by the subtle rocking of the ship. In John's hand was the telltale glitter of his knife, which he lowered to his side when he saw Teach. "Well, lookee here. The *Deliverance* won't be ready for another fortnight. Bored of the good life already, are you?"

Teach grimaced, shaking John's hand as John thumped him on the back. "I need to talk to you."

John's face grew serious, his eyes narrowing. "What is it?"

Teach led him away from the rail and down the murky stairs to the captain's cabin. The sweet musky scent of fresh pine and wood tar filled the air. The room itself was sparsely furnished with a desk, chair, and a single berth, and large windows lined one wall.

Closing the door, Teach turned and faced his friend. "I need you to take care of something for me," he said, his voice soft.

"Tell me what you want me to do, and I'll do it."

It was a relief to know Teach could count on John. "I've been accused of piracy."

"What?" John burst out.

Teach held up a hand, wary of the silent docks in the distance. "Quiet. I just found out today. The constable delivered the charges to my father."

"But that's a bloody lie."

"I need you to keep an ear out. It might have been Henry Barrett. If it was, I need you to discover what kind of evidence he has."

John spat on the ground over his shoulder. "I remember Barrett. Nowhere near as honorable as his father. Pity it wasn't him who died."

"Yes, well, if we don't get him to withdraw the charges, I might be next."

"I'm sure me and the rest of the crew would be only too happy to vouch for you."

Teach gave a weak smile. "I wish it were that simple. Others have been accused, but I'm not sure who they are or if the same person brought the evidence against all of us. I need you to find out for me."

"Right. It'll take me a bit to see what I can scare up. If you can stay with the ship, I'll be back in a spell."

"Of course," Teach said. "But you must return before dawn."

John clasped Teach's shoulder. "Don't you worry none. We'll get to the bottom of this." With a friendly nod, John opened the door and disappeared up the stairs.

Teach had been right to come here. If there was news to be learned, his friend would be able to gather it, for he was a popular figure and well-liked by all who knew him.

It only now occurred to Teach that he'd never once thought to go to William. William had returned to Bristol with Teach, and the duke was an influential man in Parliament.

But somehow Teach knew William would be of no use to him.

Teach couldn't help wondering how the meeting between his father and his solicitor was going. Anne was right. Drummond was a powerful man in the city. If he was able to disprove Henry's allegations, Teach would deal with Henry personally later.

For the next three hours Teach kept vigil at the top of the stairs, hidden in the shadows of the deck. The water lapped against the hull of the ship, comforting Teach with its familiar cadence. Despite his father's disapproval, Teach would never be sorry for the time he'd spent at sea.

If he were to hang . . .

Teach pushed those thoughts aside, his eyes drawn to a sudden movement on the docks.

John had returned.

After sliding a board into place, John was on deck within a matter of minutes. The two of them retreated once more to the captain's cabin.

"And?" Teach demanded.

"Whoever accused you isn't the same one who accused those other men. They was caught red-handed. Someone just threw your name in for good measure."

The muscles in Teach's arms and back tightened. "Was it Barrett?"

John rubbed the back of his neck. "Don't know for sure. Nobody's heard of any evidence against you, not like with those others. I've got someone watching Barrett's house, to see what he does and where he goes. You best get home, Teach. There's nothing more to be done tonight."

Frustration warred with fatigue, and Teach drew his hand

wearily through his hair. "Bring word to my house, but don't go to the front door. Come through the back, like you're visiting Mary."

"I haven't seen Mary in days."

"You can't tell anyone about this, John. Especially not Mary. You must take this secret with you to the grave, do you understand?"

John nodded. "Don't worry. I owe you my life, Teach. I'd sooner sell my own mother than disappoint you."

Having John as a friend was like having a big, vicious dog as your loyal pet. Satisfied, Teach shook John's hand and took his leave.

By the time Teach reached his father's house, the building was mostly dark, with only a few candles illuminating the interior.

After taking the stairs two at a time, he removed his coat and floppy hat and threw them across his bed. His father's door down the hallway was open, the interior of his room black. As promised, he had not returned.

Teach picked up a book from the night table and headed to Anne's room. He stopped outside the door and listened to her footsteps as she paced the floor. Teach was surprised by the pounding of his heart. He hadn't been this anxious since his father had sent him away to school for the first time. He knocked softly and waited.

Beneath the door he saw Anne's shadow cross, before she opened it partway, somewhat hidden from his view. She wore a nightdress and a velvet robe, her damp hair hanging over one shoulder. He experienced the usual shock of awareness whenever he saw her. She'd never looked more beautiful.

Her breathing was faster than normal, but she said nothing. There was a strange glow in her eyes, like compassion or sorrow. He could not be sure.

"I told you I would return," he said.

Anne nodded. "Did you . . . Did you discover anything?"

"No, not yet. But I have a friend working on it." Teach cleared his throat and held out Dampier's book, unwilling to discuss the charges any further. "I wanted to bring you this," he said, hoping his voice sounded steadier than he felt. "I thought it might help you fall asleep faster."

Opening the door farther, she reached out and took it from him, her soft fingertips touching his. He didn't let go immediately, wishing she would invite him into her room.

She did not.

"Thank you. I've been wondering what happens next." She made no move to close the door. A pulse beat at her collarbone, and he longed to run his finger along her smooth skin.

Teach took a step forward, the book still connecting them. "I could tell you what happens next," he said, his voice low. Anne swallowed. Her blue eyes shone in the candlelight, and Teach could not have turned away if he'd tried.

"Does he die?"

"He does not. At least not for many years."

"Is there any more sadness?" she asked.

He reached out and brushed her cheek with his thumb. "No," he whispered.

"Does he return to the sea?"

They both knew they were no longer discussing the book. "That remains to be seen. There might be something that could tempt him to stay."

A shadow passed over Anne's features, and she withdrew her hand while taking the book. Teach was surprised by the strength of his disappointment.

"I've heard your father say that temptation is of the devil," she said.

"Contrary to what my father believes, I do not think all enticements are wicked."

Anne gave him a sad smile, making her look older than her sixteen years. "A wise man is not the one who knows the difference between good and evil, but the one who chooses the least evil."

Before Teach could form a retort, she closed the door softly. He braced himself against the frame until the light from her candle was snuffed out.

CHAPTER 22

Anne

Wandering through the house the next morning, Anne found Teach in his father's library. He sat at the desk, tracing the wood grain with his thumbnail, but stood as she entered.

There was no sign of Drummond.

"What do you plan to do today?" Teach asked, leaning against the corner of the desk.

"I thought I might go back to the city." It had taken her a while to fall asleep, even after Teach had brought her the book. She'd been too distraught over the charges against him. If Drummond didn't find some way to have them dropped . . . Anne didn't even want to think about what might happen. No, she had to continue to believe in Drummond's abilities, for herself as well as for Teach.

For the first time in her life, she liked to think she had a friend. She admired Teach's intelligence and his drive. She envied his confidence and his ability to listen to others.

Of course, she also couldn't deny her attraction to him. Last night, when he'd given her the book, she'd been very aware of him as a man. And more than once she'd caught a certain gleam in his eyes, one that betrayed a deeper emotion than simple friendship.

In order to put some distance between them, she had decided to return to the city for the day. Every time she saw a glistening candlestick or spoon, it weighed on her. It was one thing to steal from Richard Drummond, a cold, heartless master, but it was something else to steal from the man who had opened up his home to her.

She also hoped to hear more about the charges against Teach.

"You should go. There's no reason for both of us to suffer. You are free to leave as you choose," Teach said.

Anne walked toward the desk, her skirts rustling. She knew she should leave, but his voice alarmed her. She'd never heard him so despondent. "In a few days you shall be free to leave as well."

A wry smile touched his lips. "If only I had as much faith in my father as you do, Anne." His voice was soft and tender, the sound of her name a caress.

"He obviously has faith in you. Otherwise he would never have agreed to let you spend the year at sea."

"He agreed to let me go only because I threatened to join the navy."

"You didn't," she gasped.

"Oh, but I did. Not that I would have followed through with it, but my father didn't know that. I'd sooner stay on land than be part of the Royal Navy."

Anne had heard rumors about life aboard naval vessels. "Is it as bad as they say?"

Teach nodded, his mouth turned down. "They'll take anyone, willing or not, and will use royal press gangs if necessary. On a naval ship, they rarely stock enough food and water. The only thing possibly worse is life aboard a merchant ship."

"Not my father's ships," Anne said. "I saw the way he kept them."

"No, not your father's ships. Andrew Barrett was the exception."

She noticed he didn't say anything in defense of Drummond's fleet. "I'm sure your father's aren't terrible either."

"How many of my father's ships have you seen?" Teach asked, his eyes narrowed.

Anne flushed. "None. But how bad could they truly be?"

"It depends on the captain. Anyone foolish enough to speak out on a merchant ship will most likely be punished. The same on any naval vessel. But if the crew of a pirate ship doesn't like their captain, they won't hesitate to select a new one."

"I felt pity for those men I saw yesterday, for the waste and ruin of their lives. It almost sounds as if you respect them."

He leaned back, crossing his long legs in front of him. "I don't respect them, but neither can I judge them too harshly.

If I were put in the same situation, I'm not so sure I would act differently."

"You would not become a pirate," Anne said, shaking her head. "They act without authority. They're scoundrels and crooks—"

"And is your brother so very different?" Teach asked. "I've seen some rather questionable characters who claim to be educated and well-bred act far more maliciously than any pirate. Nobles claim that the poor and uneducated cannot govern themselves, yet I've witnessed destitute men do just that, obeying their own laws like a priest obeys the word of God."

Any further argument Anne might have made was forgotten. A high-pitched scream sounded from the courtyard outside, and Anne rushed to the window, noticing a dust cloud churning near the barn.

It took her a moment to realize that it wasn't due to the wind. Two figures wrestled on the ground, while Mary and Margery stood nearby, both of them shrieking at the men to stop.

Teach was already out of the library when Anne picked up her skirts and rushed after him. He strode through the house and out the back door, toward the commotion, his expression grim. Anne recognized only one of the participants, Tom, the young groom, his shirt torn and his breeches covered in dirt.

The other individual was a stranger, but he was strongly built. Teach grabbed his arm in an effort to pull him off the prone figure of the groom, but his efforts were rewarded with a fist to the gut. Teach doubled over, and Anne rushed to his side.

Mary sobbed, clutching her apron. "Stop it! Stop it, I tell you!" she cried.

It didn't take a stretch of the imagination for Anne to realize that the other person must have been John, Mary's beau. If someone didn't act fast, who knew if the fools would stop.

Anne raced to the barn and grabbed a pail full of water. Charging out into the fray once more, she flung the contents onto the combatants. The force of her swing sent her flying, and she landed on her backside, next to Teach.

Everyone else froze, as if they, too, had been doused. Too shocked to move, Anne simply sat there. Teach heaved her to her feet and wrested the bucket from her hands. He turned on the two men—boys, Anne quickly told herself, for they couldn't have been more than three years her senior—and dragged them apart. Water was dripping down their shirtfronts.

"What happened, John?" Teach demanded, looking between the two.

John pointed a thick finger at the groom. "I caught him taking liberties with my Mary," he snarled, a pained look on his face.

Anne's heart ached for him.

Teach turned in the direction of the plump maid. "Is this true?"

Mary twisted her mouth, clearly trying to think of a way out of her present situation.

It was enough of an answer for John. He lunged for the groom once more, but this time Teach was ready. He grabbed John around the shoulders from behind, leaning back to prevent the two of them from toppling over. "You are both dismissed," he said to Tom and Mary through clenched teeth, struggling to hold John back.

Margery, seeing the need to intervene, pushed Mary toward the back door. "You heard him. Mr. Edward says it's time for you to go."

Tom stood there for a moment. "But his father hired me—"

Teach's face was bright red from exertion. "Go now!" he bellowed.

It took Tom less than two minutes to gather his belongings and leave the property. Mary quickly followed suit, in a rush to catch up to him. She left without so much as a good-bye in John's direction.

Teach released John slowly, his back tensed in case he needed to intervene again. He needn't have worried. John's shoulders slumped forward, his face crumpling with grief.

Although Anne had never lost a beau, she felt an overwhelming amount of sympathy for the young man. She could not imagine how he must feel, watching his love walk away with another.

On the other hand, she was relieved that Mary was gone. The girl had always been trouble.

Anne turned, wanting to give John some semblance of privacy. Her eyes met Teach's, and she saw the same emotions she felt mirrored in his.

"I'll go see about some food," she said to no one in particular. At the door to the house, she cast one last look over her shoulder. Teach spoke quietly to John as the first few drops of rain fell from the pewter sky.

CHAPTER 23

Teach

Teach waited patiently beside his friend as John took a deep, shuddering breath. Raindrops fell intermittently, like silent tears from the sky.

"She doesn't deserve you," Teach said.

John didn't respond. He stared at the empty courtyard that just moments before had been full of chaos.

Clapping John on the back, Teach guided him toward the stable, knowing his friend needed some privacy. He was worried John might still decide to go after Mary. "Come in out of the rain."

"You knew all along, didn't you?" John asked, dragging his feet.

Teach gave him a steady look. "Would you have believed me if I'd told you?"

After a moment of stony silence, John shook his head. "Probably not."

Teach approached Kaiser's stall and stroked his neck. The sweet smell of hay combined with the leather tack acted as a balm.

"I'm sorry for my behavior. Your life is on the line, and I acted like a fool, but when I saw Mary and that . . . I . . ." John's voice faded, his hands clenching into fists. "I'm sorry."

Teach tried to imagine how he would feel if Patience's attentions were otherwise engaged.

Relieved.

Now, if he ever saw Anne with anyone else . . .

Shaking his head to clear the image, Teach turned to his friend. "You'll find you're better off without her."

John gave him a sad smile. "Mary and I grew up together. I've known her since I was a lad and stole a pie from her father's bakery. She used to be all kinds of fun. What could make a girl change so much?"

There was no question Mary still liked to have fun, but Teach kept that observation to himself. "It happens. Some people change too much, and others don't change at all. You'll see it's for the best. You're a good man, John. You've weathered far worse, and I daresay you'll come out ahead in the end." Teach almost envied him. At the moment he'd gladly have traded positions with his friend and been rid of an unwanted betrothal.

"She didn't even look back at me," John muttered.

Teach took a long breath, disliking the thought of John

wasting another minute pining for Mary. Given time, John would forget her. "I hate to ask, but I'm assuming you're here because of Barrett."

"Aye, I am. He's gone."

"What?"

John nodded. "It's true. Word is he sold several of his father's ships to the Royal African Company, to be turned into slavers."

Teach was disgusted but not surprised. "When did he leave?"

"Yesterday, aboard a ship set for the West Indies."

"Did you hear of any evidence he might have against me?"

John lowered his head. "No. Nothing. I was about to have someone pay him a visit, but I never got the chance. He's gone."

Teach cursed, and Kaiser sidled away, snorting nervously. Leaning forward, Teach attempted to soothe the animal, his mind replaying John's words.

Barrett was gone. Barrett was gone.

"I'm sorry, Teach. I truly am."

Teach almost didn't hear him, for his heartbeat hammered in his throat. Staring at the ground, he tried to think of what his next step would be, but his mind wouldn't focus.

"Can they have an inquiry if Barrett isn't here to support the charges?" John asked, his tone hopeful.

"I don't know. I'm not even sure if Barrett was the one to accuse me, but I can't think of anyone else who would gain from it."

"I'll look into it for you," John said. "Don't you worry,

Teach. We'll get to the bottom of this, even if I have to break you out of jail myself."

The tightness in Teach's chest didn't ease, despite his friend's assurances. "Yes, well, hopefully it won't come to that."

The two of them were silent, a heavy pall hanging between them.

Eventually John cleared his throat. "I best head back to the *Deliverance*."

"Would you like to come into the house first?" Teach could do with a drink.

John shook his head, turning for the door. "I'm not fit for company. I'll keep asking around. Like I said, we'll get to the bottom of this." He raised his hand in a final farewell before striding out the door and disappearing from view.

Teach stood alone in the stable for several minutes, reluctant to return to the house. He rubbed the lower half of his jaw, considering what to do. With Barrett gone, there went any hope of confronting him, demanding answers.

Taking slow, measured breaths, he looked outside. The rain had already stopped, as if the sky couldn't make up its mind.

After several more minutes he headed in the direction of the gardens.

The wind blew and buffeted, but Teach pressed on through the manicured lawns, until he reached the trail leading behind his father's property into the nearby woods. He drew to a halt at the two weeping willows. As a child he'd loved playing near the trees, pretending he was an explorer, discovering new worlds and different cultures.

It was the same place where he had vomited on Miss Patience, and where Anne had appeared out of nowhere to help him. He liked to think that had been the start of their friendship, but it had since grown into something stronger.

As if his thoughts had conjured her, he felt her presence at his side before he saw her. She wore a dark blue cloak that fell to her ankles in long folds, and despite the mud soaking her hem, she looked every inch the queen.

"I'm going into town," she said.

"Oh?" Although he'd encouraged her to do just that, Teach couldn't hide his disappointment. There was something calming about Anne, and at that moment he craved tranquility.

"Yes, I'm going to find someone to take Mary's place." Not only was she intelligent and beautiful, but she possessed an air of efficiency. Teach had the feeling that when she set her mind to something, there wasn't anything she couldn't do.

"While you're at it, do you think you could find a replacement for the groom as well?" Teach asked, only half joking. His father hadn't been gone for even a day, and already the household had fallen apart. "I'd accompany you, but I have the feeling my father wouldn't appreciate my efforts."

"I believe I can find someone to replace the groom. Elizabeth has several siblings. I'm sure they would be more than willing to work for your father."

"Let me ready the carriage for you," he said.

"There's no need. I prefer to walk."

"You'll do no such thing. It's about to rain again."

Anne squared her shoulders. "I assure you, I've walked in the rain before. And the snow. And the ice. I'm perfectly capable of walking to town. I used to do it every day."

Teach hated the thought of Anne being exposed to all sorts of elements, both human and otherwise. "I do not doubt that, but I would prefer it if you took the carriage. And have Sara accompany you."

"Elizabeth is coming with me. And she prefers to walk as well."

In spite of his annoyance, Teach couldn't help a faint smile. She would fight till the last. "I thought we were past this, Anne."

"Past what?"

"Arguing."

"We're not arguing. I simply came to tell you where I was going. You're the one who insists on telling me what to do."

"Good. Then I'm simply telling you I will see to the carriage." Teach turned to head back to the stable, but Anne's next words stopped him.

"I saw John leave. I know he came to bring you some kind of news. What was it?" There was no mistaking the concern in her voice.

"He's gone."

Anne lifted her skirts and moved to stand in front of him, forcing him to meet her eyes. "Who is?"

"Your brother."

Looking away, she was quiet for a moment. "What does that mean? Will they continue with the inquiry if he's not here?"

Teach sighed. "I don't know. I don't know what any of this means."

"We still have to wait to hear from your father."

Teach rubbed the back of his neck. "You place an awful lot of faith in his abilities."

"And you, not nearly enough. Despite what you think, I know he loves you."

"You keep telling me that, but we must have a different understanding of the word."

"And what is your definition?" she asked.

"I believe if you truly love someone, then the most important thing should be their happiness, not yours."

"You're saying your father cares more for his own happiness."

"Yes."

Anne stepped toward him, her face flushed. "And I believe if you truly love someone, you let that person know you will always be there for them, no matter the circumstances. That is precisely what your father is doing."

"And you?"

Anne's breath was faster than usual, a pulse beating in her neck. "What?"

Reaching for her slowly, he gave her every opportunity to retreat. When she didn't, he took her hands in his and pulled her close. "Will you always be there for me, no matter the circumstances?"

"You know I only want your happiness," she said, her voice faint.

"By my definition, that means you—"

Anne tugged her hands from his grasp and moved out of his reach. "I don't think this is wise," she said, shaking her head. "You're upset."

"If I'm going to die, I might as well die a happy man. Tell me," he said, his voice soft.

Her lashes half lowered over her crystal-blue eyes. "In the short time we've known each other, I've come to bear a certain . . . regard . . . for you. Your friendship is something I could not stand to part with."

"'Regard'? 'Friendship'?" He approached her once again, and his warm palm found the curve of her cheek. "Is that all you feel for me, Anne?"

CHAPTER 24

Anne

Teach's eyes darkened, the expression in them stealing her breath. She should have pretended as if his nearness did not affect her. But it did, and instead of stepping back, she stepped closer. "Yes," she whispered, a tremor in her voice. "A very special sort of regard."

He apparently needed no further confirmation. He cradled her face in his hands, and his lips met hers, their mouths fitting together perfectly. Anne's heart fluttered in her chest like a trapped bird in a cage. But she didn't pull away. She didn't want to.

His clever fingers found the bare skin at the nape of her neck and wound into the strands that had come loose from her bun, tilting her head to an upward slant.

Anne fought to control the reckless rhythm of her pulse as he increased the pressure of their kiss. Her legs threatened to give way, and her hands traced down the fine linen of his shirt, feeling the solid strength of muscle underneath. For the rest of her life she would remember that moment. The sound of the wind rustling through the trees. The earthy scent of the moss beneath their feet, and the warmth of his breath mingling with hers. Her first kiss.

When at last he pulled away, Anne swayed forward, slightly dazed. "We . . . we shouldn't have done that," she said.

Breathing hard, his chest rising and falling steadily, Teach gave a shaky laugh. "I'm sorry, but I've wanted to do that since the first moment I saw you."

"It was a mistake."

"You cannot tell me you have not wanted the same thing, Anne."

Anne swallowed, unable to lie. It took considerable effort on her part not to lean into his embrace. She had thought about it, more than she cared to admit. Ever since he'd arrived, he had haunted her dreams. "But you're promised to another." She could not bring herself to speak Patience's name.

"Promised? What good is a promise to someone else when my heart belongs to you? What good is a promise when I might not live to see another day?"

Anne refused to think about the inquiry. In spite of Teach's scorn, Anne still believed Drummond would somehow come through for him. "What we've just done is no different from what Mary did to John."

"Do *not* compare my feelings for *you* to those of that

strumpet. Mary never cared for John. He was a lover of convenience. I do not hold out much hope for Tom, either. Give her a week or two, and she'll have moved on to someone else."

His words did little to ease her guilt. "Still, your father—"

"Oh, yes, my father. My union with Miss Patience is his will, not mine."

Anne took a step back. It was too hard to think with him standing so close. "But you agreed," she reminded him.

"I was sixteen years old and still an obedient boy! I didn't know any better. Do you think I could predict the future? Back then I saw Patience as my father wanted me to see her. She was a pretty face with a title. My father filled my head with stories of the aristocracy, how their life of leisure enabled them to cultivate their minds and improve their tastes. He spoke of their power and how much they could achieve, and like a fool, I listened to him."

Anne felt sorry for the boy Teach had once been, blindly believing everything his father had said. Her own upbringing had been so different. "You couldn't have known."

"But how I wish I had. Who would have thought that three years later, I'd care so little for appearance and prestige. I've learned so much, Anne, about people and about life. You seem to have had that understanding already, but I needed to leave this place to discover who I was and what I truly wanted. What's truly important."

"You're just upset about the inquiry. You're frightened—"

"Yes, I'm frightened, but the inquiry is only part of it. If I come out of this alive, as you so firmly believe I will, what will my future hold? I refuse to wed someone whose most pressing thoughts are about the color of her gown or what sandwiches she should serve for tea. I want a life, a partnership, with someone who has the same interests as I do. I want to share something with someone that is greater and more important than table settings and dinner parties. I want to spend my life with *you*."

"But that's impossible," Anne said, backing away from him. He had no right to speak of such things, even if, deep down, she shared the same desires. "Your father . . . Miss Patience is quite intent on marrying you."

"Of course she is. It's not a marriage as much as it is a contract."

"She is a baron's daughter. You are a merchant's son. What are they gaining from the agreement?"

"The baron has mismanaged his funds. A union with me and my father's money will benefit both families, for my father will have gained a title for his family, and the baron's estate will thrive."

Anne was quiet for a moment, his words sinking in. "All at your expense," she whispered. "You're even more of a prisoner than I am," she said.

Teach took her in his arms. "More than you could ever know. From the moment I saw you, you captured my heart and I was powerless to do anything about it."

Anne looked up, unable to bear the sadness in his voice, for it mirrored her own. He kissed her again, hesitantly at first, but when she responded, he pressed his lips hungrily to hers. Teach held her close, and Anne sighed as he trailed kisses across her face to her throat.

"A life with Patience would be no life at all," he murmured into her hair.

"Don't say that," she said.

"It's true. I would rather face the gallows than marry her. It's you I love. You with your tender heart and fierce strength."

Anne pulled away, leaning her forehead against his shoulder. "No, you'll see. Your father will have the charges dropped. And once that happens, you . . . you will do as you've promised and marry Patience. You'll still have a roof over your head and some-one to come home to."

"But that someone cares more for baubles and trinkets than she does for me. What good is a warm hearth when the heart of my future wife is as cold as ice?"

"That's a far cry more than what I will get. The illegitimate daughter of a dead merchant and a slave. Do you think anyone would have me, as different as I am? I have no prospects and no family to claim me."

"I will take you! Come away with me, Anne. Just the two of us. The devil take my father and everyone else. You and I can leave this place, together."

Hope flared within her breast at his words, but she quickly

extinguished it. As much as she wanted to leave with him, she could not. "And where will we go, Teach? Where in the world can we go where people will accept us? Until the inquiry is complete, you will be a wanted man. To leave now would only proclaim your guilt. But I cannot stay here. People will forever look at me and see our differences, not our similarities."

"What I want more than anything else in this world is to be with you."

"But for how long? Will you tire of me, just like you tired of Miss Patience?"

Teach regarded her with a mixture of surprise and outrage. "I would never tire of you. We are too alike. Even you must see that."

"It would never work," she said, desperate to stop this madness, for that was what it was.

He stepped forward, his face flushed with emotion. "Please," he whispered. "I love you, Anne. Nothing is more important than that."

Anne shook her head, shutting her eyes in an effort to clear her mind. "No. I'm sorry. It's not right."

Teach stood still, his mouth a thin line. "I'm not giving up," he muttered through clenched teeth. "You belong with me, and I will make you see that. I'll talk to my father—"

"You know he won't change his mind. Please don't make this more difficult than it has to be," Anne pleaded, tears running down her cheeks. "Please, just stop."

He studied her, anguish visible in every line on his face. Without another word he turned on his heel and strode off, ripping at the hanging branches of the willow. Anne held one hand to her stomach, sick with despair.

Teach was right. She loved him. Anne wasn't sure how or when it had happened, but she recognized as much as he did the strength of her feelings. It could have been the time they'd spent together, reading and discussing Dampier's book. Teach saw Anne as his equal, and wanted to hear her thoughts and opinions.

It could be that their visit to his mother's cottage had stimulated the first stirrings of affection. He'd been so pleased when she'd recognized its simple beauty.

Anne had missed Teach when he'd been away at the Hervey estate, more than she'd been willing to admit. It was Teach who set her heart racing. When she closed her eyes at night, he filled her dreams, and when she opened them the next morning, he filled her thoughts. All of this should have acted as a warning, but Anne was untested in the art of love.

If Anne or Teach went against his father's wishes, Richard Drummond would not hesitate to throw them out. Without a penny between them, where could they go? What kind of a life could they lead? Teach was drawn to the sea, like a willow to water, but as adventurous as Anne was, a ship was no place for a woman for an extended period of time.

She pressed the heels of her hands to her eyes, in an effort to stop the thoughts swirling through her head. She hoped to be able to talk Mr. Drummond into giving her the three thousand pounds her father had left her, more now than ever.

She could not stay here and idly stand by while Teach married another woman. Nor could she stay in the same city where she might run into him at some point. She needed to leave England. It was clear that when the *Deliverance* set sail, Anne had to be on it.

But she would have to wait until the inquiry was resolved, before she could approach Teach's father.

Drained of energy, as if her stroll through the garden had been five times the distance, Anne headed back to the manor. With a heavy heart she entered the courtyard. Hearing the sound of an approaching carriage, she turned. After pulling the two horses to a stop beside the house, the driver jumped down to open the door. Miss Patience had returned.

CHAPTER 25

Teach

Lord Hervey directed the coachman regarding the unloading of their trunks, which signified a rather lengthy stay. The Herveys were early. His father had said they wouldn't arrive until the next day.

"What is she doing?" Patience snapped, looking over Teach's shoulder.

"She lives here," Teach said, turning to see Anne approaching.

Patience shot him a sharp look, not bothering to hide her displeasure at his short remark. "Yes, I know that, but why is she in that cloak? Is that one of mine?"

"No. My father had it made for her."

"Why?"

"Because she is his goddaughter," Teach said.

"How can that be? She's a maid." Patience did not lower her voice, and there was no doubt that Anne heard her.

Teach attempted to speak in quieter tones, hating the fact that Patience spoke about Anne as if she weren't there. Neither he nor his father had told the Herveys of Anne's true identity. "She is no longer a maid. There was a misunderstanding."

"What kind of misunderstanding?"

Anne arrived at their side as Lord Hervey turned back to them, and greetings were exchanged. The four moved toward the house, but Anne allowed both Patience and the baron to separate her from Teach.

"Mr. Drummond was not given an accurate account of my family's standing," Anne said. She looked so calm walking beside Lord Hervey, as if nothing were amiss. As if the kiss near the willows hadn't happened.

Teach wondered how she managed it.

"My father misunderstood Anne's purpose for being sent here and employed her as one of the maids. Her parents were friends of his. Once we realized the mistake, it was quickly corrected."

"Has she no other family?" Patience asked.

"None," Anne said.

"My father is her guardian."

"But who are her parents? Surely they aren't English."

Anne's mouth tightened. "My parents have both passed on, Miss Patience. My father was an English merchant. But I doubt that you knew him."

Now inside, they paused at the foot of the grand staircase.

Patience looked as if she wanted to question Anne further, but Lord Hervey spoke first, clearly not interested in Anne's background. "Where is your father, Edward?" he asked.

"He was called away on business. I'm sorry he isn't here to greet you."

"Yes, well, I suppose I am to blame," Lord Hervey said. "We did arrive a day early. I'll go and rest for a bit, if you don't mind."

"And I'll go and see about the afternoon meal. Dinner will be served shortly," Anne offered.

Teach's jaw clenched as Anne hurried away, effectively leaving Teach alone with Patience. "You look well. Are you recovered?" he asked, hoping Patience wouldn't question him further about Anne.

"Yes, quite. It was nothing serious."

"How is your mother?"

"She had a friend visit unexpectedly and decided to stay behind." The relief in her voice was evident.

Teach knew Patience had a closer relationship with Lord Hervey than with Lady Hervey. It was no doubt due to the rivalry between the two women, as well as the fact that the baron was willing to grant Patience her every desire.

"But my mother will arrive in time for our wedding announcement this weekend," Patience quickly amended.

"If there is to be an announcement," Teach said, his voice low.

"Of course there will be," Patience snapped. "That was

why we returned. Our fathers will come to some sort of agreement."

Not if Teach had anything to do with it.

Patience followed Margery up the stairs, while Teach sought the seclusion of the library and dropped into an armchair before the fire.

Ignoring the book-lined walls, he closed his eyes, drawing a deep breath. He was unprepared for the Herveys' arrival and had hoped to have more time alone with Anne.

If he couldn't think of another way to get out of the marriage, he would tell Patience and her father about the piracy charges. Surely that would be enough to get them to end the agreement. If not, Teach's future stretched out bleakly before him.

His father and mother had not had an arranged match. Their partnership had been based on friendship and an abiding love, with mutual respect and admiration. Teach did not understand why his father refused to afford him the same kind of happiness.

Unable to remain seated, Teach paced the floor, pausing every once in a while to stare out at the dreary sky, the gray clouds oppressive.

One hour passed, but there was still no sign of Anne. Or Patience.

When the door to the library eventually opened, Teach turned, but it was only Margery coming to tell him that dinner was ready.

He continued his pacing in the dining room, the maps on the walls almost mocking him.

Ten minutes later Miss Patience swept in, dressed in a low-cut pink gown, a matching pink ribbon in her blond curls. Teach held out her chair as she sat down.

"It appears we will be the only ones eating together," Patience said.

Teach paused as he pulled out his own chair. "Why is that?"

Patience cocked an eyebrow at Teach. "My father is resting in his room and will have a tray sent up later."

"And Anne?"

"I asked her if she would be joining us, but she didn't answer."

"Perhaps I should see if she needs anything," he said, moving toward the door. He'd counted on Anne joining them.

"Edward, please. We both know she's fine. It was ill-mannered not to respond, but hardly surprising, considering . . ."

"Considering what?" Teach wished he'd thought of retiring to his room.

Patience let out an exaggerated sigh. "Considering her breeding."

"Anne is not ill-mannered. Nor is she unkind. It's very possible she didn't hear you," he said tightly, doing his best to control his anger. One more word, and he would walk out of the room.

Patience clearly picked up on his ire. "I did not come here to argue with you. There is something important we need to discuss. We haven't had any time together, and I . . ." Her voice trailed off. Teach couldn't remember the last time Patience had looked so uncertain. "Please."

With a heavy heart Teach returned to the table and sat down, across from Patience. The clock on the mantel ticked in time with his heartbeat. When the door to the dining room opened and Margery brought in the first course, Teach barely managed to hide his sigh of relief.

"Thank you, Margery," Teach said with a slight smile.

"It's good to see you smile," Patience said. "You're always so severe these days."

"No more severe than last year," Teach said.

Patience winced as she picked up her spoon and began eating. She waited until Margery had left the room before speaking again. "But you have changed, and no one can blame you. I know your father is constantly harping on you about one fault or another. I'm just saying that I recognize why you seem more serious than usual."

Teach gave a noncommittal shrug. The last person he wanted to discuss with Patience was his father.

"Do you remember the first time we met? You and William had just returned from school for the holidays. You teased me mercilessly, and you stood there with a mischievous look on your face, practically daring your father to rebuke you in front of his guests." Patience sighed. "I thought you were the handsomest boy I'd ever met. I still do."

A part of Teach wished he could return her compliment, but he couldn't bring himself to do it. It would be unfair to Anne as well as to Patience.

"Do you remember our first kiss?" she asked.

Teach couldn't help laughing at the memory. "It was awful."

"It was sweet!"

"How can you say that?"

"Because it was. You were so hesitant. I thought I'd given you enough hints—"

"Patience, please, stop. Whatever it is you wish to say, say it and be done with it. I, too, have something I'd like to discuss with you." If Teach couldn't get his father to listen to reason, he hoped he could convince Patience to break off their betrothal.

Patience frowned, clearly not liking the abruptness of his tone, but Teach could not let her continue.

She placed her spoon on the table and met his gaze. "All right. I had hoped to approach this subject delicately, but since you insist on bringing it out into the open, then so be it. Once we are married, you must promise me that you will never set sail again."

Teach grew very still. "Must I?"

"Yes."

"And why must I do that?"

"Because you will have no need to labor. That can be left to those most suited to that kind of work," Patience persisted. "Such as your father and others like him."

Teach stiffened at the slight. Despite their disagreements,

Teach was still proud of his father's success, and knew it had come at the cost of great personal sacrifice. "My father's hard work is making it possible for your family to keep your ancestral homes," Teach said. "I would not be so quick to reject his contribution to this world."

"I don't reject his contribution. I recognize it for what it is. A man who wants to come up in society by climbing on the backs of his betters."

"I'm sure my father would be pleased to hear how you hold him in such high esteem. Perhaps we should discuss it with him when he returns home. I wouldn't want you to rush into a marriage when you have such an obvious problem with his background."

Patience visibly paled, but she refused to back down. "She said you would do this. She said you would try to break it off."

"Who?" Teach asked, confused.

"My mother." The smile on Patience's face looked brittle enough to shatter. "She said you would lose interest in me. That I wouldn't be able to hold on to you. I told her she was wrong. And I'll prove her wrong."

Teach remembered the competition that seemed to permeate the air when the two women were in the same room together. "This has nothing to do with your mother, Patience. Or your father. This is about us not suiting each other."

"Of course we suit each other."

He almost felt sorry for her, hearing the desperation in her voice. "You know we don't, not anymore. It's time we acknowledged that. You don't care for me any more than I care for you." He hated having to be cruel, but if she wouldn't listen to reason . . .

"That's not true."

"Yes, it is, even if you're afraid to admit it. And there is something of even greater importance that I must tell you. Something that will no doubt affect our betrothal."

"Nothing will affect—"

"I've been accused of piracy." Teach hadn't meant to be so blunt, but she refused to listen.

His words hung in the air between them. The only sound in the room was the rain as it hammered the windows from the outside.

Patience blinked once. Twice. "I see."

Teach had prepared himself for a number of reactions, but her calm acceptance of his statement wasn't one of them.

Picking up her napkin, she dabbed at her mouth before placing the cloth beside her bowl. "Is that why your father is not here?"

"Yes," Teach said, unwilling to elaborate further.

Studying the table, she frowned. "Then that is all the more reason to move forward with our wedding," she said, eventually meeting his eyes. "We will announce it this weekend at William's party."

Stunned, Teach shook his head. "Did you not hear me?

I've been accused of piracy. I could be sent to the gallows."

"My father is a peer of the realm. Once you join your name with ours, nobody would dare hang you."

It was on the tip of his tongue to remind Patience that her father was merely a baron, not an earl or a duke, but he decided against it. His mother had tried to raise him as a gentleman. "I'm fairly certain Lord Hervey would not share your opinion. Once he hears about this, I'm sure he'll want to break the arrangement."

"Nonsense. I know my father. He wants this union."

Lord Hervey needs *this union.*

"Patience, it's no use. This has to end. Even if by some miracle I'm not sent to the gallows, you deserve better."

She scowled, her eyes hard. "None of this would have happened if you hadn't set sail in the first place."

Teach's own features hardened. She wasn't at all affected by the thought of him hanging, nor did she ask him if he was guilty. She simply blamed him. Just like his father. "I will never regret my year at sea, but I know we would both have a lifetime of regret if we ever married."

Jumping to her feet, she shook her head at him. "I won't let you do this. I won't!" she cried, and fled the room before Teach could stop her.

Slamming his fist down onto the table, he caused the spoons and other cutlery to jump. Some of the soup spilled out of the bowls. Pushing back his chair, he nearly toppled it to the floor.

With a sound curse, Teach strode from room, heading in the direction of the back entrance. He had to get out of the house, before he lost his sanity completely. He didn't mind the rain, and he hoped that a ride in the country would do the trick.

Near the kitchen, he stopped when he found Sara alone. "Has Anne's meal been taken up to her yet?" he asked.

"She ate before she left, sir."

"Left where?"

"She went into town with Elizabeth."

"Did they walk?"

Sara gave Teach a strange look. "No, sir. They took the carriage."

Teach didn't leave. For the next three hours he waited impatiently for Anne to return.

He retired to his room and sat in the large bay window overlooking the courtyard, as the rain continued to pour down from the skies. Although it was only four in the afternoon, it was dark and gloomy, the storm clouds obscuring any light from overhead.

He must have dozed off at some point, because the next thing he knew, he jerked awake to the sound of voices. Looking down at the muddy courtyard, he saw the carriage beside the stable and two young boys holding the horses. The boys' thin shoulders were hunched forward in a futile effort to protect them from the rain.

He recognized Anne's cloaked figure as she spoke with Margery on her way inside, while Elizabeth and another young girl, presumably Elizabeth's other sister, scurried behind.

After racing down the hall, he took the back stairs, and stopped in the doorway to the kitchen amidst a flurry of activity. Margery and Sara took the young girls' soaking wraps and placed them before the fire.

Out in the courtyard the two boys helped the driver unhitch the horses from the carriage.

There was no sign of Anne.

Teach was anxious in his search for her, his heart tripping in his chest. Less than three weeks ago he would not have believed he could need another human being this much, but the desire to see her was overwhelming.

He trailed a path of wet footprints leading to the front of the house. Anne entered the dining room, still dressed in her traveling cloak. He followed behind. "Anne?"

She whirled, an object in her hand flying until it bounced on the rug and landed on the hard wood near Teach's feet with a loud *clank*.

Looking down, Teach saw a silver goblet reflecting the glow from the fire in the hearth.

It was the goblet his father had given his mother.

And it was one of the items his father had said was missing.

CHAPTER 26

Anne

Anne watched as if in a dream while a range of emotions crossed Teach's face. Confusion, recognition, disbelief, and finally anger. He picked up the goblet, his eyes glinting dangerously in the firelight as he turned it in his hand. "Why?" he asked.

The question pulled her out of her daze, and Anne blinked, wishing she had a clever response to give. She was numb, her mind unable to respond fast enough. She should have heard him approach, but had been too intent on returning the stolen items, her pulse racing.

It had been too easy. She'd gone to Elizabeth's house and spoken with her mother, explaining Mr. Drummond's need of a groom and another maid. Elizabeth's two brothers, David and Ian, had both volunteered for the job, as well as their sister Kate.

Leaving Elizabeth to help her siblings pack their meager belongings, Anne had made a quick trip to the shop. There

264

they had lain, behind the counter. The two spoons as well as the goblet. Anne hadn't been able to believe her good fortune.

It appeared her good fortune had now run out. "Margery said you and the Herveys were in your rooms resting." She could not help the accusatory note in her voice.

"Aye, I was, but when I saw you arrive, I came down because I wanted to speak with you."

"About what?"

His eyes were those of a predator. "I wanted to know if you would accompany me on a ride."

"In this weather?"

Teach ignored her question. "Were you aware that this goblet was among the items my father believed had been stolen?" He stopped, his dark eyebrows peaked, but when she didn't respond, he pressed on. "Did it magically appear in the cupboard? Did you find it somewhere in the house? Some dusty corner of the attic?"

She looked down as shame washed over her, but she wouldn't embarrass herself further with a poorly told lie.

"Tell me that you found this," he said with quiet menace.

Shaking her head, she forced herself to meet his gaze. It raised gooseflesh all over her. "I did not find it. I knew exactly where it was."

"And where was that?"

"At a shop. Near the docks."

"That was why you didn't want me to accompany you yesterday."

"Yes."

"Why? Why did you do it?"

Something bleak and angry rose within her, a memory of how she'd first felt when she'd arrived at the Drummond estate. "My life here was a prison, a drawn-out death sentence. You of all people should understand that."

"Perhaps, but I never stole from anyone."

"You stole from Henry Barrett."

"He deserved it."

Anne didn't wish to discuss the differences between their crimes. She simply wanted to make her point. "In order to escape this house, you threatened to join the navy."

"But I would never have followed through with it."

"Which makes you either a coward or a liar." As soon as she'd spoken, Anne realized she'd made a mistake, but it was too late to take the words back.

Teach went still, his face hard. They stared at each other in wordless challenge. What seemed like an eternity passed.

Letting loose a string of foul words, he stalked toward her, his broad shoulders blocking the warmth from the nearby hearth. "My father must *never* find out about this, do you understand?"

Anne nodded, determined not to shrink from him. "Believe me, I have no intention of telling him."

Gripping her by the arms, he gave her a slight shake. "How could you be so reckless? Do you have any idea what could have happened to you if he'd discovered it was you who'd stolen from him? Or worse, Margery?"

Breaking free of his hold, she went to stand before the fire, trying to chase away the chill she'd felt since he'd first discovered her. "I did think about the consequences, but it was a chance I was willing to take. A quick death was preferable to a slow suffocation of my life with Margery or your father—"

"Tell me, do you still regard this house as a prison?"

Whirling around, she glared at him. "At the moment, yes. It feels as if the very walls are closing in, and it's all I can do to stop myself from running away."

Teach approached her again, his normally healthy complexion ashen. "Don't. Please don't ever run away from me. I understand why you did it. Do you think I don't know how stifling this house can be?" Cupping her chin, he tilted her head back. "You must promise me never to do anything that foolish again."

Anne took a steadying breath, grateful she'd been able to retrieve the three pieces and that she hadn't sold any of the others. "I won't."

"Is there more?"

Picturing the chest hidden by the two willows, Anne was nearly smothered by the weight of her guilt. She did not want Teach to know the extent of her stealing. She could not stand to see the look of hurt and betrayal in his eyes again. If she could find the right moments, the other items should be easy enough to return.

Realizing that Teach still waited for her answer, she hated her denial even as she spoke it. "No, nothing."

She felt Teach studying her, and returned his gaze, trying to convince herself that it wasn't a complete lie. If she had her way, Mr. Drummond would give her her inheritance, and then she wouldn't need any of the stolen goods.

But until she was sure . . .

"Will you please join us for supper this evening?" Teach asked. "I cannot endure another meal alone with Miss Patience."

"And if I choose not to?"

Teach snorted. "I'll come to your room and drag you to supper myself."

"You wouldn't dare make a scene to that extent."

"When it comes to you, Anne, I would dare a lot of things. I told Patience about the piracy charges."

Torn between hope and despair, Anne swallowed around the tightness in her throat. "What did she say?"

"Not much."

"Does Lord Hervey know?"

"Patience might have told him, although I haven't spoken with him myself. He hasn't left his room since he arrived."

Anne took a moment to gather her thoughts. "I wish there were something I could do to help you." It was in her nature to form some plan of action. Her father had often said that it was better to walk aimlessly than to sit idle, but in this instance she did not know how to change the situation.

"There is something you can do."

"What?"

Margery came in, preventing Teach from answering. "Master Drummond has returned. He would like to speak with you, Mr. Edward."

Teach's head swung around. "He's back already?"

"Aye, sir," Margery said. "He's waiting for you in his room."

"I'll be there shortly," Teach replied.

Margery left as quietly as she'd entered. Anne reached for the watch in her pocket, her fingers shaking. Teach's eyes held hers.

"Come with me," he said.

"He asked only for you." As much as she wanted to find out what had happened, a small part of her was afraid of the outcome. Either way, he was lost to her.

Teach rubbed the back of his neck, his irritation and anxiety clear.

"I'll wait for you in the library. Come and find me," she said.

"Always."

CHAPTER 27

Teach

"It's over," Drummond said, holding a glass of brandy in his hand. He sat in an armchair and gazed up at the ceiling.

Teach's heart gave a lurch. "What's over?"

"The charges against you have been dropped."

For a moment Teach was too shocked to respond.

"You will not be hanged for piracy," his father said, giving him an expectant look.

All the tension Teach had kept so tightly constrained was released in a long sigh of audible relief. "How? How did you do it?" he asked.

"My solicitor and I consulted, and I simply explained that you had been aboard one of Andrew Barrett's ships. You could not possibly have committed those crimes. I prepared a list of character witnesses for you, which took some time, but in the end that wasn't necessary."

"And the constable believed you?"

"He was interested in justice being served," was his father's curt reply.

"What kind of evidence did they have against me?"

"The constable didn't say. Nor did he say who had brought the charges against you. But no matter. It's over."

Warmth radiated throughout Teach's limbs, and he smiled, knowing that his death sentence had been lifted. He understood the unspoken part of his father's comments. Constables were unpaid volunteers, and Drummond's pockets were deep. He'd said he would do whatever it took to see the charges dropped, but Teach hadn't been sure whether his father would have been willing to pay the constable, or if the constable was even the kind of person willing to take a bribe.

But there was no doubt in Teach's mind that that was what had happened.

"I . . . I don't quite know what to say, except . . . thank you. Thank you, Father."

Drummond waved his hand, looking ill at ease from Teach's gratitude. Teach knew better than to embrace him. It would only make him more uncomfortable.

"It's in the past. Don't give it another thought."

Within twenty-four hours his father had been able to avert disaster. It seemed there was truly nothing his father could not do.

"And now there is nothing to stop you from marrying Miss Patience."

Any feelings of euphoria were suffocated by his father's statement.

"Did you hear me, Edward?"

"Yes."

Drummond rose and poured himself another glass of brandy. "Good. Then we will announce your wedding date this weekend at your friend William's party."

"But we haven't settled on a date."

"Which is precisely why I asked Miss Patience and the baron to come here. I understand they arrived early."

"They did."

"I should have been here to greet them." His tone implied it was yet another grievance against Teach. Sitting down, Drummond pinched the bridge of his nose, a sure sign that the conversation was over. But Teach wasn't willing to end it just yet.

"Father, I don't want to set a date for the wedding."

Lowering his hand with exaggerated deliberateness, Drummond pinned Teach with a glare. "What did you say?"

Teach refused to back down. "I don't want to set a date for the wedding. There's no need to rush."

"There is also no reason to wait."

"Yes, there is. I told Miss Patience about the charges."

"You should have waited for me to return. I had planned to tell Lord Hervey myself, once your name was cleared."

"Don't you think he might change his mind now?"

"The baron is not in a position to change his mind. He is on the brink of financial ruin."

"But I just arrived home."

"Yes, from a year at sea that very nearly cost you your life. Do you have any idea what I did for you today?" his father demanded, his voice rising with each word.

"Yes, and I've already told you that I'm thankful, I truly am. But I think it would be best to wait. My feelings for Patience have changed. She is no longer the girl I wish to spend my life with, and I am quite sure she feels the same about me. If you forced us to marry, we would both be miserable."

"That is not your decision to make."

"How can you say that? It's my life we're discussing, not yours."

"And you have proven that you are incapable of making good decisions."

Turning from his father, Teach caught sight of the portrait hanging above the fireplace, his mother's kind eyes smiling down on him. "If mother were alive, she would let me make them. Why can't you?"

The air seemed to escape his father's lungs at the mention of his wife. "I will not argue with you. Not now. I am too tired for this. We will continue this conversation after I have rested. I do not wish to be disturbed until supper this evening. Please instruct Margery that I would like my tea to be delivered to my room and left by the door." He headed in the direction of his dressing room, his weary footsteps echoing in the chamber.

Clutching the back of the chair in his hands, Teach barely managed to stifle his shout of aggravation. He knew very well that his father would not discuss it with him further. If Drummond was to rest until the evening meal, Teach would have no opportunity to speak with him privately. It was as if the older Teach became, the more Drummond tightened the noose.

If only they had a few days, Drummond might have time to mull over what Teach had said. Then they could speak reasonably, just like they had when Teach had convinced his father to let him sail on Andrew Barrett's ship.

After closing the door to his father's bedchamber soundly behind him, Teach headed down the stairs. His heartbeat roared in his ears as he struggled to understand how he had so completely lost control of his life, and when he would get it back.

Anne, unaware of his presence in the doorway of the library, sat in a chair with a book in her lap. She stared out at the rain as it continued to fall. A log broke in the fireplace, and part of it fell from the grate, sending a plume of white sparks into the air.

Teach paused, watching her until she turned. Setting the book aside, she stood and took several quick steps forward. Teach met her in the center of the room. Before he could say anything, she smiled.

"I heard. I'm sorry, but I stood outside your father's door for a moment and listened." Anne reached for one of his hands, and her fingers warmed the chill in his. "I heard him say it was over."

Teach looked down at their clasped hands. "Yes. It's over." Glancing up, he saw her smile fade.

"What's wrong? What else did he say?"

Teach's only reply was grim silence. It was clear she hadn't listened for long.

Anne stumbled back a step, her skirts rustling. She gave a slight shake of her head, her brows furrowed as she looked about the room. "I should go."

"Do you wish to retire? I'll escort you to your—"

"No. I must leave England. At once."

Pain unfolded in Teach's chest. "You can't leave. I won't let you."

"Once I have the three thousand my father left me, you won't be able stop me. I will not stand idly by and watch you marry her. If I can leave before that happens, I will."

He knew it would do him no good to argue with her, but he couldn't help himself. She was his only source of pleasure at the moment, and it frightened him how much he depended on her to achieve his happiness. "Don't do it, Anne."

Their gazes caught and held. Her blue eyes, usually so bright, were now bleak.

"Don't do anything rash," he said.

"I have no other choice."

"Yes, you do. Come away with me. I'm no longer a wanted man. We could leave, just the two of us."

"And then what? I won't be a kept woman like my mother

was. And where could we possibly go where people won't look at me and immediately assume that's what I am? Or worse."

"Marry me, then. We'll leave England and find a place. We'll *make* a place." Teach watched her intently, hoping for a sign of consent. But she took another step back, her shoulders straight, her lips set.

"You might want to leave now, but in time you would come to resent me. You would be giving up your inheritance and this lifestyle. I won't have you blame me for losing everything."

"I would never resent you. Or blame you. I just spent a year at sea. I've seen what it's like to be without."

"Yes, but it was an adventure. You always knew you would come back. I've experienced what it's like to truly be without, and I would not wish that on anyone. Least of all you."

"That's my choice to make, not yours."

"I'm sorry," Anne said. "But when I leave, I will go alone."

"It's too dangerous."

Anne stepped around him, heading for the door.

Desperation caused his voice to rise. "I'll tell my father about us. I'll tell him I wish to marry you."

She stopped with her hand on the knob and turned, her blue eyes flashing. "If you do that, he will not hesitate to throw me out. He tolerates me now, but if he believed I came between you and Miss Patience, he would not be kind. Or merciful. You should not wish his wrath on anyone. Least of all me."

◇◇◇◇◇◇◇◇◇◇◇◇◇

Sitting in the darkened captain's cabin of the *Deliverance*, Teach toyed with an open bottle. It had been several hours since he'd left the estate. After the disastrous evening meal, he hadn't trusted himself to stay under the same roof as the others.

Despite his request, Anne had retired to her room and stayed there. Teach had been forced to share a tense supper with Patience, Lord Hervey, and his father.

"Remind me, if I'm ever in trouble, your father would be a handy one to have in a pinch," John said.

Teach had told him the outcome of the inquiry.

"Yes, well, my father might have cleared up that problem, but he's the reason for another, even greater problem. He and Lord Hervey set the date for the wedding. In two weeks, they say I am to wed, the day after the launch of the *Deliverance*."

John studied Teach's expression, a sympathetic look in his eyes. "You fancy her, don't you?" John said. "This Anne you've mentioned. The one who tossed the bucket on me."

Teach trusted his friend well enough to tell him the truth. "Lord help me, but I do."

"I could tell. You haven't stopped talking about her since you arrived."

Teach took another sip from the bottle.

"And yet your father expects you to marry a fancy peacock with a pea brain."

Perhaps Teach had been a bit harsh in his criticism of Patience, but she offered little in comparison to Anne. "I can't do it, John. I can't go through with it," Teach muttered. "My father has already lived his life. Mine has just begun, and yet he would sentence me to death, for my every breath shall be stifled if I am forced to spend the rest of my days with that girl."

It was John's turn to take a sip from the bottle. "Have you told your father you don't want to marry Patience?"

"Yes."

"And what did he say?"

Teach scowled, his anger stirring at the memory. "He said it wasn't my decision to make."

John gave a low whistle. "What other options do you have?"

Teach held up the bottle.

"Sorry, mate, but that won't solve anything."

Taking a large swig, Teach shrugged. "Perhaps not, but it can make me forget for a while."

"What does Anne have to say about any of this?"

"What can she say? She's living in my father's house, as his guest. How can she go against his wishes?"

"Does she love you?"

"I know she does."

"Well, then. You're your father's son. Let's see you do something about it."

CHAPTER 28

Anne

The next morning Anne opened the door to the dining room, only to discover that Mr. Drummond and Teach were both already seated. Neither of them spoke, which was why she had assumed the room was empty. The house was silent, except for the occasional noise coming from the direction of the kitchen.

She stopped, cursing herself for not ordering another tray to be sent up to her room. So far she'd done a fair job of avoiding the other members of the household, but she knew it couldn't last forever.

Teach looked up and saw her, his mouth tightening. Tension thickened the air. She should have gone for a walk in the gardens instead.

"Good morning, Anne," Drummond said, motioning her in. "I wished to speak with you. Come, join us."

Nodding in Drummond's direction, she walked to the

buffet and took a plate. Bypassing the poached eggs and the crisp fried bacon, she took only a handful of blackberries and a hot scone, not sure if she could even stomach that much. She had not slept well, and her insides were tied in knots.

"Bring me some juice, would you?" Drummond asked, his question intended for her.

Anne bristled at his words, as Teach pushed back his chair. "Father, she's no longer a maid. I will get it for you."

"Nonsense. The other maids are busy. You don't mind, do you, Anne?"

He would never have asked Miss Patience to fetch him a glass.

After a moment's hesitation Anne set her own plate down, tempted to walk out of the room altogether. But she intended to ask for the three thousand pounds, and so she remained, reaching for the pitcher at the same time that Teach did. His fingers covered hers.

I'm sorry, his gaze seemed to say.

Anne picked up her plate once more as Teach poured the juice. Once they were seated, she looked at Drummond, her hands clasped in her lap. "Yes?" she asked, wondering what he could possibly wish to discuss.

"I would like you to go to the party with Edward tomorrow night," Drummond said.

It was the last thing she'd expected to hear. "I had not intended to attend—"

"Nevertheless, you shall go. You are of age."

Alarmed, Anne glanced in Teach's direction, but his expression was masked. She turned back to Drummond, determined to plead her case. "Please, sir. I prefer to stay home—"

He shook his head. "No. I've already given it much thought. At the party we will announce that you are coming out."

"But I don't want—"

"Father, you cannot announce Anne's coming out at the same time that you declare an engagement. It wouldn't be appropriate."

Anger flared in Drummond's eyes. "How else will she find herself a husband? You can't expect her to stay here for the rest of her days. *That* would not be appropriate."

Anne barely managed to keep her own anger in check. "I have no intention of staying here. *When* I choose a husband, I would like it to be when *I'm* ready. I'm not ready now. And I have no desire for it to be announced this week."

"Nonsense. You are . . . lovely." Anne noticed his hesitation. Miss Patience was clearly Drummond's ideal of beauty. "And your father has left you not without means. Edward is to marry a baron's daughter, and your association with him will be advantageous."

She braced herself against the ache caused by his words.

"You cannot make me," she said, no longer caring about holding her tongue. All she could think about was the agony of having to watch Teach swear his allegiance to Patience publicly.

"Father, it's too soon," Teach said, his voice louder.

"Your mother was seventeen when I married her," Drummond said, shooting his son a silencing glare, before turning once more on Anne. "When do you turn seventeen?"

It took her a moment to answer. "I . . . In two months' time."

"There, you see. This is for her own good."

"And if no one will have me?"

Drummond didn't meet her gaze when he answered. "Once I attach a handsome dowry to your head, someone will speak for you. Tell her, Edward. Tell her she'll make a fine match."

Teach looked Anne straight in the eyes as he spoke. "The man who wins Anne's heart will recognize in her the answer to his dreams."

The color was high on Teach's cheeks, but his father didn't pay attention. He merely waved his fork at Anne after taking a bite of his eggs. "There, you see. Edward believes you will not have a problem."

Anne felt trapped, caught between the two men who appeared to hold the happiness of her future in their hands. It was time to take control of her own fate.

An icy calm overcame her, and she sat back. "All right. I'll go."

Drummond smiled, clearly pleased, but Teach was motionless.

"But I would like the money my father left me to be transferred to an account with my name."

A muscle worked in Teach's jaw, but Drummond nodded. "Of course. When you turn eighteen—"

Anne was sure they could hear the pounding of her heart.

"No, not when I turn eighteen. I would like the money now."

"But that's not possible," Drummond said.

"Then I request that you make it possible. I will attend the party. All that I ask in return is that you do this for me." It wasn't as if he needed the money. She did.

Drummond studied her, clearly surprised by her boldness.

For the first time since entering the house, Anne was not afraid of Richard Drummond. She had nothing left to lose. "I'd like to at least know that I can purchase a small cottage somewhere, sir. I have no desire to inconvenience you any further."

"All right," Drummond said, after another moment of silence. "Given your past experience, I can understand why you make such a demand. I will contact my solicitor to have the funds transferred to an account in your name. You will have access to it. I will not stand in your way."

"But, Father—" Teach began, but Drummond held up his hand.

"No, Edward. The girl is right. It's the least I can do, to help her on her way."

Anne gave a small nod, her pent-up breath threatening to explode. "Thank you, sir. Now, if you will excuse me, I find I'm not as hungry as I first thought," she said, coming to her feet.

Drummond waved her away. "Yes, you may go." Teach looked as if to follow suit, clearly intent on chasing after her, but Drummond wasn't finished. "I ask that you stay, Edward," he said. "We still have things to discuss."

Anne shot Drummond a grateful look, aware of the blaze burning in Teach's eyes. Now was a good time to make her escape.

As she closed the door behind her, Anne could still feel the heat of Teach's gaze on her back.

Two hours later he found her in the library.

Teach entered, and then used his foot to close the door behind him. Anne stood abruptly, the book in her hands dropping to the floor. If she'd wished to avoid him, she could have gone into town, or retired to her room, but she had decided it was time to stop running.

"Why did you do it?" he demanded.

Anne thrust out her small chin. "You know why."

A swallow rippled visibly down his throat, and he ran a hand through his already disheveled hair. This was a new version of Teach, one she'd never seen before. He reminded her of a caged animal, and it pained her to think she was partly responsible for it.

"How can you stand there so calmly?" he asked, his voice rough.

If he only knew. Her head ached. She'd spent the past two hours trying to convince herself that leaving was the best for everyone concerned, even Teach, although he couldn't see it at the moment.

Now that her funds were secured, she hoped to find a place

where she belonged. She would see firsthand the places her mother had told her about in the West Indies. It was both exciting and terrifying at the same time.

But without Teach at her side, her plans felt somehow empty and hollow, as if she would leave a piece of herself behind.

"My father and Lord Hervey have gone to toast my father's acceptance into the aristocracy. Strangely enough, they didn't ask me to join them."

"I know." She'd heard them leave.

"And my future bride has gone to pick up her dress for William's ball this weekend." There was no disguising the bitterness in his voice.

"I'm sorry," she said.

"Are you?"

"Of course. I don't wish to see you suffer. I like to think of you as my friend."

Teach moved forward, and then was standing so close to Anne, she could feel his body heat, even though they were not touching. "We're more than just friends. You know that."

She shook her head, her eyes fixed on the floor. "I'm afraid we shall never be more than friends as long as I'm frightened."

"You once told me I didn't frighten you."

"Perhaps it's not you I'm afraid of."

Teach reached out and caressed her cheek with his finger.

"Please," she whispered, her breath catching in her throat.

"Whether you acknowledge it or not, Anne, we belong

together. We could be on opposite sides of the world, but you would still be mine, as I am yours."

Anne closed her eyes. Deep down she knew he was right. Fighting for composure, she moved toward the desk and began gathering the papers scattered across its surface. They were her father's, the ones Mr. Cogswell had given her.

Teach bent and retrieved the book from the floor, then came to stand by her side. "You're not the only one who can run away, you know. If you truly wish to leave England, I will accompany you. It's far too dangerous to travel by yourself."

Clutching the papers in her hands, she glared at him. "You think I'm running away?"

"Aye, I do. You're afraid to trust someone. But you have the means to be independent, and I have no desire to hold you back. If you truly wish to find your mother's family, I will help you search for them."

Struggling against the pull of his words, Anne looked once more at the desk and the papers on it. Everything he said was true. It would be hazardous for her to travel alone. Even if she secured a lady's maid, they would be on a ship for several months. The uncertainty of the weather alone was enough to give her pause.

And once she reached her destination, who knew what kind of circumstances she would find herself in? Even if Mr. Cogswell was in a position to help her, he didn't have time to send a message to any contact before she left. It would be a relief to know she didn't have to undertake this daunting task alone.

But the most important reason for her to agree with him was that she could not think of anyone else she'd rather have by her side.

"Let me come with you," he said, his voice soft. Urgent. "Please."

Anne sighed. "All right," she said, looking up. "If that is what you truly wish."

Teach's eyes glowed with triumph, and he slid his arms around her. He bent his head to kiss her, but she stopped him, her fingers on his lips.

"But we will wait until after the ball to leave. I do not want your father to go back on his word. Once my money is secure, then we will go."

"Agreed."

"And you will not kiss me until that time."

Teach drew back, his eyes wide. "What?"

Anne pushed at his chest. "Technically, you are still betrothed to another."

"Yes, but—"

"Those are my conditions." She felt a small sense of victory at the flash of irritation in Teach's eyes, glad that she was able to unsettle him as well.

"All right. We will wait until after the ball tomorrow night. But I will secure our passage on a ship."

"Shouldn't we wait until the *Deliverance* sets sail?"

"Why?"

Guilt caused her voice to be sharp. "Because you are your father's only son. It's bad enough that you're leaving him. I would hate for our departure to ruin his moment of glory."

"The *Deliverance* sets sail in twelve days, Anne. I have no intention of waiting that long."

CHAPTER 29

Anne

Anne drew in a deep breath, wishing Sara hadn't pulled the stays so tight in her ivory gown. Now that Anne didn't work her fingers to the bone every day, her shape had softened. She had curves in places that before had been sharp angles. She waited dutifully as the maid pinned the last pearl clip into her hair, the design matching the pearl choker around her neck. Her hands were slick with perspiration.

"You look beautiful, Miss Anne," Sara whispered, taking a step back to look at the girl before her. "Don't pay attention to what anyone else says about you. You're a lady, no doubt about it."

Anne had confided some of her fears to Sara about the upcoming ball. There would be no way to stem the tide of gossip and speculation her appearance would create, but in order to gain her inheritance, Anne was willing to face the vultures.

Turning toward the looking glass, Anne's eyes widened in surprise. Her skin glowed against the creamy fabric, while her hair hung in luxurious black curls that Sara had painstakingly set and pinned. The combination was mesmerizing, and Anne couldn't help the surge of pleasure that ran through her, as she involuntarily wondered what Teach would say.

She'd not seen him since they'd agreed to leave together. There had been several raised voices and slamming doors from the Herveys. No doubt the conflict had to do with Anne's presence in the house.

She'd kept to her room, reading over her father's papers and writing a list of things she would take with her when she left. It still seemed unreal to her.

Giving herself a slight shake, Anne turned. "Thank you for your help, Sara. I shall miss you while you're gone." She was glad Sara had agreed to spend some time with her mother. She was leaving tonight, and John would escort her home, since Sara lived in an unsavory part of Bristol.

Anne had no wish to say good-bye, for she'd grown genuinely fond of Sara.

Following the maid out the door, Anne heard the sound of voices in the entryway below them.

"I still don't understand why she has to come," Patience hissed.

"What does it matter?" Lord Hervey replied. "They simply wish to announce her coming out."

The baroness, who had arrived the evening before, spoke

up. "I knew this would happen. If you want your daughter's evening to be ruined—"

Teach's terse voice interrupted her. "Nobody's evening will be ruined."

"It will be if your father doesn't return soon," Lady Hervey said sharply. "His obsession with that ship is disturbing. You'd think he cares more for it than for his own son."

"My father regrets being called away, but it's early yet. He will still be able to make the ball later in the evening. We will not announce the wedding date until he is present."

A sad smile touched Anne's lips as she descended the stairs. Teach would fight this wedding until the bitter end. "Good evening," she murmured. "I'm sorry I kept you waiting."

The four individuals in the entryway turned to look. Both Patience and Lady Hervey glared at Anne. Lord Hervey's mouth dropped open. Teach stared openly, looking splendid in a crisp white shirt and black coat with breeches. The yearning in his eyes reached across the space between them.

He helped Anne with her matching ivory cloak, the color a perfect foil for her skin. His fingers brushed her collarbone as he clasped it for her.

Patience quickly grabbed Teach's sleeve, pulling him closer to her. As they exited the house, Teach allowed the Herveys to precede him, his eyes skimming Anne from head to toe once more as he helped her into the carriage.

Anne sat next to the baron, as his wife and daughter had

taken the other side. She expected Teach to sit between the two women, but their dresses took up too much space. Instead Teach settled himself beside Anne.

It was a tight fit. Miss Patience and her mother glowered at Anne the entire way. Beside her, Anne felt Teach's thigh pressed against her own, the heat reaching through the layers between them. His nearness stole the breath from her lungs, and she was painfully aware of every move he made. She stared out the window in an attempt to distract her thoughts.

It was no use.

By the time they pulled up in front of the Cardwell estate, Anne was dizzy. Torches lit the stairs leading up to the grand entrance. The house itself was aflame with lights, the windows full of people milling about in the interior.

The baron and his wife exited first, followed by Patience. Clutching the arm Teach offered, Anne lifted her skirts and stepped forward, her heart fluttering wildly in her chest. Her initial reaction to the invitation had been correct. She should have stayed alone at the Drummond house.

Anne hadn't even accompanied her own father when he'd been entertained elsewhere. Instead she and her mother had stayed at home, content to read or sew by the fire.

This would be her first real social gathering, and she felt ill equipped to manage it.

Patience grabbed Teach's arm and attempted once more to

disengage him from Anne's side, but Teach held back. "It would be in poor taste to let Anne enter alone. My father is her guardian, and he asked me to look after her tonight."

"But . . . but," Patience sputtered. "We are to wed."

"Your father is waiting," Teach said.

Patience gave Anne a look of pure venom before joining her parents.

"You shouldn't have done that," Anne said, although inwardly she was pleased. She was quite sure no one had ever put Patience in her place like that.

"She deserved it. She acts as if we're already married," Teach muttered. "Which we never shall be."

Not daring to think about their secret departure, Anne took in her surroundings, trying not to gape at the luxurious setting. The air was heavy with the scent of hothouse flowers. Inside the grand manor, women floated along in their beautiful dresses. The men all wore breeches and waistcoats, their shirt collars starched and standing at attention.

At the entrance to the ballroom, their names were announced. Teach paused, glancing around until he saw the Duke and Duchess of Cardwell. He advanced, giving Anne a gentle tug when she held back.

"Come along now," he said briskly. "Let me introduce you to our hosts."

"I wish you wouldn't," she replied beneath her breath.

"Nonsense. It would be rude not to acknowledge their hospitality."

"But what if William has said something to them about me?"

"What could he have said?" Teach asked.

Anne gave a short laugh, surprised by his obstinacy. "That I used to be a maid in your house."

"But you're not anymore."

She still refused to move. He made it sound so simple.

Looking at the duchess, Anne was intimidated by both her elegance and her beauty. The older woman wore a gray gown covered with the most exquisite lace Anne had ever seen. And her eyes were as hard as the strand of diamonds around her neck.

"Anne, these people are not any better than you. There's no reason to hide," Teach whispered.

"I'm not hiding," she hissed. He had no idea what he was asking.

"Then come with me. Please. I secured your invitation. I've known them for years."

Taking a deep breath, she accompanied Teach as he strode forward. She envied his confidence.

It wasn't long before they stood in front of the impressive pair.

"Mr. Edward, it's nice to see you again."

"Thank you so much for your invitation, Your Grace. Allow me to introduce you to Miss Anne Barrett. Miss Barrett, the Duke and Duchess of Cardwell."

The duke tipped his white-haired head. "And where are you from, Miss Barrett?"

"I was born here in Bristol, Your Grace." Although it was the first time she'd ever met a duke, Anne could not help wondering if he always asked his guests where they were from.

The duchess's eyes widened in surprise. "Really?"

Anne fingered the pearls at her neck nervously, her face burning beneath the intense scrutiny. Teach had sent the pearls to her room, and Anne had been touched by the gesture.

"She is the daughter of an old family friend, Your Grace," Teach said.

"Who are these old friends?" the duchess asked archly.

"I'm afraid they are both deceased, Your Grace," Teach said, no doubt sensing Anne's unease.

Anne was grateful there were other guests waiting to greet the host and hostess, and Teach led her away. They approached the buffet table, but Anne was too anxious to eat, aware of the many glances that followed her advancement through the room. Nobody said anything, because she was with Edward Drummond, but she could see the disapproval in several faces, curiosity in others.

Anne had never felt so exposed, and firmly gripped Teach's arm. "I wish to leave."

"Do not let them win, Anne."

"*Win?* Do you think this is a game?" she asked, bristling when she saw William approaching. She did not understand how Teach could be his friend.

"Ah, I see you've brought 'the maid' for me," William said, taking Anne's hand in his and bringing it to his wet mouth.

Anne's toes curled with disgust. She could not escape his grasp fast enough, and slid her hand behind her back, wiping off on her dress the touch of his lips.

She did not imagine the steely gaze Teach gave his friend. "She is not for you," he said tightly.

William's eyebrows rose. "Do I detect a hint of possessiveness in your voice? You can't keep them all for yourself, old friend. You are as good as married. Leave something for the rest of us."

Teach stiffened at her side. "I am not yet married, and Anne is my father's goddaughter. She is therefore off-limits. Unless you would like to take it up with my father."

William faked a laugh, but Anne could see the resentment in his eyes. "Always so superior, aren't you, Teach? And yet I am to be a duke and you are simply a merchant. When will you learn to relax a little?"

"When I am sure you mean Anne no harm, Lord Lorimar," Teach said coldly.

Anne was surprised at the animosity between the two friends. She and Teach were William's guests, after all, and yet Teach had just insulted his host.

He led her away and joined a small group of people with varying titles. They were courteous, and she didn't notice any censure in their expressions as Teach introduced her. It was obvious he felt at ease among them, and Anne felt herself relax somewhat.

It didn't take long for Teach to be caught up in a conversation about the end of the Nine Years War and the treaty between France and the grand alliance of England, Spain, and the Holy Roman Empire. The treaty had brought no real resolution to the deeper issue of the balance of power between the warring nations, but at least the fighting had stopped.

Anne listened as they debated what kind of an impact such an event would have on the shipping industry. Of the individuals present, Teach appeared to be the most knowledgeable on the topic. "I cannot predict the future," he said tersely.

Anne hid a smile, for she had said the same thing to him.

"But I foresee some troubling times ahead," he continued.

"Why is that?" one man asked.

"With the war over, think of the soldiers and sailors who will no longer be employed. What will they do now that they are no longer fighting for a united cause? You cannot tell me they will be content to return to the fields or attempt to learn a new trade."

"What do you think they will do, Edward?"

"They will take to the seas, doing what they do best," Teach said.

"Do you mean they'll become privateers?"

Teach looked at each man carefully. "Either that—or pirates."

"Are you concerned about your father's new ship? Once the *Deliverance* sets sail, every pirate on the seas will be after it."

Anne broke away from the group as their discussion continued, keeping to the side of the room so as to avoid the dance floor. A manservant walked by, and she accepted the goblet he offered, savoring her first taste of champagne as she observed the small clusters of landed gentry and wealthy merchants, each intent on their own conversations.

A few men attempted to approach her, but Anne quickly learned that if she turned away, pretending interest in a nearby group, they lost their nerve and left her in peace. Her father had taught her many things, but how to dance was not one of them. The last thing she wanted was to embarrass the Drummonds.

One set of French doors was opened to the balcony, allowing the brisk October air to blow through the crowded hall. Anne slid outside and found an unoccupied bench hidden behind a potted plant. Closing her eyes, she ignored the muted voices coming from the interior of the house, wondering if it was too early in the evening to return to the Drummond household.

The moon overhead was full, giving light to the manicured gardens and casting long shadows across the lawn.

Anne watched the graceful figures dancing inside, their movements smooth and flowing. She wished she could join in the festivities, but knew she would stand out like the interloper she was.

"Your Majesty," a familiar voice muttered into her ear.

Anne jumped up, nearly dropping the goblet in her hand, and glanced over her shoulder. Teach stood beside her, a sly grin on his face.

"Why do you insist on frightening me?" she demanded, irritated at his smirk.

"Why do you insist on being alone?" he countered, folding his arms across his chest. "Do you not know a solitary woman wandering through the garden unaccompanied will quickly develop a reputation?"

Anne blushed at her own ignorance. "No one was concerned for my welfare when I was a maid and walked to the market alone."

Her words found their mark, and Teach winced.

"Besides, it was too crowded in there," she said.

He glanced behind them before raising his eyebrows at her. "What did you expect at a ball?"

Anne smoothed her gown, her fingers reaching automatically for the gold watch in her pocket. She'd had a pocket sewn into every dress. "I certainly would never have agreed to come if I'd known it would be like this," she said. "I don't belong here."

"Of course you do. There are visitors inside from around the world."

"You don't understand. You grew up this way. I did not."

"You forget, I'm just the son of a merchant."

"Yes, who is invited to balls hosted by a duke."

Teach made an impatient sound in his throat. "I would much rather spend my time with you than with any of them. Come back inside with me."

"I don't know how to dance," she said.

"I'll teach you."

She glared at him. "Do you wish to make a fool of me?"

"No, I simply wish to dance with you. Nothing more. Nothing less. Just a simple dance."

Looking down, she nodded slowly. "I'm sorry," she whispered. "It's just . . . I . . ." Her voice trailed off, finding it difficult to put her feelings into words. No matter where she went, she felt out of sorts.

She was unable to prevent the tears shimmering in her blue eyes, and Teach muttered something under his breath. "Why are you always so sad?" he asked.

Noting the tenderness in his features, it was difficult to speak around the lump in her throat. "I'm not."

"Yes, you are. When we are married, I shall make you smile, every day for the rest of your life."

She pulled away, wiping her damp cheeks. "Do not speak of such things."

"Why not? I only speak the truth."

"Yes, but I asked you not to."

He gazed at her from head to toe. "No, you asked me not

to kiss you. Can I help it if I want to tell the world how I feel about you? You're my queen."

"Beneath these trappings I'm still just a simple girl," she said, her voice barely above a whisper.

Something in Teach's expression changed, and his eyes flicked to her lips.

Anne's breath hitched in her throat. "You promised—"

"I lied." Lifting a strand of her hair from her collarbone, Teach leaned in close.

"Edward, your father has arrived and is looking for you!" A sharp voice cut through the night air, splitting the two apart as effectively as a knife. The potted plant provided just enough shelter that whoever it was did not see the look of frustration crossing Teach's face, nor Anne's look of chagrin.

Teach stepped out, hoping to shield Anne from the curious onlooker. "Tell him I'll be there shortly."

Footsteps headed in the other direction.

"I don't want to leave you," he said, adjusting a curl at her temple.

"I'll be fine."

"At least come back inside where it's warm—"

"Go, Teach. Come and find me after." In truth, Anne could not bear the thought of hearing Drummond say that the marriage would still take place, for there was no way she would be able to hide her feelings then.

She slid toward the end of the balcony and escaped down

into the gardens. Even though the air was brisk, she preferred it to the stuffy interior. She knew it was too cold for anyone else to venture outside as well.

Walking along a path, she followed Teach's progress through the window as he returned inside, and watched as he was led to what appeared to be a library beside the ballroom. Drummond waited for him there, and the two sat down. Teach listened intently as his father began to speak.

Leaning against a short wall, Anne continued to observe the conversation, knowing she should return inside, but loath to do so. Her stomach was in knots, and her hands clenched the cold stone balustrade.

The sound of approaching footsteps along the gravel path startled her. Instinctively she ducked behind a tree, unwilling to have anyone find her pining after Teach.

Moments later she was glad she had, for William came into view, illuminated by the full moon. His arms were wrapped around a figure dressed in an elegant cloak. The pair stopped beneath the shadow of a nearby tree and embraced. Anne's insides protested as she listened to them kiss, quietly professing their love for each other. As usual, William was effusive in his admiration.

The girl's face was obscured in the shadows, but she appeared to enjoy William attention.

"Darling," he said, his thick lips making slurping sounds against his companion's unfortunate neck. "How long must I endure your continued courtship with that fool? You know we are destined to be together. Please do not torture me and let him raise my child as his own. Call off the wedding."

"Yes, well, my father didn't care enough to break off the engagement. The next time you accuse someone of something, make sure the charges stand." It was Miss Patience!

Anne gasped, and immediately placed her hands over her mouth to prevent another sound from escaping. She froze, afraid to move.

Patience was pregnant with William's child! And William was the one who'd accused Teach of piracy! It hadn't been Henry after all.

The two lovers were quiet. Had they heard her? Anne's pulse raced, wanting to confront them, but an inner voice held her back. She would not do it alone, for she did not trust them. They were both as crooked as the day was long. She needed to find Teach first and tell him what she had discovered.

Her heart soared. Surely now Teach would not be forced to marry Patience. And Anne and Teach would not have to leave immediately. If at all.

The couple moved on, but Anne waited until the sound of their footsteps disappeared. Her fingertips and toes were numb, and she slid silently out from her hiding spot. She saw from her vantage point that Teach was still conversing with his father.

Anne had just stepped onto the balcony when a fleshy hand grabbed her wrist. She shrieked as William leered at her.

"I thought it was you!" he snarled, dragging her along behind him.

Fighting desperately against his hold as he attempted to yank her back toward the gardens, Anne looked frantically over her shoulder, trying to catch Teach's attention. But the balcony was in shadows from the large trees surrounding it. Even in her ivory dress, it would be hard for Teach to see anything while the library was lit from within.

"Let go of me!" Anne yelled, hoping her voice would carry, but the sound of the orchestra in the ballroom drowned her out.

"I'll not have you running off to tell Teach about us," he said. "You will keep your mouth shut."

"If you love Patience, why don't you marry her yourself?" Anne cried. It didn't make sense. Upon his father's death, William would become a duke. Surely he had more to offer a baron than a merchant?

William did not respond, but Anne managed to escape, lifting her skirts and flying back the way she'd come. William tackled her from behind, and Anne fell forward, her head narrowly missing the edge of the balcony stairs.

If she didn't get away, he might kill her. She searched the ground, looking for something, *anything*, to throw that would capture Teach's attention, but there was nothing at hand.

The watch in her pocket.

Anne kicked out, her foot connecting with William's face. He fell back, his hands clutching his nose as blood spurted everywhere, like a fountain. Jumping to her feet, Anne reached into her pocket and grabbed the watch.

Taking aim, she threw with all of her might. Both she and William remained motionless as the watch sailed through the air. It pierced the window in the library, shattering the smooth surface and breaking the reflection of the moon into a thousand shards.

CHAPTER 30

Teach

Glass rained down from the window, and a familiar gold object landed on the carpet near Teach's feet. It was Anne's pocket watch. Alarmed, he scooped it up and looked out, to where he saw a flash of ivory in the gloom. Two figures battled outside, and an overpowering rage swept through Teach as he realized it was Anne. And William.

"What the devil?" Drummond snapped.

Throwing open the French doors, Teach nearly pulled them off their hinges. The cold air rushed in, as well as the sounds of Anne's struggle. Teach flew across the balcony, his arms outstretched as he reached for William's throat.

He would kill him for this.

Teach's blood roared in his ears, and he tackled William to the ground in a confusion of limbs and cloth, his fists pummeling his former friend with coiled strength. William could only lie there, trying to protect himself as best he could.

"Edward, stop this at once!" His father's hands gripped Teach around his shoulders, attempting to pull him back, but Teach was not prepared to stop. After one particularly hard hit, William caught his breath in a gasp of agony.

Only Anne's voice was able to break through the haze, piercing Teach's rage as she cried out to him.

Slowly, like a man waking from a dream, Teach fell back, his chest heaving, finally aware of a number of people surrounding them. William lay curled in a ball, openly sobbing, his clothes bloodied and soiled.

"Get her out of here," Drummond said. "I'll deal with this."

Teach scooped Anne into his arms and carried her away from prying eyes. The rips in Anne's dress along with the grass stains painted a condemning picture.

He set her down once they were out of sight, his eyes and hands running over her, trying to assess how much damage had been done. She trembled uncontrollably, clearly in shock.

"Are you all right? Did he hurt you?" Teach asked.

Anne shook her head. "No, no," she whispered, her voice quivering. "I was trying to get to you—"

It was all Teach could do not to return to beat the remaining life out of William. If Teach ever saw William again, he swore to himself he would finish the job.

But not now. Right now Anne needed him.

Teach gathered her close, pressing his lips against her hair, desperate to convince her that she was safe. "Let's get you home," he said, taking off his longcoat and placing it around her shoulders.

As they neared the front of the house, Teach was careful to shield Anne from curious looks. He hailed his driver and then climbed into the carriage beside her, shutting the door soundly behind him. Once inside, he brought her close, running his hands up and down her arms in an effort to stop her shivering. The carriage pulled away.

"I have to tell you—" Anne began, but Teach silenced her.

"Shhh, no, don't," he said, unable to bear it. If William had indeed harmed her . . .

"No, it has n-nothing to do with me. He . . . he did not hurt me." Teach snorted, but Anne remained firm, even as her teeth chattered from shock. "He might have, if . . . if you hadn't come. He was frightened I would tell you about them."

"About whom?" Teach asked.

"William and Patience. William is the one who accused you of piracy. And Patience is pregnant with his child."

Teach froze, his hands resting on Anne's arms.

"I'm so sorry," she said, concern for him evident on her face.

Teach stared at her. "You're sorry? Why would you be sorry?" he asked, incredulous.

Anne swallowed. "Because William is your friend. And because I was the one who had to tell you. I overheard them in the garden." A look of disgust filled her eyes. "They deserve each other. I don't understand why the two of them don't just marry."

"After tonight they will have no choice," Teach said.

"But why didn't they simply do that in the first place? Does Patience truly love him?"

"I believe she may. William makes her laugh. The two of them have much in common, caring more about parties and appearance than books or learning. It seems that while I was gone, their attraction to each other merely increased."

"Then why didn't the baron choose William to marry her? Why you?"

"Because the Duke and Duchess of Cardwell would never agree to it. On more than one occasion, I overheard them talking about her. They see Patience for what she really is, a spoiled, manipulative girl. And they wanted more than a baron's daughter for William."

"But William is no better," Anne said bitterly.

"But he is their *son*. They've spoiled him and are too afraid to admit that they were wrong to supply his every whim." Teach exhaled loudly. "I should have suspected something."

"William believed charging you with piracy would get Lord Hervey to change his mind about your match. But it didn't."

"No, it didn't. And knowing Patience as I do, I believe she was torn. She loves her father and knows how much he needs my father's money. That was why she couldn't break off the betrothal outright."

Anne leaned into him, and Teach closed his eyes, relishing the warmth of her body against his.

"Will they claim the baby is yours?" she asked.

"They might try. That was why they were rushing the engagement." Looking back, everything made sense. The note Anne found had been intended for Patience.

"What will you do now?" she asked.

"Marry you," was his simple response.

Anne met Teach's gaze. Her mouth tilted up at the corner, and a bright glint entered her eyes. "And if I'm not ready to marry?"

"Then I will wait."

"Is that a proposal?" she asked softly.

Teach grinned. "Perhaps. Will you accept?"

"Perhaps."

"What would it take to convince you?" he asked.

"It's not me you have to convince. It's your father."

Teach brushed her hair behind her ear. "My father can have no objections now. You're Andrew Barrett's daughter and more of an equal match for me than Patience ever was."

Anne appeared unconvinced, but remained silent.

In the shelter of the carriage, Teach held her close, her heart beating against his chest.

"You're going back there, aren't you?" Anne asked.

Teach frowned. "I should. I wish I could leave it until tomorrow, but I'm afraid of what Patience and William will say if they're given enough time to concoct some other story. The best time to catch them in their lies is now, when they haven't time to regroup. I must go and explain my case."

The carriage pulled to a stop. Teach jumped out and walked Anne up to the entrance of the house. "I'm sorry for leaving you so soon."

"I'll be fine. You must tell your father what I heard. Come and find me later."

"Always," he said.

Teach waited until Elizabeth appeared and took Anne to her room before he bounded back down the stairs toward the carriage. This would not take him long. Word of what had happened had no doubt spread throughout the party.

Teach instructed the driver to return to the Cardwell estate.

By the time he arrived, the last of the guests were entering their carriages, no doubt disappointed that the grand party had been cut short. The lanterns out front flickered in the wind, and the green garlands and topiaries looked forlorn instead of festive.

Inside the large house, Teach followed the butler down the long, deserted hallway. He heard the loud voices before he entered the drawing room. Both the duke and the baron were crouched over William where he sat in the corner of the settee. A bloody cloth was pressed to his nose, and his head was tipped back to staunch the flow.

"How is Anne?" Drummond asked, reaching his son's side before the others were aware of his presence.

"Recovering, thank you. What have I missed?"

Before Teach's father could respond, William's eyes widened. The duke turned, his face red with rage.

"There you are. Would you care to explain why you attacked my son in the middle of a party held in your honor?"

Drummond stepped in front of Teach. "As I told you, your son attacked my goddaughter, Your Grace. I saw it with my own eyes. Edward was merely protecting her."

The duke spread his hands wide. "Where is she, then? Hmmm? The only victim I see here is William. You could have killed him!"

If his father hadn't been standing in front of him, Teach might have gone for the duke's throat as well. "I took Anne home for her own protection. She happened to overhear a conversation between the earl and Miss Patience."

"What did she expect, skulking about the gardens like a common street— Ahh!" William's words were cut off by his own high-pitched squeal as Teach lunged for him.

It took the combined strength of the duke, Lord Hervey, and Drummond to hold Teach back.

"You bloody coward!" Teach spat, straining against the three men who prevented him from delivering more damage to William's face. "The only sullied reputation is Miss Patience's. Does your father know he's about to be a grandfather?"

"What?" the duke cried.

"What the devil are you talking about?" Lord Hervey demanded.

Teach stepped out of their grasp. "Oh, didn't Lord Lorimar tell you? In the garden he professed his undying love for Miss Patience. She's carrying his child."

The silence in the room was thick, and for a moment time seemed to stand still.

Turning to his father, Teach pointed an accusatory finger at William. "And it was Lorimar who accused me of piracy. He did it hoping the baron would hear about it and break the betrothal, for the earl hopes to marry Patience himself."

"Is this true?" the duke asked, piercing his son with an astonished glare.

William cowered in the corner, his mouth opening and closing, but no sound came out.

Lord Hervey sputtered protestations, his face and neck turning an alarming shade of red. Drummond looked between the three men, his brows drawn together in a frown.

"Is this true, Edward?" he asked, turning to his son.

Teach nodded. "Yes. I suspect Miss Patience is several weeks along already. They have only to ask Miss Patience to confirm it."

The duke strode to the door and barked out orders. In just a few minutes Patience arrived, along with Lady Hervey and the duchess.

"What is the meaning of this?" the duchess asked. "William should be in bed." Glancing at the assembled group, the duchess saw Teach, and her eyes narrowed. "Why is he still here? Are you going to press charges?" she asked, turning on her husband.

"If anyone is going to press charges, it will be me," Drummond said. "Your son attacked an innocent girl, who happens to be under my protection." Turning to Lord Hervey, he nodded in Patience's direction. "The betrothal is off. My son will no longer marry your daughter." His voice rang throughout the room, and Teach's chest nearly burst with the relief he felt at his father's words.

"And why not?" Lady Hervey asked.

"I believe that is a conversation best left between you and your husband. My business here is concluded. Edward, it's time for us to go."

Teach was only too happy to exit the room as the aristocrats started flinging accusations at one another. He gathered it wouldn't take long before objects followed.

CHAPTER 31

Teach

For the next three days Teach couldn't wipe the smile from his face. He hadn't been this happy since he'd first set sail on Andrew Barrett's ship more than a year ago, bound for adventures untold.

He was grateful and extremely relieved that his involvement with Patience Hervey and her family was at an end. It had been an ugly confrontation, one that had no doubt turned uglier the moment he and his father had left.

Drummond had actually apologized to Teach. It was now widely known that Patience was several weeks pregnant, and since Teach had only recently returned, there was no conceivable way he could have fathered the child. Instead of announcing Teach's and Patience's betrothal, William's and Patience's names were tied together publicly.

Teach didn't care if he never saw William or Patience again.

When he thought how close he had come to marrying her . . . his stomach twisted at the thought. If they had married, when the child had been born, would he have recognized that it wasn't his? Or would he have assumed the baby had simply come early, and raised it as his own?

If it hadn't been for Anne— Teach pictured her struggling against William. He had a hard time controlling his anger when he thought of it.

He and Anne had decided not to tell his father about their plans to marry. Not yet, at least.

She was the daughter of a respectable and admired merchant, not to mention Master Drummond's closest friend. She would be a worthy match, and with time Teach was sure his father would see it.

Without a wedding to plan, Drummond had thrown himself into preparations for the launch of the *Deliverance* and was hardly ever at home. Teach was glad, for it left him time to spend with Anne alone. They dined together at the house and took walks through the garden, talking about everything and nothing. When they were silent, it wasn't the awkward silence of two who had exhausted their conversation. It was simply companionable, each one at peace with the other.

Now Teach hurried his pace, oblivious to the busy city streets. He was supposed to meet up with Anne and Elizabeth within an hour, and nothing was going to make him late.

Anne had been reluctant to go into the city, ever since the

party, and he'd told her he would meet her near the docks in an hour. Anne had shaken her head at him. "I shouldn't have let you talk me into this. You're like a young boy on Christmas Day."

"And you are my gift. Just so you know, I was never very good at sharing." Laughing at the shocked look on Elizabeth's face, Teach had left the two of them at the dressmakers.

He could not wait to see Anne again. She was more honorable than most landed gentry he knew. Including his ex-fiancée. Once he and Anne were married, he would show everyone just how remarkable she was. The fact that Anne's skin was a shade darker than most should not exclude her from anyone's drawing rooms.

Teach quickened his pace as he neared his destination, unwilling to let anything ruin his plans or his mood. He pulled the heavy wooden-and-glass door open and stepped inside.

The shop gave off a clean, sharp scent of linseed oil. Teach glanced around at the simple interior. Several chairs were arranged in groups of three at small desks, a curtain hanging between each grouping, giving the occupants privacy.

Teach nodded to the shopkeeper, who withdrew into a back room, only to return with an ornate velvet box in his hands and a shiny gold object.

"Please sit down," he instructed Teach.

Teach settled into his chair, his heart racing. Anne was right. He hadn't been this excited since he used to wake up on Christmas morning, waiting to see what gifts he'd been given.

"Here is the watch you asked to be repaired."

Teach held the familiar object in his hand, clicking it open. "Thank you. Excellent work." He slipped it into his pocket.

"Now for the other matter. I took the liberty of picking these out myself, once I read your message." With a deft movement the shopkeeper opened the velvet box, and Teach smiled at what lay before him.

Rings in all shapes and sizes lined the interior, covered in diamonds and pearls. "Which one shall it be?" the jeweler asked.

Teach was momentarily overwhelmed and shook his head, wondering if he should have brought Anne along with him. "I can't pick. They're all so beautiful. That would be like picking a favorite child."

The shopkeeper smiled indulgently, no doubt used to such astonishment. "Perhaps it would help if you held them up to the light." He reached out and picked up a gold ring with a large pearl, then slipped it into Teach's hand.

Teach held it up, admiring the ring as it shimmered in the sunlight streaming through the windows. "It's . . . quite large," he said at length.

The jeweler's eyebrows drew together.

Teach sensed his displeasure and placed it back in the tray.

"How about this one?" the jeweler asked, picking a large diamond ring.

Teach frowned and held it up as well. It didn't feel quite right for her. "I'm afraid she would cut me with this," he said after a moment. "Or scar me for life."

The shopkeeper was clearly not amused. "I have some other rings I could show you," he said haughtily.

Teach nodded. "Please."

The jeweler probably thought Teach was too cheap to buy anything this extravagant. Quite the contrary. He wanted to show the world how much Anne meant to him, but he also wanted to prove it to *her*. A large ring might impress the residents of Bristol, but it wouldn't impress Anne.

She already had several new dresses and gowns. Teach was even worse than his father when it came to dressmakers. He'd gone so far as to have an ivory gown made, to replace the one that had been ruined at the party. She'd protested the entire time, but Teach had managed to override her objections.

As the shopkeeper left, his back stiff with his displeasure, Teach drummed his fingers on his knee. He couldn't wait to see her reaction when he presented her with a ring.

The jeweler was back. He set the box down in front of Teach and snapped open the lid. "Perhaps these are more to your liking," he said.

The rings were decidedly less ornate, but no less beautiful. Teach's eyes settled on a gold band, carefully handcrafted, with a braided centerline framed by twisted ropes. Holding it up for inspection, he breathed a sigh of relief.

"This is the one," he murmured.

The jeweler nodded.

As much as Teach would have liked to buy her the biggest,

fattest ring, this one suited her, much more than the other garish choices. "How long will it take for you to size it?" he asked, handing him a circular thread. He'd used it to measure Anne's finger.

The jeweler tilted his head to the side. "You may return to pick it up in two days' time."

Teach smiled. "Excellent." He shook the jeweler's hand and headed outside, into the brisk fall afternoon.

At the top of the hour, he met Anne and Elizabeth at the entrance to the docks, the sharp scent of fish and brine assailing their nostrils.

Teach pulled Anne into an alcove, leaving Elizabeth standing a few feet away. "I missed you," he whispered. Someone laughed quietly behind them. Teach looked and saw young Ruth and a friend pointing and giggling, with Elizabeth nearby. Teach reached into his pocket and took out two coins. "Here. Go and bother someone else," he said to the little girls.

They took off, running down the street.

He threw one to Elizabeth as well. "What's this for?" she asked.

"For you to leave us," Teach said.

"But it wouldn't be proper—" Elizabeth began, but Teach handed her another coin.

"I just need you to go shopping for a minute or two. Miss Anne will be quite safe with me."

"Won't your father be expecting us for lunch?" Anne asked.

"No. He's too busy."

"He works much too hard."

"You're right." Turning to the maid, Teach waved his hand. "Elizabeth, go and see if my father needs anything."

"You're impossible," Anne muttered. "Elizabeth isn't going anywhere. Now hurry and show me what you want so that we can return home."

Sighing, Teach held out his hand, motioning to Elizabeth. "Hand over the coins."

Elizabeth clutched them to her chest. "No, sir. I need these. You gave 'em to me fair an' square."

Teach's mouth dropped open. Anne smiled.

"This is your doing," Teach said, pointing a finger at Anne. "I'm not sure if you deserve this." Withdrawing the pocket watch, he held it out for Anne to see.

She grabbed for it, but he raised it above her head. "It comes with a price," he said.

While his attention was focused on Anne, Elizabeth jumped up and caught the watch in her hands.

Anne laughed. "Thank you, Elizabeth. Who knows what kind of price he would have demanded of me."

Recognizing that he was outnumbered, Teach accepted defeat and turned toward the docks.

The *Deliverance* bobbed gently in the water before them, the waves lapping noisily against its polished hull. The square-rigged main and topsails were crisp and white, while the bowsprit jutted out like a spear from the foredeck.

Elizabeth stopped in her tracks. "I'm not going on that."

Teach's heart lifted. "Fine. You stay here and wait for us. This won't take long."

He couldn't help his surge of pride as he helped Anne onto the plank, leading the way as they boarded. Anne didn't display any of Elizabeth's fear. He'd asked his father if he could show Anne the ship, and his father had arranged for the crew to be absent during that time.

The deck gleamed beneath the sunlight. Teach knew that after a few days at sea, the ship would not resemble its current state, but for now it was spotless. Ropes and barrels lay nearby, waiting to be used.

Anne ran her fingers along the railing, apparently taking in every detail of the massive ship. They strolled the entire length, ending on the starboard side facing out to sea.

"Do you like it?" Teach asked.

"It's magnificent," Anne said. "I've never seen a ship this large before."

Teach wrinkled his nose. "Trust Father to attempt such an undertaking."

"But won't it make a large target? Think of all the pirates who will come after this ship, hoping to claim it for their own."

Teach leaned against the main boom, his arms above his head. "Father has thought about that. He made sure that enough cannons are aboard, making a direct assault on the ship difficult."

Anne made a face. "Difficult, but not impossible."

"You need not worry. Father has said he's hired the most experienced sailors and soldiers. He pays them well."

Anne walked across the quarterdeck, down the steps, and through the long hallway into the captain's cabin.

She twisted her hands in the folds of her dress. "You know, before you arrived home, I planned to leave on the *Deliverance.*"

Teach's eyebrows rose. "Did you?"

She nodded, blushing. "Yes. Looking back, I realize how foolish I was. I had planned to steal away, or else pay someone to let me on board."

Teach smiled. "Not so foolish. I planned to be captain."

"Did you?" Anne asked.

"Yes. My father doesn't like to hear me say it. Even if everything hadn't worked out in our favor, I had no intention of marrying Miss Patience. I had no idea how to approach the subject with him, but I was determined to be on board when the *Deliverance* left port."

"If our plans had worked, we would have been together anyway," Anne said.

Teach took her hand in his. "Always."

Now it was Anne's turn to smile.

CHAPTER 32

Anne

"I'm sorry, but I have no desire to return to the city," Anne said. It was late afternoon two days after their visit to the *Deliverance*, and her breath came out in soft puffs of white. Her fingertips were numb.

She and Teach had gone for another walk in the garden, the grass beneath their feet long dormant. The limbs of the bushes and trees appeared lifeless, suspended in their frozen states.

"Are you sure?" Teach asked.

"Quite sure, but thank you," she said. It was time to return the last remaining items to the house. For the past few days she'd risen early and gone to the two willows, hid the stolen silverware in her skirts and cloak, and returned them to their original places when no one was looking. Only a small number of objects remained, as well as all of the coins she'd collected. She'd decided to give the money to Elizabeth and her family, as well as to Sara.

"It won't take me long. I promise to return soon," Teach said.

"You can't go into the city like that," Anne protested.

"Like what?"

She eyed the dark scruff on his chin. "You look like a pirate. Has your father seen you?"

"No, my father is too concerned with his ship at the moment, and I have had more important things to do in the morning than to bother about my appearance."

"Oh, really? And what was so important?"

"Coming to see you," Teach said, pulling her toward the shadow of the garden wall.

"We live under the same roof. You see me every day," Anne pointed out.

"Trust me, I'm well aware of that fact." His arms wrapped around her, and his mouth covered hers.

Anne felt a surging tide of warmth that left her breathless, and she kissed him back.

Eventually he lifted his head, his eyes bright. "When I return, perhaps we can go for a ride. Is that all right with you?"

Anne managed to nod.

"Good." After one last lingering kiss, Teach turned and strode toward the waiting carriage.

As it pulled away, Anne paused, an uncomfortable feeling settling inside her. The sooner she completed this task, the sooner she could relax. There would be no more secrets between them, and Anne could begin her new life with Teach, for she could not imagine spending it with anyone else.

Glancing back at the house, she paused and scanned the windows. She couldn't help feeling as if someone were watching her, but there were no movements anywhere.

She was being ridiculous. It was her guilt that made her feel this way, for surely she was the only one foolish enough to remain out in this cold.

Shivering, Anne ducked beneath the archway and entered the wilder realm outside the Drummond grounds. With brisk steps she approached the willows, grateful to put this part of her time in the Drummond house behind her.

As Anne swiped aside the long branches, her heart stopped at what she saw—or, more important, her heart stopped at what she didn't see.

The chest was gone.

Rushing forward, she looked around the base of the two trees and at the surrounding ground, but the chest was not there.

"Is something wrong?"

Anne spun to find Margery standing several feet away, a flicker of triumph lighting her cold eyes.

The buzzing in Anne's ears started low but grew sharper, more piercing. "No, I . . . I just needed some fresh air."

Margery smiled. "Aye, you often seem to require quite a bit of fresh air, don't you?"

"I'm sorry?"

"Your early morning walks. You enjoy rising early, before

the rest of the house. You were never that industrious as a maid."

"What do you want?" Anne asked, wishing she felt as fearless as she sounded.

"Master Drummond would like to see you. He's waiting for you back at the house."

Anne turned even colder, and her mouth went dry.

Margery stepped away but stopped when she noticed that Anne hadn't moved. "I suggest you come with me now. He's not in a favorable mood."

This time Margery waited for Anne to precede her. Anne's mind raced with each step. Her pulse drove in erratic surges, and her chest was tight with fear.

He knew.

What could she possibly tell Drummond about the chest?

He stood in the back door, waiting for her approach. Margery nodded at him before she disappeared into the kitchen.

Motioning for Anne to follow him, Drummond led the way to the drawing room. He closed the door behind her, the look in his eyes hard.

"I wished to speak with you about my son."

Anne's face grew warm, but she managed to meet his eyes. It was not what she had expected.

"Sir?"

"What are your plans?" he asked bluntly.

"My plans?"

"Yes."

Anne shook her head, perplexed. What kind of game was he playing? "I don't know what you mean."

"Margery tells me that you and my son spend a great deal of time together. Is this true?"

"We dine together, yes. But that is only to be expected."

"And is it *expected* that you take walks together in the garden, or that he show you my ship?"

"Teach asked for permission. *You* arranged that." Too late, Anne realized her mistake. Drummond's mouth turned down at the corners at the use of his son's nickname.

"*Edward* did ask me. But I would not have given my permission if I'd known about the nature of your relationship."

"Sir, under the circumstances, you can hardly expect your son and me to ignore each other. If you would like, I will take my meals in my room."

"What I would *like* is for you to quit my house."

Although she'd tried to prepare herself for the dismissal, the sting of his words was severe. "Please, let me explain."

Drummond ignored the pallor of her face, looking ready to attack. "In light of the circumstances, I think it would be best if you left. I've arranged passage for you on the *Deliverance* when it sets sail."

"Please—" she began, but he ignored her.

"I have hired a lady's maid to accompany you. You have the money your father left behind, although you certainly don't deserve it. That should be enough for you to start a new life somewhere else. I'm prepared to give you more, to ensure that you leave."

Anger quickly replaced Anne's pain. "Money is your answer for everything, isn't it? If you want to become a member of the aristocracy, you have only to throw money at a baron. If someone falsely accuses your son of piracy, by all means, pay for the constable's silence. If someone falls in love with your son and wishes to marry him, you pay her off and send her packing, because you don't approve of the match. You think that just because you have money, everyone else has to bow to your every whim."

The irony of the situation wasn't lost on Anne. It wasn't that long ago that she had planned to do that very thing, leave Bristol and everything behind her, to search for her mother's family. But her situation had changed, and the last thing she wanted was to leave now. Especially without Teach. She'd thought that perhaps, once she and Teach were married, they could visit the islands together.

"Do not make this harder than it needs to be."

"Harder than it needs to be? You're asking me to leave everything I know and love behind."

Drummond was unmoved by the tears in her eyes and the desperation in her voice. "So you refuse to leave on your own?" he demanded.

"I do not wish to."

"I didn't want to resort to this, but I can see that you leave me no choice. There is another matter."

Anne closed her eyes.

"It has been brought to my attention that several objects in the household have gone missing."

"I was going to return everything," she said, meeting his condemning gaze. "I never meant to steal from you."

"What, precisely, did you *mean* to do?"

"The only reason I took anything was because I was treated unfairly here and I wanted to escape. I took nothing more than you owed me. Or my father."

Drummond looked decidedly uncomfortable at the reminder. "Yes, well, you will have a hard time convincing the constable of that."

"Are you going to contact him?" Anne asked, desperate to wake up from this nightmare. How had everything gone so wrong in such a short amount of time?

"Not if you go willingly. You will leave within the hour."

"But I can't—"

Drummond held up a warning finger. "Unless you wish to go to jail, you can and you will. Margery will help you. She has already gathered your things. I will have your solicitor send part of your inheritance to the White Stag Inn. Once you reach your destination, you may let him know where he may send the rest."

"But that could take months."

"You should have thought of that before you stole from me.

I will allow you to pack all of the dresses I have given you, but nothing more. You will stay at the White Stag near the docks for the next few days. When the *Deliverance* sets sail, you will be on it. My debt to your father has been paid in full."

Anne pressed the knuckles of her clenched fist against her stomach, a fierce pain slashing her heart. "And Teach—" she said, almost afraid to mention his name.

"You will write Edward a note, telling him you harbor no genuine feelings for him and that you only used him."

"But that's not true!" she cried, her blood turning to ice water. She didn't want to believe he could be that cruel.

"Regardless of whether it's true or not, you will declare it so."

"He won't believe it," she said.

"Yes, he will. Oh, I know he was fond of you, but that was before he knew you were a thief and a liar. In time he will get over you. As he did Miss Patience."

Anne flinched at his words, but anger and hurt pride drove out some of the pain. She'd once accused Teach of the same thing. Now, of course, she knew better, but there was no way she could convince Mr. Drummond of Teach's feelings for her.

"After you are gone, he will go on and marry someone else, someone who will bring out the best in him."

"You mean someone with a title."

"Yes, someone with a title. Someone more suited to him."

"If you knew him, you would know that he doesn't want that."

Drummond snorted. "And you know my son so well?"

"I do. I know he understands and accepts people, regardless of their circumstances or backgrounds. He's independent and forthright and appreciates it when others are as well. And the last thing in this world that your son cares about is marrying into the aristocracy."

He glared at her, his eyes hard. "I admit, I made a mistake with Miss Patience. Thanks to you, that disaster was averted. But I believe I know what's best for him, and that person is most certainly not you."

"Have you ever thought to ask your son what he wants?"

Drummond turned from her. "I have hired two gentlemen to see you to the docks and then safely onto the *Deliverance*. They will make certain you arrive at your destination and nowhere else. Once you are gone, my son will once again become the boy that I remember."

Anne shook her head incredulously, wondering at his conceit. "You can't continue to control his life. At some point you will lose him."

"On the contrary. When you're gone, everything will return to normal. When he saw William attack you, Edward was . . . wild, half-crazed. I've never seen him act like that before. He was clearly not himself. *You* brought out those primitive responses in him. At the time, I was angry with William as well. I had no idea of the depth of Edward's feelings for you."

"And you are obviously opposed to such feelings."

Master Drummond spun to face her. "Of course! How

could I be otherwise? Such a union would be impossible."

"Why is that?" Anne shot back, her voice laced with acid.

"Because of your position in society."

Anne was beyond caring what she said. In that moment, she realized there wasn't anything from the outside that could beat her. If she let it, it would come from within, but not if she fought against it. "My position in society?"

He pulled at his collar but remained silent.

"Despite what you think, I'm not a criminal. I made a mistake, yes, but what makes you think you're so superior to me? You're a merchant, just like my father."

"Yes, but your mother was a—a . . ." He clearly couldn't bring himself to say the word.

"A slave," Anne said proudly. She would not allow him to slander her mother. Jacqueline, at least, had done nothing wrong. "You would blame her for the color of her skin?"

"I wasn't going to say it," Drummond snapped. Going to the door, he called for Margery.

Suddenly Anne's desire to act was like a physical pressure, pushing from within. The rope that she felt around her neck when she was under this roof had tightened into a noose.

She raced for the door, but was brought up short by the appearance of two men. They caught her arms in a painful grasp. Anne almost wished Mr. Drummond had contacted the constable. She fought against the men's hold, but they simply tightened their grip.

"After you write the letter to Edward, these men will escort you to the White Stag, where you will stay until you set sail. Once you reach the West Indies, I'm sure your mother has some relatives who would take you in. Where you can be with your own—with people who are your family," he quickly amended.

"You mean where I can be with people of my own kind."

"I said 'family,'" he said, his voice terse.

If Anne had had something to throw, she would have. Preferably at his head. "If I do have any living family, they're even more of a stranger to me than you are. But I would sooner stay with them than spend another night in this house."

There was an awkward moment of silence, until Drummond nodded. "Good-bye, Anne. I wish you luck." With that, he motioned for the two men to take her. Anne was led out of the room, her shoulders back and her head held high.

CHAPTER 33

Teach

Teach stared out the carriage window at the pouring rain and blackened sky. The ring in his pocket was practically burning a hole through the material. His insides bubbled like a pot boiling over, and he couldn't wait to give the ring to her. His Anne. Sweet, strong, beautiful Anne.

Teach's mother had often told him that good people brought peace. That was precisely what Anne did for him. Oh, she could arouse his temper like no other girl ever had, but it was her strength and depth of character that had attracted him to her in the first place.

That and her unmistakable beauty.

Teach's pulse picked up as he neared his father's house. The large, gray exterior no longer filled him with dread. Ever since his mother had died, Teach had felt trapped, unable to do as he chose.

But now his father could not prevent him from marrying Anne.

The *Deliverance* would set sail within six days, but he would not be on it. There was no need. He was as happy as he'd ever been, and nothing was left to stand in the way of his happiness.

He sprang from the carriage and tore up the stairs. Inside the house all was still. *Anne must be upstairs, changing,* Teach thought. He headed for her room on the second floor, but stopped in his tracks when he discovered Margery on the landing. She stood in the dim light, a dour look on her face. "Your father is asking for you, sir."

"I'll be right there," Teach said quietly.

"He wishes you to come immediately."

"I will, as soon as I've spoken with Miss Anne."

"It has to do with her," Margery said, the distaste in her tone obvious.

If the old woman wasn't careful, Teach would still talk to his father about sacking her. Following Margery to his father's room, Teach placed Anne's ring in his pocket. Now would be as good a time as any to approach his father about marrying Anne.

The room was ablaze with candlelight, and his mother's portrait above the fireplace seemed to smile serenely at him.

"Good evening, Father. You're looking well."

"Thank you, Edward. Please, sit down."

Teach noticed the tense lines in Drummond's shoulders,

and his instincts told him something was wrong. Not wanting to argue, he took a seat and waited.

Drummond stepped to the side, and it was then that Teach noticed a small coffer on his father's dressing table.

"Did you know of Anne's propensity to go for long walks?" Drummond asked.

"Yes," Teach said warily. What a strange question.

"Did you ever follow her?"

"No, I never followed her. There were times when I accompanied her."

"Have you ever observed her doing anything . . . out of the ordinary?"

Anxiety settled in Teach's stomach, like an unwelcome guest who would not leave. He remembered the time when he'd caught her returning the items she'd stolen. "Never."

"Do you recognize this chest?" Drummond continued.

"No."

"Her name is engraved on it."

"Then it belongs to her."

Drummond made an ugly sound. "But the contents inside do not." He unhooked the latch and flipped the lid back before tipping the chest forward. Inside were a few pieces of household silverware and coins. There was even an ornate spyglass, one Teach recognized as his father's favorite. The one his father had claimed was missing.

His heart thundering anxiously, Teach shook his head.

"There—there must be some kind of explanation," he stammered, staring at the objects like they were a poisonous serpent.

"Yes, there is a perfectly good explanation. Anne stole them."

Teach ran his tongue over dry lips, trying to fight down a rising sense of panic. "We don't know that." But he did. Hadn't he caught Anne red-handed?

"Edward, it's useless to pretend otherwise. Margery followed Anne and discovered the chest hidden among the willows. While I have been quite generous, I have not given her leave to take anything from this house. Please, do not do me the disservice of trying to pretend otherwise."

"I'm not trying to pretend anything. I'm simply trying to understand it from Anne's perspective. You treat your employees only marginally better than someone else would treat their slaves, and yet you seem surprised that someone would steal from you. Perhaps she did it because you barely gave her enough to survive on."

His father's face turned a deep shade of puce. "I have never had trouble with my servants before now."

"That's not true and you know it," Teach said.

Drummond went to the decanter near his bed. He poured a glass of brandy and downed the contents. "It doesn't matter. The damage is done."

Teach tried to come up with a reasonable explanation he could give his father. She'd told him there was nothing else.

He'd believed her. If he'd known she'd taken this much . . . What would he have done?

It didn't affect the way he felt about her. He was disappointed, yes. And frightened for her. If only she'd confided in him. He could have returned everything himself, and his father would never have found out.

Drummond placed his hand on his son's shoulder. "I know this must come as quite a shock to you, Edward, and I'm sorry for that. I've seen how you look at her. I know that you care for her. There is no denying she's attractive. Not as attractive as Miss Patience, in my opinion . . . But the fact remains that Anne is nothing more than a common crook." He shook his head ruefully, turning back to the damning chest and closing the lid with a loud bang. "And to think I offered her shelter. To think I somehow felt obligated to watch out for her."

Teach jumped to his feet. "You're wrong. Anne deserves our protection. And our love. If it hadn't been for her, you would have made me marry Patience. You said so yourself."

"When it comes to Anne, I am often—mistaken," Drummond said gruffly. He made a face, as if the word left a bitter taste in his mouth.

"What are you going to do?"

"I should contact the constable."

"You can't," Teach said. "She's Andrew Barrett's daughter. You promised him you would take care of her."

"I did, but that was before I knew she would behave like this. She should be hanged, but I won't have her blood on my hands. She's gone now." His father's voice wrapped Teach in its destructive web. "She used you, Edward. I hope you see that now. She doesn't care for you."

"What have you done?"

Drummond retreated a step, his hands raised in a defensive gesture at the look on Teach's face. "If you don't believe me, see for yourself. She left you a note."

A cold fist clenched around Teach's heart as he grabbed the paper Drummond pulled from his pocket.

Dear Edward,

By the time you receive this, I will be gone. I'm sorry I did not get the opportunity to say good-bye, but it's for the best. We're not right for each other, and it was wrong of me to allow you to believe otherwise. I regret my actions, for I never had any intention of staying. We both know what my greatest desire in life was, and now I am achieving it. You deserve a queen, Edward. Go and find her.

Always,

Anne

Teach shook his head, hoping to clear his thoughts. He reread the note, stumbling over the clumsy phrasing, trying to piece it together with the girl he knew in his mind. *We're not right for each other.* Teach knew she didn't believe that.

You deserve a queen, Edward. Go and find her.

Something wasn't right. She'd never called him Edward. Why would she suddenly— His breath hitched in his throat. The clever, beautiful girl. She loved him. She was *his* queen, and she wanted him to find her.

Her goal had always been to search for her family. And she'd always planned to leave England by ship. On the *Deliverance.* That meant he had to get to the docks. John would help him.

Aware that his father watched him, Teach forced the muscles in his shoulders to relax, resisting the temptation to race from the room. He would have to be careful. Drummond must never suspect that Teach intended to go after her.

"She was not for you. In time you will see that."

"Just like Miss Patience," Teach said in a low voice.

"Yes, just like Miss Patience."

Except Anne was nothing like Miss Patience. Knowing that she was out there somewhere, alone, filled him with ice-cold fear.

And knowing that his father had done this filled him with a burning hate.

After an uncomfortable silence, Drummond cleared his throat. "As difficult as it may be, I need you to do something, Edward. Something very important."

"What?" Teach asked tersely.

"I need you to go to London for me."

"When?"

"Tomorrow morning. I'll need you to stay there for at least a week, if not more."

Teach turned and faced him. "If I do that, I'll miss the launch."

Drummond hesitated. "I know that. And while it is an important event, I would like you to visit with my solicitor in London."

"Why?"

"You've always shown an active interest in my business dealings. I was wrong not to let you pursue your dreams."

"My dream was to be captain of the *Deliverance*."

"That's impossible. But perhaps, in time, you might take command of a different ship."

By offering Teach this olive branch, his father clearly hoped to take his mind off Anne. But once again his father's plan backfired.

Teach knew exactly when and how Anne was leaving the country. "I can't give you my answer now. I'd like to be alone."

"You mustn't wait long. My solicitor in London is expecting you."

"Of course," Teach said, and strode to the door.

"Will you be joining me for supper this evening?" Was it Teach's imagination, or did his father sound uncertain?

Teach paused with his hand on the door handle. "Not

tonight. I have a lot to think about. Please have my meal sent up to my room instead."

"I'm your father. I would still like you to join me."

Teach met Drummond's eyes. "And I would like you to leave me bloody well alone."

CHAPTER 34

Anne

Anne lay on her back, surveying the small room where she had been brought. The gloomy sky outside did little to brighten the space. Despite what Drummond had told her, she knew for certain this was not an inn. She'd heard of the White Stag, and this place was most certainly not it.

The coarse mattress beneath her smelled of dried sweat and urine, and Anne tried not to think about what had caused the ring of stains marring the surface. The room itself was chilly and drafty, with several boards broken and missing from the walls, allowing a stiff breeze to blow through the cramped space. Anne shivered, her dress still damp from the rain. She pulled at the ropes that secured her cold hands and feet, hissing as a sharp pain pierced her side. The two men had trussed her up like a turkey after she'd tried to escape. She'd waited for the carriage to slow down before she'd jumped from the interior. If it hadn't been for her skirts, she could have outrun them.

As it was, they'd knocked her to the ground, and Anne was sure she'd cracked a rib when she'd landed.

There had to be some way out of this mess. She hoped the hints in the note she'd left for Teach would be enough for him to come after her.

If only Anne had returned the stolen items sooner, none of this would have happened. Margery wouldn't have become suspicious and followed her out to the trees. Drummond would never have evicted her, and Anne would be with Teach.

But for how long? Drummond had said that he still intended for Teach to marry someone with a title. And he'd made his prejudice against Anne all too clear.

It was late in the evening, and she had been gone for hours. Teach would have noticed her absence by now. She should have accompanied him to the city. Would Drummond have confronted her in front of Teach when they'd returned? Or would he have waited?

She squeezed her eyes shut against the prickle of tears. It was no use getting upset over what might have been. Right now she needed to concentrate and wait for an opportune moment to get away.

The door opened, and Martha entered, her silhouette illuminated by the candle in the hallway. Drummond had told Anne he'd hired a lady's maid for her, and Anne had been surprised that he'd gone to the trouble of securing her a companion.

When Anne had first seen the aging woman, she'd thought it was Margery, the resemblance was so striking.

Martha had clearly been an efficient lady's maid in her youth. But with her hunched shoulders and poor vision, Anne wondered why she had accepted Drummond's request. No doubt he had decided to employ her because she was old and frail and he wouldn't be required to pay her very much.

"I have some broth for you to eat," Martha said, her cloudy gray eyes searching the gloomy interior.

Anne shrugged, forgetting momentarily that Martha's eyesight prevented her from seeing very clearly. "I'm not hungry."

Martha's hands shook slightly as she carried the broth. "It won't do you any good to starve yourself. You'll need all your strength when we take you to the ship shortly."

Anne held out her hands. "I can't eat tied like this."

"You can sip it at least. It's your fault, you know. If you'd just come quiet like, instead of jumping out o' the carriage, my Bartholomew wouldn't have had to use the ropes. He didn't mean to hurt you."

"Then why didn't *your* Bartholomew take me to the White Stag like Mr. Drummond told him to?" Anne asked.

"Stop your fussing."

"What do you think Mr. Drummond will say when he finds out you didn't do as he said?"

An ugly smile crossed Martha's lips. "He won't never find out, now, will he? He won't know we kept the money he gave us for the White Stag. If I was you, I'd mind my words. I'd hate for such a pretty thing to meet with an accident. These parts of the docks are dangerous. Girls like you go missing all the time."

Part of Anne longed to fly into a rage, but she knew it would not help her cause any. It would be much better to retain her wits and try to think of a way out of the situation.

"It was very kind of Master Drummond to secure your passage," Martha continued. "He's a generous man, not turning you over to the constable. Any other master woulda done just that, and you'd be swinging from the gallows. My sister, Margery, warned me about you. She said you're a crooked one."

That was how Martha had come to be Anne's lady's maid.

"It was Margery's idea not to take you to the White Stag. Says you didn't deserve it, not after what you done."

Not even Margery was above stealing from Drummond.

Martha continued to speak, rambling on about merchant ships and how none of them could compare to the grandness of the *Deliverance* and how a large crowd would no doubt come to watch it set sail.

Lying back against the small pillow, Anne tuned Martha out, closing her eyes against the physical discomfort. Anne had tried to loosen the ropes that bound her but had been unsuccessful. Her side still throbbed from where she'd fallen, as did her hands and knees.

Anne needed to conserve her strength if she wanted to escape. If there was indeed a large crowd when the ship set sail, that might be to her benefit if she could not get away earlier.

If she was unable to flee . . .

The *Deliverance* was bound for the West Indies, but Anne was not sure where it would call ashore first. She knew the island her mother was from, but she did not know if she had any living relatives there.

Which brought up the question of where she should go. Drummond had said he would send part of her inheritance along to the White Stag. What would he do if he discovered Anne wasn't at the inn? Would he search for her?

And did Martha and Margery know about that arrangement? They would surely steal the money if they did, and Anne would be left destitute once more.

Unfortunately, Anne did not know the answer to any of these questions, and despite her best efforts, tears formed once again in her eyes.

Anne's stomach churned, and her palms were slick with perspiration. She eyed the bowl Martha had brought, but doubted she'd be able to keep anything down if she tried.

The sound of Martha's voice brought her out of her reverie.

"I'll leave the broth here in case you change your mind, and I'll check back in a bit. I wouldn't turn my nose up at it if I was you," Martha said, a sneer pinching her lips. "If Bartholomew hears you're not eating, he might not feel so inclined to give you anything again."

Fire surged through Anne's blood as she watched the old

maid quit the room. Only when she was alone and Martha's footsteps had faded in the distance did Anne once again fight to free herself from her bonds.

Martha might come back, but by then Anne hoped to be long gone.

CHAPTER 35

Teach

Teach went straight to his room to gather his clothes. He intended to search the docks for Anne, and when he found her, they would leave on the next available ship. It didn't matter where it was headed, as long as it took them far away from England. And his father.

A soft knock at the door halted his movements. He ignored it.

He rolled up a shirt and threw it into the small bag he would take with him. He would not be returning.

The knock became more insistent. "Sir! Please! It's urgent I speak with you."

That was not his father's voice. The amber glow from the candlelight flickered as Teach strode to the door. Opening it, he saw Elizabeth's pinched face as she wrung her hands.

"What do you want?" Teach demanded.

"Please, you have to come with me, sir. Miss Anne needs you."

Gripping Elizabeth's wrist, he pulled her into his room and checked the hallway before closing the door. "Where is she?"

"Your father had her taken away, sir. By two mean-looking men. They were supposed to take her to the White Stag, but my brother heard them talking and changing their plans. He followed them. Miss Anne tried to escape, but they caught her. I think she's hurt, sir. And they're keeping her in an awful place."

Shaking his head, Teach closed his eyes briefly against the surge of white-hot rage. "Who took her? Can your brother show me where they are?"

Elizabeth nodded, her eyes wide with fear. "Yes, sir. He's waiting downstairs with your horse—"

"Is my father in the dining room?"

"No, sir. He asked for his meal to be sent up. You must hurry. If Margery finds me here . . ."

Teach didn't need to be told twice. Throwing the bag across his shoulder, he silently headed for the back stairs. Elizabeth didn't carry a candle, and there was no moonlight to illuminate the way. Although the rain had stopped, the night was still dark, and they crept noiselessly along the stairwell.

In the courtyard Teach saw the outline of the young groom where he held Kaiser's reins in his hands. Teach's breath escaped in small puffs, the chill in the air biting. "What's your name?" Teach whispered, swinging up into the saddle.

"David, sir."

"And you followed the men when they took Miss Anne?"

"Aye, sir. I saw her being taken to the carriage. It didn't look like she was very happy about it, so I jumped on the back once they left the premises. They didn't suspect a thing," he said, his chest jutting out with pride.

Teach pulled David up behind him. "I'll see that you're rewarded. Now show me where they are."

Fearful that Kaiser's hooves would alert Drummond to his escape, Teach kept to the strip of grass lining the side of the drive.

Once he reached the city streets, he urged Kaiser on. Teach was only vaguely aware of the lanes they rode along, bloodlust racing through his veins. If she was injured . . .

Forcing himself to breathe regularly, he followed David's directions, Kaiser's hooves clattering along the cobblestones. The closer they got to the docks, the fewer people they encountered. Most workhands had returned to their families at this time of day, and Teach was grateful for the abandoned roads.

David led him through a labyrinth of small alleys and back-streets. Teach sincerely hoped the lad knew where he was going.

"It's just up ahead, sir. That building there on the corner."

"You're sure?"

"Aye. I'm sure."

Teach slowed Kaiser to a walk, Teach's eyes long accustomed to the dark. The two-story structure David had pointed to was a ramshackle house, with several boards missing on the second story and its front door hanging forlornly on its hinges.

The skeletal remains of the surrounding buildings appeared to lean against the other for support, blackened by a recent fire. It was far enough away from any main thoroughfare that no one would think to look here. For anything.

Teach pulled Kaiser up short and slid to the ground, with David following close behind. One of the charred buildings had a small courtyard and the remnants of a stable nearby. After leading Kaiser off the street, Teach hid him from view.

They crouched for a moment in the shelter of a stall, waiting for any sign of movement to come from the building next door.

"There are two men with her, sir. And an old woman. The two men stay here, but the old woman comes and goes," David whispered.

Teach gave David an appreciative look. "How did you know to follow them?"

David grimaced. "I was in the barn when the two men took Miss Anne away. They mentioned something about the White Stag and your father's ship, the *Deliverance*."

"And you've watched them?" Teach asked.

"Aye. I like Miss Anne. The men your father sent her with didn't look like the sort you'd want to send a lady to, so I stayed here."

"Good lad," Teach said, slipping several coins from his pocket and handing them to David.

The boy's eyes grew large, but he handed the coins back to Teach. "I didn't do it for payment, sir. Miss Anne's looked out for my family, and I didn't like the thought of her suffering."

Teach refused to take the coins. "Even more reason for you to keep them."

Before David could argue any further, they heard voices as the door opened and out stepped a woman. From the slant of her shoulders and her slow gate, she appeared to be elderly. As Teach peeked through the scorched wooden slats, his pulse raced. For a moment he thought it was Margery, but the woman before him didn't limp. And Margery was still at the estate.

"I'll be back soon. Make sure you have everything cleaned up," the woman said to some unseen person holding the door open. "We don't want to leave a trail." Where was she going at this time of night?

"Nobody could blame us for what we did," a man's voice answered, followed by a hollow laugh. "She deserved what she got, thinkin' she's better than the rest of us."

He's a dead man, Teach thought as the door closed and the old woman walked away, mumbling to herself.

"Would you like me to go with you, sir?" David asked.

Teach was already standing, his muscles tensed. "No. You go after that woman. Tell her Master Drummond found out what they've done and Margery sent you to warn her."

"But, sir, do you intend—"

"Yes, I do," Teach growled, heading for the door. Tempted to kick it in, he instead opened it carefully, not wanting to alert anyone inside to his presence.

A single candle cast an eerie glow in the dim hallway. The floor was scarred and buckled, the corners laced with webs. Dust covered everything, and a faint acrid smell still hung in the air. Teach heard a soft scuffling sound and the telltale squeak of a rat.

The first room he encountered was empty. The sound of movement came from the back of the house. Stealing forward, Teach came face-to-face with a large man, his physical stature almost equal to Teach's.

"What the devil do you want?" the man demanded.

"To take back what you took from me."

The man charged at Teach, but Teach flipped him over his shoulder and slammed him to the ground, the force of it shaking the house to its rafters. Clipping Teach's ankle, the man pulled him down. The two wrestled and grappled, until Teach managed to catch the man in the stomach with his elbow. Moaning, the man rolled to his side. Teach reached down, gripped him by his hair, and pulled him to a kneeling position before delivering a crushing blow to his face. His opponent fell back and didn't move again.

Teach heard a tread on the floor above and hurtled up the shadowy stairs, his heart hammering. He'd just turned onto the landing when a shot rang out and the wood paneling near his head splintered. Dropping down, Teach saw another man, equal in stature to the first, fumbling to reload the pistol in his hand.

Jumping to his feet, Teach rushed at him and slammed him

against the wall. The pistol fell harmlessly to the floor. "Where is she?"

"Don't know who you're talking about," the man spat back.

Teach drove his fist into the man's stomach. "Try again."

"Bugger off!"

Once more Teach connected with the man's middle. Doubled over, his opponent barely managed to gasp his reply. "She's—gone. To—sea."

"I don't believe you," Teach said, delivering a swift right to his jaw.

Blood dripped from the man's lip where it had split. "She is. I swear it."

Grabbing the man by his shirtfront, Teach smashed his head against the wall. "You were told to take her to the White Stag and then to the *Deliverance*. That ship still sits in the docks."

The man stuck out his jaw, his lips pressed tightly together.

Teach felt his self-control slipping. "Tell me where she is," he growled, pressing his forearm against his opponent's windpipe. "Or I swear I'll kill you."

"You'll—never—" the man gasped, his eyes bulging from their sockets as Teach leaned all of his weight into his choke hold. "The *Prov—i—dence*."

"She's on the *Providence*?"

Nodding, the man drew in a deep breath as Teach released the pressure slightly.

"If you value your life, you'll take me there."

Giving Teach a surly scowl, the man's gaze shifted, looking over Teach's shoulder. Teach ducked, but it was too late, and a crushing blow was delivered to his head. As he staggered backward, the darkness swirled around him, and he sank to his knees before falling forward, face-first.

"Sir! Sir, wake up!"

The earnest voice pierced Teach's clouded mind. Stirring in confusion, Teach cracked his eyes open. In the dark a young face swam in and out of focus.

"Are you all right, sir?" It was the young groom, David.

Teach's ears rang. He rolled over, and white and blue sparks obscured his vision as he attempted to sit up too quickly. His stomach felt as if it were caught in a vise, and the pounding in his head was incessant.

"Help me up," Teach mumbled, cursing his body's weakness.

David clasped one of Teach's wrists with both hands. He was surprisingly strong for one so small. Bile rose in Teach's throat, but by the time he was on his feet, the room had stopped spinning.

"We have to find the *Providence*," Teach said, moving toward the door. It was still dark out. He wondered how much time had passed.

Stumbling down the stairs, David followed in Teach's wake. "That ship is gone, sir. It sailed out with the tide."

Stopping abruptly, Teach turned and caught the young

boy by his shoulders, preventing him from plowing into Teach. "What?"

"I did as you said and told the woman the master knew about her plans. Then I came back to see if you needed help. The two men were leaving. I heard them mention the *Providence*. Since I couldn't wake you immediately, I went to the docks. The ship had already left, sir." Even in the dim light, Teach saw that David's chin quivered, and his eyes filled with tears.

Anne was gone.

An animal sound ripped from Teach's throat, and he slammed his fist into the wall. "Do you know where it was headed?" Teach asked, his voice rough.

"To the West Indies, sir."

Taking a steadying breath, Teach closed his eyes briefly against a wave of fury. Anne was unaccompanied, bound for foreign seas. In his own travels he'd witnessed many women, alone and destitute, suffer indescribable harm and degradation. The thought of Anne suffering like that was nearly his undoing.

"What do you plan to do, sir? Can I help?"

"I'm going after her. And if anyone dares harm her, I will have my revenge."

CHAPTER 36

Anne

The floor of the small dank cabin crawled with movement, and the sound of hundreds of tiny legs scurrying across the boards made the hair on the back of Anne's neck stand up. The *Providence* was teeming with rats and cockroaches, each creation vying for precedence, and clearly outnumbering the human cargo on board.

It was too dark to see anything in the cramped space. Her father had often explained that open flames were forbidden at sea unless attended to in the galley, and the light from the massive stern lantern mounted on the back of the ship did not reach into the ship's belly.

The smell of wet canvas and mold permeated every inch of the filthy vessel. With tears running down her cheeks, Anne wondered how she would possibly endure several weeks aboard. Her cabin was like a coffin, for she truly felt as if she would die.

Lying in the protective cocoon of the hammock, she turned onto her side, pulling her knees up to her chest. Her forehead was damp with perspiration, and her head pounded. What had been the contents of her stomach now swilled around in the bucket on the floor as the ship rose and fell with every surge.

Anne had lost track of time. Each wave that crashed against the hull of the ship seemed to count every second with never-ending precision.

Her fingers shook as she reached for her pocket watch, the cold metal an anchor against a rising tide of despair. Her side still hurt from when she'd fallen in Bristol, but by the time they reached their destination, it should be healed.

Her heart, on the other hand, was an entirely different matter.

She'd written the note, just as Drummond had instructed. She'd almost expected him to stand over her shoulder while she'd performed the task, but thankfully he'd left her to her duty.

She hoped Teach would understand what she'd written. If he couldn't find a way to get to her . . . then she would find a way to get to him.

I will make it out of this alive. I will, she vowed silently.

But not if she remained in this cabin much longer.

Stumbling to the door, Anne wiped furiously at her cheeks. She tried not to think about what was underfoot, even as she felt the telltale squelch of several insects through the thin leather soles of her walking boots. Pulling the door open, she took a deep breath of the briny air, and tripped in her haste to reach the deck.

The ship continued to roil beneath her feet, and more than once Anne staggered against the railing of the stairs as she made her way up to the deck.

The slate gray of the sky matched the choppy waves of the sea, both extending in an unbroken line to the horizon. The wind whipped her hair about her face, and wrapped her skirts around her legs.

The port of Bristol had been left far behind. And with it any hopes of seeing Teach.

Choking back a sob, Anne clenched her hands to her stomach, her nails biting into her palms.

She had always planned to leave England, she reminded herself. Together she and her father had often looked at maps and sketched their course, an expanse of open sea the only hindrance between them and their destination.

But from where Anne stood now, the stretch of water appeared wider and vaster than she could have imagined. And she was alone on a strange ship, without a single coin to her name.

"Don't go too close to the sides," said someone on her left.

Startled, Anne whirled around, clutching a nearby rope to keep her balance. Before her stood a boy and a girl, each perhaps twenty years of age. They were both blond, with wide blue eyes, and they were clearly related.

The boy was stout, with sturdy shoulders and a thick neck.

His sister, although not as large, had a full figure. Her brown dress and shawl were threadbare, hardly sufficient to protect her from the biting wind. And she was far too cheery for being aboard such an unworthy sea vessel.

"I had no intention of doing that," Anne said.

The girl smiled, her eyes warm. "Good. My brother, Coyle, here, says it's dangerous and that I shouldn't come up here without him."

Anne glanced at Coyle. People would definitely think twice about approaching if he stood by your side. Anne had already felt several crewmen eyeing her, their gaunt expressions hardened by years of strenuous labor. She planned to ignore them, hoping they would afford her the same courtesy.

"My name's Cara Flynn. What's yours?"

"Anne Barrett."

"Pleased to meet you, Anne Barrett. Would you mind if Coyle and I kept you company? I have no wish to spend any more time in my hammock than necessary."

"I wouldn't have minded," Coyle muttered.

His sister frowned. "Then you can go back down. I told you I'd be fine up here."

"I couldn't remain in my cabin any longer either," Anne said, shivering at the thought of the rats and cockroaches.

"You're lucky you have a cabin. Coyle spent the whole night making sure no one harmed us. But the only thing that came close to bothering me was a cheeky rat who took a liking to my ankles."

Anne grimaced. "Lucky" was not a word she'd use to describe her present situation, but having her own cabin was far better than sleeping with the rest of the passengers in hammocks belowdecks.

Excusing herself, Anne moved away from the siblings as they continued their discussion of the numerous dangers on board the ship. Despite the chaotic running and shouting of the crew, Anne felt strangely removed from everyone and everything around her.

She drew a deep breath, her stance wide to maintain her balance. Looking toward the stern, Anne watched the white-capped waves that seemed to form a path trailing behind the back of the ship. That path led to Teach.

Even as Anne tried to block out the seriousness of her situation, it continued to plague her thoughts. The fact that she sailed on the *Providence* instead of the *Deliverance* made her ability to reunite with Teach incredibly difficult.

Difficult, but not impossible.

It would not be an easy journey. For either of them. But he would come for her, of that she was certain. And she would not give up until he found her or she found him.

Lifting her head, Anne turned and studied the open ocean in front of the ship. The initial shock of leaving England was beginning to wear off. Admittedly, she'd hoped to leave under different circumstances, but she would survive this voyage.

She had to.

And one day she and Teach would be together again, for it was just as he'd said. They could be on opposite sides of the world, but she would always be his, and he would always be hers.

CHAPTER 37

Teach

The congested dock fairly groaned beneath the weight of the assembled crowd. Anticipation was everywhere in the city, on the streets and in the water. Children cried, parents bickered, and clever tradesmen called out their wares for sale. With a group this large, there were sure to be several hungry individuals.

Everyone had come to see the launch of the largest galleon ever built. The *Deliverance* rocked in the swell under full canvas. It was an awesome sight, like a preening peacock, as if aware of all the attention. The eager men of the crew stood at attention, squinting against the morning sun, small arms draped from their shoulder belts.

Richard Drummond himself stood before the group, dressed in a velvet coat and silk waistcoat. On his head he wore a powdered wig, and the silver buckles of his shoes glinted in the sunlight. The mayor of Bristol droned on and on about the importance of this day and how proud the city was to have such an esteemed merchant in their midst.

For his part, Drummond's eyes searched the crowd, a cheerless look on his face. Despite this being one of the most anticipated days of his life, he appeared unable to muster even the slightest hint of a smile.

Teach stood back, his square jaw once again covered with several days' growth, his hair pulled into a knot beneath his hat. He stared at his father, as one would stare at a stranger. Teach had always felt affection for the man. Even when Drummond had been at his most demanding, deep down Teach had yearned for his father's approval and affection.

Not now. Not after what Drummond had done.

Teach and John had spent the past six days searching the docks and ships of Bristol for the two men, but they hadn't been able to find them. Teach and John had also made more inquiries into the *Providence*. It belonged to another merchant but was nowhere near as large or grand as the *Deliverance*. It would call on several ports in the West Indies. Teach refused to believe he was too late to catch up to it.

He would have set sail on another ship if he'd found one heading out sooner, but the journey often took months to prepare for, and the *Deliverance* was the next vessel leaving port.

Teach had given Kaiser to David. He could not take a horse with him where he was going.

That morning, as Teach had wandered the city streets,

people had drawn back in fear and revulsion when they'd seen him, for he was covered in mud and grime. They'd whispered behind his back, pointing fingers at the unsightly figure before them.

Teach had been numb to it all. He hadn't had any feelings left. Until he'd seen his father.

Teach's was one face among hundreds on the docks, and Teach did not fear discovery. On his feet he wore stout calf-hide boots. He had the old jacket and floppy hat John had given him. Once again his face and hair were unkempt, and his father would have a hard time recognizing him.

Teach watched as his father addressed the crowd briefly. There was a haunted look in his eyes, and his was the face of a man suffering.

Teach knew instinctively that if he would simply show himself, his father would recover, but Teach was unwilling to move. His father would make him stay in Bristol, and Teach could not accept that fate. Everywhere Teach looked he was reminded of Anne. The pain of her absence hadn't dulled. He was constantly aware of the knowledge that she was somewhere far away and he couldn't reach her.

Teach's eyes moved over the crowd, but they paused briefly on the familiar sight of William and Patience standing together, William's arm draped protectively around her. Teach's mouth tightened slightly, but he gave no other response.

Swinging his bag of belongings onto his back, Teach pushed

through the throng. In his bag were the things he'd packed from the house, and in Teach's pocket was the ring he'd planned to give Anne.

As Teach approached the boarding plank, he reached for the papers in his waistcoat and handed them to the stocky young man near the plank. On Teach's instructions, John had paid the original first mate a tidy sum not to report that morning, allowing Teach to take his place. The first mate was a representative of the merchant owner, and in most cases, he could not be removed from his office by the captain of the ship.

A cheer went up as the assembly dispersed, people jockeying for a better position to watch the mighty *Deliverance* set sail.

"You're late," the man said, giving Teach a once-over.

"I know," Teach said shortly. It hadn't taken much for him to mimic his father's signature on his papers. He'd mastered the art when he'd been a schoolboy and Drummond had taken Teach to his office once in a while, before Drummond had decided that a merchant life was no life for his son.

"I wonder what Richard Drummond would say if he knew you cared so little for your post," the man said doubtfully.

Teach nodded. "You're free to go and ask him yourself, . . ." He waited for the young man to supply his name.

"Jack Thurston."

"Well, Jack Thurston, you're free to go and ask him yourself, but he's a very busy man. If you want to waste his time—"

Jack shook his head. "No, that won't be necessary."

Teach was an imposing figure, and he knew how to use his size to his advantage. He was quickly learning that he didn't need to employ force to get what he wanted.

"Are you as good a first mate as they say?" Jack asked.

Teach didn't know what kind of rumors John had spread, but he could imagine they'd been slightly exaggerated.

"Aye, I am." There was an undercurrent of danger in Teach's nearly blank expression.

Jack obviously assumed that Drummond had employed Teach at the last minute, knowing what a target the *Deliverance* would provide out on the open sea. Any sloop out there would have heard of the galleon's maiden voyage and know what a coup it would be to capture such a ship. Most of the *Deliverance*'s crew was former soldiers, prepared to fight if any pirates dared show themselves. "Well, then, what's your name?" Jack asked. "I can't read this chicken scratch."

Teach studied Jack for a moment. "The name is Edward Teach."

Jack nodded. "Good enough, although I think 'Edward' is too fine a name for you. If you intend to look like a street urchin and smell like a sow, I shall have to call you something else." He looked Teach over from head to toe, noting his shabby black hair and beard. "You're no dandy. I'll call you Blackbeard. Welcome aboard."

AUTHOR'S NOTE

I am a self-diagnosed history nerd and I'm not afraid to admit it. Trivial facts, random dates, and important battles are fascinating to me. So when my family decided to take a trip to Charleston, South Carolina in August 2012, I did what I always do: studied the history of the place. Did you know that Blackbeard the pirate actually blockaded the port city of Charleston and held it hostage in May 1718? His only demand was medication. That discovery got me thinking—what kind of man was Blackbeard? And what made him become one of the most notorious pirates to sail the seas?

And so the spark of *Blackhearts* was ignited.

Apparently, only the last few years of Blackbeard's life are documented. He went by the name of Edward Teach, although no one knows if that was his real name. Some records indicate his last name was Drummond, but nobody can truly verify this fact. Pirates often changed their names to protect their families at home. It's believed that Blackbeard was educated, because he could read and write. That meant he had to come from a wealthy family, because only the prosperous could afford tutors or any form of schooling at the time.

He was large in stature and changed his appearance to

intimidate people. Some records indicate that Blackbeard was amiable and almost forgiving and generous with those who cooperated with him, but he could be ruthless and merciless to those who fought or challenged him. Despite reports of his cruelty, there are no reports of his having killed anyone until the last battle that eventually took his life. Unlike other pirates at the time, he didn't torture victims for fun. I don't mean to imply that he was a good person. He wasn't, but many of the rumors surrounding him were exaggerated because of the demonic appearance he himself tried so hard to cultivate.

Blackbeard's flagship was named the *Queen Anne's Revenge,* so I knew that I wanted the female lead to be called Anne. An image of a beautiful girl with striking blue eyes, thick black hair, and copper-colored skin came to mind, and she stuck with me. I needed someone who would be able to hold her own against such a compelling figure as Edward Teach, and I think Anne is the perfect companion for him.

The idea for Anne's background was inspired, in part, by my husband, Miguel. Miguel was born in Uruguay, but his family moved to Germany when he was nine years old. (His father was Uruguayan, his mother German.) My husband has often said that he feels like a man without a country. In Germany, people called him "the Uruguayan." In Uruguay, they called him "the German." Here in the States, people expect him to look a certain way, because his name is Miguel, but physically, he favors his German ancestors. This was the impetus for part of Anne's identity—someone caught between two cultures— although Anne's conflict is far greater than my husband's.

I chose to have Anne's mother come from an island in the West Indies. The island of Curaçao was originally inhabited by the Arawak peoples who migrated from South America. When Europeans first landed there, they brought with them diseases that killed a number of the indigenous people. The Arawaks who survived were forced into slavery. Eventually, the Spaniards left the island because it lacked gold deposits, but the Dutch quickly claimed it for themselves in 1634. In 1662, the Dutch West India Company made Curaçao a center for the Atlantic slave trade, often bringing slaves there before taking them to other Caribbean islands for sale.

I decided to make Anne's father an English merchant who traveled extensively and who tried, in part, to shield Anne from the prejudices of the population. In England at the time, the notions of race were hopelessly confused, as any person of color was routinely and wrongly categorized: Africans with Arabs, Indians with South Asians. Indeed, blacks and Indians were often interchangeable in the popular mind. There was already a large division between the aristocracy and the poor inhabitants of the country. Records show that historically, people of color had long been part of the English court, but in contrast to the rest of the population, their numbers were significantly smaller. The majority of slaves who survived the horrific transatlantic journey from Africa were forced to work in the American colonies or the islands in the Caribbean under unspeakable conditions. Very few were actually taken to the British Isles.

The British led the Atlantic slave trade for more than one hundred years, and the port cities of Bristol and Liverpool thrived during this time. Between 1700 and 1800, Liverpool's population rose from five thousand to seventy-eight thousand. The money earned from the slave trade helped finance the Industrial Revolution.

Ironically, there was a ruling made in 1697 by Chief Justice Holt of the King's Bench that claimed that as soon as a slave lands in England, he is free. Not everyone heeded the ruling and people of color were often left to beg in the streets, and were refused positions because of their race.

I wanted part of Anne's inner conflict to be the desire to see more people like her, to have a sense of belonging and connection with them. Not only had her father tried to shelter her from prejudice and racism, but he had often promised to take her to the West Indies. With his death, that link was lost, until she ultimately determined to make the journey herself.

I admit to taking a few liberties with this story. I do think of it as a Blackbeard origin story, but it's Anne's story as much as it is Teach's. It's my idea of what would lead someone to leave everything he knew and set out on a life of piracy. *Blackhearts* is about two young people trying to find their way in the world and discover where they belong. It's also about how those two people meet and fall in love. I hope readers love the story as much as I do.

ACKNOWLEDGMENTS

It's both incredible and humbling to think of all the people who helped make this book possible. First of all, an enormous thank-you goes to my amazing editor, Sara Sargent. Working with you has been a privilege and an honor. You understood what I wanted to write from the beginning, and without your valuable insight, Anne and Teach's story wouldn't be what it is today.

To the remarkable publishing team at Simon Pulse, who helped make this dream of mine come true: Mara Anastas, Mary Marotta, Liesa Abrams, Kayley Hoffman, Carolyn Swerdloff, Teresa Ronquillo, and Nicole Ellul. Thank you so much for all of your support! Karina Granda, you rendered me speechless with the beautiful design for the cover. I couldn't have asked for a more accurate symbol of Anne and Teach's struggle. And to Sarah McCabe, Rio Cortez, and Danielle Esposito, thank you for taking the time to read the manuscript and making sure I told Anne's point of view the way it should be told.

Quinlan Lee, I will never forget the day I received your e-mail asking if we could have a chat. You were an answer to my prayers and I will always be grateful to you for being such a huge champion of this book.

ACKNOWLEDGMENTS

Thank you also to Tracey Adams, agent extraordinaire, who took me on. Your knowledge of and passion for the industry lets me know I'm in very capable hands. A special shout-out to Josh Adams, who came up with the brilliant title for this book. And to Samantha Bagood, your feedback was greatly appreciated. I'm incredibly blessed to be a part of the Adams Literary family.

There have been many writerly friends who've supported me on this journey. I'm grateful to Anne Perry, über-talented murder-mystery author and longtime family friend. I'll never forget your encouragement and our discussions about characterization and plot. To my sister from another mister/critique partner, Becky Wallace: I wouldn't have made it this far without you, cyber best friend. One day we will get to hang out together. Thank you also to Caroline Richmond and Lynne Matson for being awesome betas.

Thank you to the many book bloggers who've already shown incredible support and excitement for *Blackhearts*.

I have several nonwriterly friends who've helped me along the way. Dionne Matthews, Brandee Hammett, Andrea Stroud, Sam Loveland, and Becca Castleton, thank you for taking the time out of your busy schedules to read for me. Of course I couldn't have written as much as I did without the help of Janine, Sydney, and Jake Simpson, as well as Holly and James Loveland. Thanks for being there for me throughout this entire process and entertaining my kiddos while I pursued my dream.

To my mother, Doris S. Platt, you always encouraged me

to write. You knew I would love it, because you taught me to love books. You were right! To my father, James S. Platt, you taught me the importance of getting up every day and going to work, no matter what. To my siblings Andrea Christiansen and Cameron Platt and their families, thank you for listening to me when I talked about my story ideas. For my twin sister, Kirsten Major, I'm so glad I had you by my side. Not everyone is as lucky as we were to come with our very own best friend. Your family is lucky to have you! To my in-laws, the Castroman/Perez clans, thanks so much for all your support.

And finally to my beautiful family: Sophia and Anthony, you are my everything and I'm proud to be your mother. You always believed in me. Thank you for understanding when I said, "Mommy has to write." And to my Miguelo, I knew when we first met that you were the one for me. Without your encouragement I wouldn't have made it this far, and I'm thankful for every day we spend together. *Te amo mucho.*

Teach and Anne's story isn't over yet.
Flip the page to get a sneak peek at *Blacksouls*,
the swashbuckling sequel to *Blackhearts*.

BLACKSOULS

The sequel to *Blackhearts*

NICOLE CASTROMAN

Anne

Anne's father had often told her that a smooth sea never made a skilled sailor, but this morning she was grateful for the tranquility as the *Providence* cut the surface like a finger trailing in the water. The blue sky overhead stretched to the horizon with lazy white clouds floating on the breeze.

She tried to convince herself that her calm surroundings made her present task somewhat less repellant, but the expressions of her fellow passengers told her otherwise, which was why the duty had fallen to her. No one else had stepped forward to help.

Kneeling on the deck, the skin on Anne's arms and face was tight from prolonged exposure to the sun and seawater. The dull needle in her hand pierced the bloody canvas with a gentle pop as she pulled the edges of the hammock closer together to create a makeshift shroud.

She avoided looking at the dead man's eyes as they stared sightlessly up at the heavens. Holding her breath against the rancid smell of his rotting teeth and gums, she said a silent prayer, hoping he had not felt the rats gnawing on the soles of his feet as he lay dying.

The sailor standing beside her shifted, momentarily blocking the sun. "That's only twelve stitches. He'll come back if you don't have thirteen."

"Perhaps you'd like to do the last one," Anne snapped up at him, unable to hold her tongue any longer.

The sailor took a hasty step back, shaking his head, his eyes wide with fear. These men and their silly superstitions, she thought.

Bracing herself, Anne pushed the needle through one side of the canvas before passing it through the dead man's nose. She winced as she tugged at the thread to complete the last and final stitch to close the hammock. The sailors claimed that the law of the sea demanded it, a way to make sure that the person wasn't simply sleeping.

Anne knew for a fact that the man before her was dead, for she was the one who had found him. Hidden behind a large crate on the quarterdeck of the *Providence*, he had crawled away to suffer the scurvy alone and in silence. He'd had no family on board, no one to claim him.

Her task complete, Anne sat back on her haunches, waiting as a few sailors lifted the body. Gaunt and exhausted themselves, they rested it briefly on the railing before rolling it over the edge into the serene sea below.

Anne closed her eyes when she heard the splash, knowing the cannonball they'd placed in the hammock would drag the emaciated form down to the murky depths of the ocean. A small part of her couldn't help thinking that perhaps he was the lucky one. His suffering was over. For the rest left on board, their hardships would continue.

In the four weeks since they'd left the shores of England behind, he was the sixth person to succumb to the disease, and unless they reached their destination soon, he would not be the last.

From the beginning, the vessel had been plagued by exceptionally bad luck.

A lack of foresight or funds had left them with an inadequate supply of provisions. Their salted-pork and dried fish had long run out, with only hardtack remaining. The biscuits themselves were barely edible, teeming with beetles and weevils. After her mother's death, Anne had thought she'd known hunger. That was nothing compared to the famine she endured now.

The weary people surrounding Anne wore threadbare clothes and haunted expressions, resembling the ship on which they sailed. It was a miracle the *Providence* had made it this far, with its tattered sails and slowly leaking hull.

While the other onlookers drifted to different parts of the deck, Cara helped Anne to her feet. "How do you do it?" Cara asked, her freckled face pale underneath her sunburn. Her once plump features had significantly thinned in the weeks since their departure.

Anne had told Cara and her brother, Coyle, how she'd been taken from the Drummond estate and put on the *Providence*, against Richard Drummond's instructions. In turn, Anne had learned that Coyle and Cara's uncle had sent them enough funds to sail on a grand ship, but someone had robbed them and the two were left to sail on the *Providence* as well. Anne was grateful for their friendship.

Looking up from the needle in her hand, Anne gave Cara a sad smile. "It's not much different than mending the sails." Cara had a fine hand for stitching and had been invaluable to the crew of the *Providence* for patching and repairing the old canvas sails ripped during the storms they'd encountered. Cara hoped to earn a living as a seamstress one day, and put her talent to use.

"I don't believe you. Some of these lads have been sailing for years and none of them offered to help the poor man."

"It was the least I could do. I like to think that if anything happened to me, someone would take the time to give me a proper burial at sea."

Cara crossed herself before shaking her head at Anne. "Don't be talking like that. Nothing's going to happen to you. Coyle won't allow it. And neither will I."

"Aye, she's right," Coyle said, coming toward them. His blond hair, so similar to his sister's, had lightened considerably in the sun, while his fair skin had darkened. He'd lost at least two stones since they'd set sail. "We're glad you're here, even if we were all supposed to be on the Deliverance."

Cara linked her arm with Anne's. "And when we get to Nassau, you can stay with us. I'm sure our uncle would welcome an extra hand in his tavern. From what we've heard, he seems to be doing well, with plenty of thirsty folk on the island."

"It will only be until I can earn enough to continue my journey. I don't wish to be a burden," Anne said, hating the fact that she was once again penniless, with no way to send word back to Teach. Every time she thought of him, the pain of his absence was like a cruel fist squeezing her heart.

It would take weeks for any letter to reach Bristol, but she had to try something to get in touch with him. Perhaps he'd left word with her father's solicitor. It was quite possible Teach had quit the country, in an attempt to find her.

If she closed her eyes, she could almost picture him aloft in the rigging of a ship, adjusting the sails and making repairs. The work of a sailor was physically demanding, yet Teach would never shrink from his responsibilities. He wouldn't have hesitated to sew the dead man up in the hammock. Not because he was unfeeling, but because Teach knew there was enough filth and disease on a ship without a decaying body adding to the misery.

A part of Anne couldn't help being grateful that she would soon reach land and have to stay there for some time. The trip across the Atlantic had been more challenging and difficult than anything she'd imagined. They'd endured unending hours of monotony, only to be surprised by storms so violent and fierce that Anne had been convinced the ship would send her to a watery grave.

Cara gave Anne a comforting squeeze. "You could never be a burden. If you hadn't allowed me to share your cabin, I would still be forced to sleep with the passengers below and Coyle would never get any rest."

"I still don't get any rest. But at least I don't worry as much," Coyle said, striking the small biscuit in his hand on the railing. Several weevils fell out and he brushed the tiny black insects overboard, before dipping the hardtack in a mug of diluted brandy. "Care for some?" he asked, offering it to Anne.

She shook her head. They'd all learned the hard way that the simple wafers were unbreakable and had to first be immersed in liquid in order to make them edible. Hardtack might be inexpensive to make and long-lasting for a voyage, but flavorful it was not.

Coyle shrugged and took a bite. Cara wrinkled her nose at him. "Aren't you going to offer me anything?" Cara asked.

"No. George ate your portion."

"Which George?" Cara had taken it upon herself to try to name every rat on the *Providence*. An impossible task considering how many there were, but it was a simple game that helped fight the monotony of the voyage.

"How should I know?"

"Was he missing a hind foot? If so, it was George III. If part of his tail was gone, then that's George I."

"I'm too bloody tired for this, Cara," Coyle muttered, rubbing his weary eyes.

Anne shook her head at him. "You don't need to sleep outside our cabin, Coyle. You've heard Captain Oxley. He's said no harm will come to us." After weeks observing the coarse crew, Anne had come to realize that the sailors mostly kept to themselves, leaving the passengers alone. Cara's outgoing nature bordered on flirtatious, but the men were too busy trying to keep the ship afloat to pay much attention to her. Especially with Coyle remaining nearby.

"I want to be close by in case anything does happen," Coyle said, looking off the port side.

Anne followed his gaze, a thread of unease winding its way through her chest. In the distance, two ships cruised the open waters, their dark outlines visible against the stark blue of the sky. For four weeks, the *Providence* had sailed along, separated from familiar landmarks without a glimpse of another vessel on the horizon.

But two days ago, as they neared their destination, the call had gone out that a ship had been spotted. And shortly after, a second ship had appeared. Like two shadows, they followed the *Providence*, but made no move to get any closer.

Anne drew a deep breath. "Have they shown their flags?"

"No. We're too far for them to raise an ensign," Coyle said.

"What do you think they want?" Cara asked, her eyes narrowed. "We don't have anything worth taking." The *Providence* was a pitiable merchant vessel. With rotting timbers and old rigging, the ship transported more people than cargo. Whatever goods she *did* carry, it couldn't have amounted to more than a few hundred schillings at best.

"I don't know," Coyle said, downing the rest of his brandy. "But it's not normal."

"It seems to me that they're waiting for something," Anne said.

"Like what?" Cara asked, her voice sharp.

Coyle wiped his mouth with the back of his hand. "Don't know, but I think Anne's right. See how they keep their distance?"

Cara looked between her brother and Anne. "But we're only a few days away from Nassau. It's to be expected that we see other ships."

"Yes, but they should move on, shouldn't they? If they're merchants, they would be heading to their next port," Anne said. "Do you think the tales are true?"

A few of the crew members had claimed that life was difficult for many settlers in Nassau. The Spanish had burned and destroyed the town in 1684. English settlers had arrived two years later and more continued to arrive each year, but stability was difficult to maintain, even with a governor in residence. In order to survive, many in the population had turned to piracy to earn their living. Nassau was rumored to be a lawless nest of adventurers and thieves.

"Surely they wouldn't attack a ship flying under the English flag," Cara said.

Anne remained silent, the *Providence* rising and falling gently beneath her feet. Was it possible that the life she'd left behind in Bristol was better than the one she now faced, living among thieves in Nassau?

The first part of their journey was nearly complete. In a few days' time, they would make port. But what kind of future awaited her?

"Sail ho!"

Looking up, Anne raised a hand to shield her eyes, squinting against the brightness of the sun. In the distance, the unmistakable outline of another vessel could be seen.

A murmur spread across the deck like a wave approaching shore as other passengers and crew crowded along the railing. If they hadn't been so spooked by the two ships already following them, Anne doubted the appearance of a third would have caused such a stir.

But cause a stir it did.

The downy hair on Anne's nape prickled. Glancing back up at the cloudless blue sky, she saw that there was no sign of an approaching storm, but she sensed danger on the horizon nonetheless.

Teach

The briny air was tainted with the coppery scent of blood. Across the slick deck of the *Deliverance* a thin trail of red spread. The cat-o'-nine-tails whistled once more, striking the young boy's back with parallel stripes and lacerating the skin. He let out an anguished cry as tears ran down his grimy cheeks.

"Captain Murrell, surely that's enough," Teach ground out, his shoulders tense as he watched the agony on the boy's face.

The thin man at Teach's side gave him a stern look, his cold gray eyes unforgiving. "If I don't maintain discipline on this ship, then someone else might try to steal from you."

"I realize that, sir. But perhaps the punishment does not fit the crime. After all, Matthew didn't get away with it."

"Because I saw him when he exited your cabin. Would you have reported the theft if I hadn't caught him in the act?"

If Teach had caught young Matthew stealing the small chest of coins, he would have dealt with it in a different manner. Scarcely twelve years old, Matthew did not belong at sea.

"If you don't have the stomach for disciplining the crew, perhaps I should have Peter replace you as first mate?" Murrell said, his thin lips curled in a sneer.

Peter weighed the whip in his hands and gave Teach an impassive stare. Teach suspected he enjoyed the whippings as much as Murrell did. In truth, Teach was not supposed to be second in command, but back in Bristol, it had been a simple task to forge his father's signature and falsify Teach's papers. A significant bribe had helped the real first mate decide to stay behind and Teach had assumed his responsibilities on board the *Deliverance*.

At times, Teach had regretted his decision. He detested Murrell, but Teach had been desperate to be on the first ship leaving Bristol to go in search of Anne. His father's vessel had been his only option, with Nassau as its first port in the West Indies. Since the *Providence* was also scheduled to stop in Nassau, Teach had had no other choice.

Peter raised his arm once more, ready to deliver another blow to the small figure bound to the main mast. He was one of the few men loyal to the captain. With his pale blue eyes and equally pale skin, Peter reminded Teach of a fish.

Teach stepped forward, his pulse pounding in his ears, but Captain Murrell caught Teach by the arm, halting him.

Teach glared down at the offending appendage before meeting the captain's eyes. "Do not touch me again," he said, his quiet voice filled with malice.

Murrell slowly removed his hand, his nostrils flaring. "Do not interfere with my orders again."

The man grasping the whip looked askance between the two, and the crew seemed to be holding a collective breath, waiting to see who would win the confrontation. It had been like this for weeks, the will of the captain at odds with the will of the first mate.

A soft whimper came from Matthew, and Teach clenched his fists at his sides. Murrell caught the slight movement and a wicked gleam entered his eyes.

"Do you have something you'd like to say?" Murrell asked.

"No, sir," Teach said, fearing more punishment for the young boy.

After an interminable pause, the captain gave a negligent flick of his wrist. "Cut him loose. I have no wish to have his death on my hands."

Teach muttered an oath, sliding his knife from the scabbard in his boot, before moving forward to free the boy.

Matthew's breathing was ragged, his eyes narrowed from pain and fear as Teach knelt at his side, slicing through his bonds.

"Take him to my cabin," Teach murmured to the two sailors who also came forward to help. "I'll be there shortly to see how he fares."

"Aye, sir."

Grabbing a bucket, Teach filled it with sea water from a nearby barrel and splashed the deck where Matthew had knelt. The crew, including Murrell himself, watched silently as Teach filled bucket after bucket, dousing the spot until the blood was gone. Teach wished he could make Matthew's pain disappear just as easily, but he knew from experience that it would take several days for the welts on the boy's back to heal.

There was a much larger stain still visible on the deck, one Teach hadn't been able to wash away. Beneath the baking sun, it had darkened to black, but it too had started out a bright crimson.

"Would you rather I had him keelhauled?" the captain asked.

Teach replaced the bucket before turning. "I don't think dragging Matthew beneath the ship is necessary. Since he stole from me, I'd rather you let me determine the punishment, sir," he said, wiping the sweat from his brow. Although it was November, the weather was warm, indicating their proximity to the West Indies. Teach could not wait to get off the ship, and be rid of Murrell once and for all.

"Yes, well, I've taken control of the chest and had it locked in my cabin."

Teach froze. "That's not necessary, Captain."

"The name on the inside of the chest reads Anne Barrett. How did you come by it?"

Hearing Anne's name spoken by Captain Murrell caused Teach's stomach to clench and his heart to contract painfully. Robert Murrell was one of the most repulsive men he had ever had the misfortune to meet, and he sincerely hoped Anne's passage to the West Indies had been easier than his.

"The chest belongs to my betrothed," Teach said tightly.

Murrell's eyes widened. "Waiting for you back in England, is she?"

Unwilling to let the captain know the truth, Teach gave a short nod. Teach would never forget the last time he'd seen Anne in Bristol. He'd asked her to go into town with him, but she'd refused. He'd kissed her, a kiss that still haunted his dreams. By the time he'd returned to his father's house, she was gone.

Every time Teach thought about her, it drove him mad not knowing how Anne fared. Was she frightened? Did she suffer from seasickness?

Did her fellow passengers leave her in peace? It was the uncertainty of her situation that caused Teach the most pain. He would withstand a hundred lashes if only he could be sure that she was safe.

Murrell opened his mouth once more, but a cry from overhead arrested everyone's attention.

"Sails ho!"

A murmur went up around the deck as sailors lined along the rails. They'd been too preoccupied with Matthew's whipping to keep a proper lookout.

"I spy three ships, Captain. Two sailing port side, the other to star-board."

Captain Murrell held out his hand for the spyglass at Teach's waist. Now that young Matthew was out of harm's way, Teach slapped it into Murrell's outstretched palm, wishing he could break it over the captain's head.

"They're most likely English or French," Murrell said, studying the distant ships. "It's to be expected. This is one of the busiest shipping lanes in the Atlantic."

"Aye, but we're still a good distance from Nassau. They could be Spanish," Teach said.

Murrell's head whipped around. "We're too far from the Spanish main. They wouldn't attack us here."

For the hundredth time, Teach wondered how Murrell had ever secured his post as captain of the *Deliverance*. He was a skilled naviga-tor, with an uncanny ability to sail close to the wind on a course that led him directly to his destination. But his conceit often got in the way of his logic. Instead of inspiring his crew's respect, Murrell resorted to violence and fear to maintain control. "Sir, the *Deliverance* is one of the largest merchant ships ever built, and this is its maiden voyage. We've been a target since we left port," Teach said, unable to control the disdain in his voice. Teach was surprised they hadn't been attacked before now.

Frowning, Murrell seemed to consider Teach's words before glanc-ing around at his crew. When they'd left Bristol, the men had stood straight and eager, most of them former soldiers and proud to be chosen for such a grand vessel. But after four weeks under Murrell's leadership, they were now skittish and tense, never sure when they would be on the receiving end of the captain's brutal tirades.

"Ready the ship," Murrell said.

"For what, exactly, sir?" Teach asked, studying the captain. If the vessels were friendly, there was no need to ready the *Deliverance* for anything. Did the captain wish them to fight? If so, then it was *Murrell's* job to rally the men. He needed to give the final order. Teach had learned that to assume anything under Murrell's command was a grave mistake. Although it had been two weeks, the wounds on Teach's back had not fully healed. He'd carry the scars for the rest of his life.

"If they're Spanish, we'll try to outrun them," Murrell said dismissively.

"That won't work. The *Deliverance* is too large and sits too low in the water," Teach said.

Captain Murrell flushed a dull shade of red. "Then we'll throw some of the cargo overboard. And some of the cannons if we need to."

"We can't outrun them, Captain. They're most likely in sloops that are swifter and more maneuverable than we are." Teach's gut told him a fight was coming. Although they were still some distance away, the other ships were clearly smaller. They had most likely spotted the *Deliverance* some time ago and were now giving chase.

Murrell pursed his lips. His eyes traveled once more over the crew, as if gauging their loyalty, before coming to rest on Teach. The anger in his eyes was palpable. "Ready the ship for battle."

Teach nodded. "We'll need all hands on deck, sir. That includes the men locked in the hold."

Murrell glared at Teach. Once more, there was a strained silence as the two men regarded each other. "Fine. Let them out." Turning, the captain stalked away, leaving Teach and the rest of the men to stare after his departing back.

The gun crew on the *Deliverance* rushed to roll the twenty-two cannons into position in their lower deck ports, stacking twelve-pounders by their sides. Above, others raced to secure ropes and check the masts and mainsails.

The two men Captain Murrell had locked in the hold joined in the activity, but the four days they'd spent below in the cramped quarters had taken their toll, especially on Teach's friend, John. Built with a broad back and stout legs, John winced every time he moved.

Teach had met John the previous year on board one of Andrew Barrett's merchant ships. The two had been fast friends ever since. It was John who had help secure Teach's position on board the *Deliverance* by bribing the original first mate to abandon the voyage, and Teach was grateful for John's presence.

"Murrell's addled," John muttered to Teach as he readied his flintlock pistol. "Punishing us for a game of dice. How else does the fool expect us to spend our time? Perfecting our rope work?"

Cleaning his own firearm, Teach shook his head. "He didn't lock you away because of the game. It's because you and Thurston came to blows."

John scowled. "We meant no harm."

"That's not how it looked to the rest of us," Teach said. Jack Thurston was built much like John. Thurston had accused John of cheating at the game. Naturally, John hadn't taken kindly to the insult, and the pair had seemed like two bulls charging at each other.

"I s'pose I should be glad he didn't have me whipped. How's young Matthew?" John asked.

"He'll live. But it will take several days for him to heal," Teach said, his voice grim.

"How are you faring?"

The tightness across Teach's back was lessening as his wounds healed. "I'm fine."

"You should be in control of this ship. Not that fool captain."

"Careful what you say, John. That smacks of mutiny," Teach warned in an undertone, glancing over his shoulder. After years of living under his father's control, Teach was less than heartened to find himself under the command of a tyrant even worse than his father.

John followed Teach's gaze.

At the moment, Murrell was berating the helmsman for the direction he had chosen. "I don't care if they are leeward. I want you to stay on course."

John rolled his eyes. "The man's daft. He doesn't know the first thing about fighting."

"We have no choice. Those ships are going to attack."

"Aye, and when they do, he won't have any idea how to respond."

"Then it will be up to us to make sure they don't board us." During his year at sea, Teach had developed some skills with the saber, but he wouldn't stand a chance in a close fight with more experienced swordsmen. He simply relied on his size to intimidate any opponents.

"Don't know if we can stop them. We'll be exposed to their shot between wind and water and with Murrell leading us, we won't stand a chance."

"Yes, we will."

John looked at Teach. "How do you know?"

"Because I know this ship. And I have a plan."